"From the first page you are immersed in the life and loves and losses of Elijah Campbell. A great story pulls you in and doesn't let go until you see yourself—this book is like looking into a mirror."

Chris Fabry, author and radio host

"Stunning. Through eloquent prose and exquisite storytelling, Flanagan invites us into the unraveling of another's false self. Yet we enter not as strangers but as friends, caring deeply for the unhiding of Elijah, for the unhiding of us all. The scenes will linger with you, as will wise words to nourish the movement toward your true self. Recommended for all who seek to journey into the deep waters of their own transformation."

Bethany Dearborn Hiser, director of Soul Care at Northwest Family Life and author of *From Burned Out to Beloved: Soul Care for Wounded Healers*

"I knew from the first page that Elijah Campbell was a special character. Every chapter, paragraph, and sentence that I read proved me right. This novel is infused with gentle storytelling that reminded me of Wendell Berry, elegant prose that brought to mind Marilynne Robinson, and salt of the earth characters reminiscent of Leif Enger. The great delight that I found while reading, however, was what Kelly Flanagan brought to this story that only he could—a deep insight into what makes us human and how that makes us worthy of being seen and known."

Susie Finkbeiner, author of *The Nature of Small Birds* and *All Manner of Things*

"A captivating story illustrating the power and redemption in knowing oneself and being known. Kelly Flanagan weaves together wisdom, humor, faith, and relationship to beautifully portray a path for Eli to wholeness and healing, and a path all of us need to take. Numerous times while reading this novel I was convicted regarding my own areas of hiding and the need to take additional steps into the light."

Michael MacKenzie, executive director of Marble Retreat and author of *Don't Blow Up Your Ministry: Defuse the Underlying Issues That Take Pastors Down*

"*Tuesdays with Morrie* meets *The Shack* in *The Unhiding of Elijah Campbell*. A pitch-perfect page-turner of a story about one man's dismantling and reconstruction as he collides with his past. Authentic, heart-rending, absorbing, and wise, this book hits the bull's-eye of psychological and spiritual relevance. I closed the cover with new clarity, new conviction, and, I hope, new capability to forgive and love."

Cheryl Grey Bostrom, author of *Sugar Birds*

"Through the captivating and poignant voice of Elijah Campbell, Flanagan takes us to the depths of brokenness and on the slow climb toward healing. This story invites us not only to unhide from one another but also to see in every glory and specter of our past the grace-filled presence of the One who keeps company with us through it all."

Diana Gruver, author of *Companions in the Darkness: Seven Saints Who Struggled with Depression and Doubt*

THE UNHIDING OF ELIJAH CAMPBELL

A Novel

Kelly Flanagan

An imprint of InterVarsity Press
Downers Grove, Illinois

InterVarsity Press
P.O. Box 1400 | Downers Grove, IL 60515-1426
ivpress.com | email@ivpress.com

InterVarsity Press® is the publishing division of InterVarsity Christian Fellowship/USA®. For more information, visit intervarsity.org.

All Scripture quotations, unless otherwise indicated, are taken from The Holy Bible, New International Version®, NIV®. Copyright © 1973, 1978, 1984, 2011 by Biblica, Inc.™ Used by permission of Zondervan. All rights reserved worldwide. www.zondervan.com. The "NIV" and "New International Version" are trademarks registered in the United States Patent and Trademark Office by Biblica, Inc.™

Published in association with Creative Trust Literary Group LLC, 320 Seven Springs Way, Suite 250, Brentwood, TN 37027, www.creativetrust.com.

While any stories in this book are true, some names and identifying information may have been changed to protect the privacy of individuals.

The publisher cannot verify the accuracy or functionality of website URLs used in this book beyond the date of publication.

Cover design and image composite: David Fassett
Interior design: Jeanna Wiggins

ISBN 978-1-5140-0228-5 (print) | ISBN 978-1-5140-0229-2 (digital)

Printed in the United States of America ♾

Library of Congress Cataloging-in-Publication Data
A catalog record for this book is available from the Library of Congress.

29 28 27 26 25 24 23 22 | 8 7 6 5 4 3 2 1

He said, "We all got secrets. I got them same as everybody else—things we feel bad about and wish hadn't ever happened. Hurtful things. Long ago things. We're all scared and lonesome, but most of the time we keep it hid. It's like every one of us has lost his way so bad we don't even know which way is home any more only we're ashamed to ask. You know what would happen if we would own up we're lost and ask? Why, what would happen is we'd find out home is each other."

FREDERICK BUECHNER

To Kathryn Helmers, my agent, who kept asking,

"What if?" until if came true.

PROLOGUE

THE PAST IS BEHIND US, but it is also, always, within us. Which means the past can feel dead and gone one moment and then, in the next, it can be very much living and breathing and *here*. My past came back to life in the form of a nightmare I hadn't dreamed in over thirty years.

When I was a child, the nightmare always began the same way, with me standing at a river's edge, watching it rush by, brownly opaque with mud, swollen with storm debris, and foamy with turmoil. It was the kind of cataclysmic river in which a kid could disappear without warning, carried downstream to rot in some unpredictable destination. An old wooden bridge spanned the river. Though it had probably been a feat of humankind at its creation, its glory days were clearly behind it. The railings were gone. Most of the walkway had been torn away by storms long forgotten. The remaining planks were rotted and loose and spaced out, some resting where they were originally placed, some resting at angles. Large gaps in the walkway revealed the roiling waters just a few yards below it.

Beyond the bridge, the other side of the river was always cloaked in fog. I had no idea what the fog hid, and yet—with the kind of certainty that can only be called faith, the kind of anticipation that can only be called hope, and the kind of longing that can only be called love—I wanted to find out. So I'd look down, preparing to take my first step, and I'd see on my feet a pair of worn-out blue sneakers with yellow trim. They were so dirty the yellow looked almost brown and the blue looked almost black. The shoe on my right foot had a hole at the front of it, and my big toe protruded, covered by a dusty sock.

Every night, the dream seemed to contain all its previous renditions, so I knew exactly how it was going to end. I knew I would step out onto the bridge and the water would rise and it would be impossible to escape it and, as it reached me, I would silently scream myself awake. However, I also knew I'd step out onto the bridge anyway, yearning so much for the opposite shore that I was willing to endure the familiar terror at least one more time.

Sometime around middle school, the dream seemed to die. I went to sleep one night, and it didn't go with me. Weeks passed. No nightmare. Then months passed, then years, and somewhere along the way I forgot about that old nightmare altogether. It turns out, though, it hadn't died. It had simply gone dormant. Or maybe it *had* died, and almost three decades later, on the cusp of my fortieth birthday, it was resurrected.

I don't think the future is ever predetermined, but I do think our futures are *eventually* determined by what we do with these moments of resurrection, especially when such moments cluster together, forming a sort of bridge in the middle of our life, one we may cross to new ground or one we may turn back from, retreading the ground from which we came. My bridge was made of that old nightmare. It was also made of a secret I kept from everyone so long I eventually began to keep it from myself, and a secret that was kept from me for so long I never knew it existed. My bridge was made of a bunch of lost loved ones who came to life again within the magic of memory and the mystery of imagination. It was made of a God I once loved who went silent, and then one day started speaking to me again through those beloved ghosts of mine.

In the Bible, Jesus dies on a Friday, and there's a lot of talk about that. Then he's resurrected on a Sunday, and there's even more talk about that. No one talks much about Saturday, though. Death and resurrection. No one talks much about the *and* that bridges the two. Sometimes, though, all of life can begin to feel like an *and*. Every day can start to feel like the Saturday between what happened to you and what you will—or will not—do with it. And once you recognize your bridge for what it is, you have to decide whether you'll cross it with no guarantees of surviving the passage, just the merest of hopes that it will deliver you to more graceful ground. It took me a long time to recognize my *and*—my Saturday, my bridge—for what it was. Too long. It began with a leg in my lap, more than a decade before the nightmare resumed.

My name is Elijah Campbell, and this is the story of my unhiding.

SOMETIMES YOU DON'T KNOW YOUR LIFE has been on pause until someone or something hits play. My someone was Rebecca. My something was that leg of hers, lifted from the cracked and crumbling concrete of the old patio where we sat facing each other, and lowered onto my lap, bridging the gap between us.

It was beautiful and it was brash and it completely blindsided me.

We'd met a month earlier on the first day of orientation for our graduate program in clinical psychology at the University of Pennsylvania. She'd spent most of the month going out of her way to connect with me, sending me signals that had gone well over my head. Finally, she'd decided to send me one that landed right in my lap.

The day had begun typically enough. A morning of study followed by a hot dog in the microwave for lunch, carried on a paper plate to the back patio of the dilapidated duplex I was leasing for the year. The patio was just outside some sliding glass doors that didn't look very glassy with all the grime caked on them and, for that matter, didn't so much slide as grind upon opening.

It was a Friday in October, a fall afternoon poised so perfectly between summer and winter that the former seemed a distant memory and the latter an impossibility. I was sitting in a plastic forest-green deck chair left behind by some previous renter of the duplex—the half-eaten hot dog perched on my lap, my face turned to the sun, eyes closed—when Rebecca walked around the corner of the building. Her shadow darkened the backs of my eyelids as she cautiously said my name, and I startled so dramatically the flimsy chair nearly toppled backward, the hot dog rolling to the ground where it collected flakes of fallen leaves.

She picked up the gritty frank, examined it theatrically, and said with bemusement, "Campbell, I'm not sure if I should apologize to you for ruining your lunch, or if you should thank me for saving you from this mystery meat."

My embarrassment about being seen in such an unguarded moment was momentarily relieved by her playfulness. I paused for effect, then folded my hands into a namaste pose before bowing and saying with exaggerated solemnity, "Thank you."

She laughed, and her laughter sounded like the autumn light.

Then she dragged the only other deck chair—a white one originally, now soiled and aged into a dull khaki color—so it faced mine, and she sat down with our knees almost touching. As we made small talk about our classes and our classmates, I asked her casually what she was doing that evening. Cue her leg in my lap. And her response:

"I don't know, Campbell, what are *you* doing this evening?"

The whole thing sent a surge through me, twin threads of hope and fear intertwined—the conflicted response of someone whose loneliness is both their greatest wound and their most dependable defense. I stared down at the tattoo of a great egret on her ankle, framed by skin still bronzed by summertime, and I suddenly felt like an understudy called into the spotlight on opening night. The heat of her attention brought out prickles of sweat on my brow.

"I, uh, well, you know, I'm not sure. Actually, I think I do have some plans, but, uh, yeah, they're no big deal. I could probably cancel them. But, well, probably not, so, um, yeah . . ."

The truth was, my roommate had set me up on a blind date for that evening.

I took a deep breath and tried to recover my most reliable way of responding when my walls were about to be breached: a smile so bright no one's scrutiny had ever survived its wattage. It wasn't a calculated smile; it was instinctive—the closest cousin to sincerity—which is probably why it had always been so effective. I often paired it with some charismatic question or another and, voilà, the spotlight would swing away from me. Leaving me in the dark again, but safe at least.

I beamed, but the reiteration of my original question—"What are *you* doing tonight?"—came out sounding a little too desperate.

Rebecca studied me thoughtfully with her hazel eyes. The brown waves of her hair glinted in the sunlight, revealing natural auburn highlights. The prickles of sweat on my forehead threatened to become beads as I waited for her to judge me with those hazel eyes, lower her leg, and move on to a guy who could field a simple question about his whereabouts without acting utterly exposed.

Instead, she doubled down, lifting her other leg and crossing it over the first.

"It wasn't fair to start with such a difficult question," she announced matter-of-factly. We both knew it wasn't a hard question. Yet in her tone I could hear full permission for it to have been difficult for *me*. That felt like a gift. No one had given me a gift like that in a very long time.

"I tell you what," she went on, "if I'm not going to get to know you better tonight, we should get to know each other better right now. Let's play Two Truths and a Lie."

It sounded like the kind of game I'd be about one-third comfortable with, but I was so grateful for the gift she'd just given me, I was hesitant to turn her down. "I haven't heard of that one. How does it go?" Trying not to sound too cautious and mostly succeeding.

"It's simple," she answered, a smile in her voice and on her face. "I tell you three things about myself. Two of them are true, and one isn't, and you have to guess which one isn't. Then it'll be your turn. Cool?" She held out her knuckles for a fist bump.

I focused on how the spotlight was about to swing to her while ignoring that it would eventually swing back to me. "Cool," I agreed, reaching out and tapping her knuckles with my own. When they touched, it closed some kind of circuit between us, and a current ran right through me. Suddenly, I was awake.

I had no idea I'd been asleep.

"Okay. Hmmm," she said, and as she contemplated what to say, she used a forefinger to tug her lower lip down before releasing it with a *plop* as it returned to her upper lip. Over and over again. *Plop. Plop. Plop.* It was both very innocent and exceptionally attractive.

"Got it!" She looked me in the eye. "I once lost my passport while illegally squatting on an abandoned vineyard in the hills of Italy and got back to Maryland without any help from anybody.

I've been skydiving, twice. And I have three tattoos. Okay, which one is a lie?"

She recrossed her legs. The color of the great egret on her ankle changed from blue to purple as it shifted from light to shadow.

"I'm guessing the last one is a lie; you only have this one tattoo."

She smiled again, rotating her right arm to expose a tattoo of a cross on the underside of her wrist. "Wrong. I do actually have three tattoos."

She didn't show me the third. It made me wonder.

"The lie," she revealed, "was that I've only gone skydiving once. Okay, your turn!"

She leaned forward and rested her chin on her fist like Rodin's *The Thinker*, settling in to fully listen to me, and the scrutiny was like a thousand spotlights—no smile of mine could outshine it. I decided the quickest way to get out of the spotlight was to get my line over with, so I barreled ahead.

"I'm from a small town in Illinois called Bradford's Ferry. Pretty much everybody calls me Eli—yes, that rhymes with belly. And," I paused, trying to come up with a lie, "both of my parents are dead." That, of course, was a terrible way to get out of the spotlight. The guy who'd been voted Most Socially Skilled by his graduating class appeared to have exited stage left.

Rebecca's eyebrows creased and the hand she'd been resting her chin on covered her mouth. "Oh no, I hope it's the last one?"

I ran my palm over my forehead and it came away damp. "Yes, it's the last one. I'm sorry. It was thoughtless of me to insert that into a fun game. My dad passed away almost seven years ago, but my mom is alive and well in Bradford's Ferry." I saw the question in her eyes. "Heart attack while shoveling. Right before I got home for Christmas break, sophomore year of college."

"I'm so sorry," she said, and she sounded like she really was.

"It's okay. I mean, thank you. But I'm okay now, and my relationship with my dad was complicated . . ." I stopped, appalled by my apparent eagerness to tell her something I'd planned to take to the grave. "There I go again, getting all serious. Okay, your turn to be a buzzkill!" Self-deprecation. It worked. Perhaps Mr. Most Socially Skilled wasn't completely AWOL.

Rebecca smiled again and reluctantly but graciously stepped back into the spotlight. After taking a moment to collect herself, she offered her next round. "Someday, I want to be a therapist for underresourced children. I once found a two-legged turtle and nursed him back to health and he became my pet. I named him Geppetto. And I think I really like you, Elijah Campbell."

My smile was easier to find this time, and every lumen of it was for real. My rejoinder also came naturally. "Well, I certainly hope the last one isn't a lie."

"It's not," she replied, instantly yet gently.

"Then, I'm going to guess it's the second one."

"Correct you are, sir. Geppetto had three legs, not two."

At this, a genuine laugh escaped me, and the look on Rebecca's face suggested a laugh from me was the reward she'd come for.

"Okay, your turn," she said, returning to her *Thinker* position. But I was saved by a buzzing in her backpack. She pulled out her cellphone, flipped it open, and tilted her head to talk to the caller. More red highlights shimmered like the red leaves in the maple next to the patio. She slapped the phone shut.

"Gotta go," she announced as she lowered her legs and stood up. "My roommate and I are shopping for a used couch this afternoon, and she thinks she has a lead."

She held out her knuckles again. Again I tapped them. Again the electricity.

She turned on her heels and hollered, "See you, Eli!" over her shoulder, pronouncing my name correctly. She'd actually been listening. Her spotlight was already seeming a little safer than all the rest. And suddenly it was the prospect of her leaving that made me feel uncomfortable and impulsive. The impulse was to prolong the conversation just a little longer.

"Hey!" I called. She stopped and turned. "Do *you* go by any nicknames?"

She shook her head. "Nope. Just Rebecca. The whole name. I've always wanted it that way. It reminds me to show up with my whole self." She paused, thoughtful. "I guess I expect others to show up with their whole self too. Even if they *have* shortened *their* name." She smiled mischievously. "Well, if I don't see you tonight, I'll try to swing by again next Friday, maybe catch you sunning yourself like a turtle again."

Like a turtle.

The phrase got into me. And a theory about Rebecca's interest in me began to form: like a turtle I had a shell, and like Geppetto she sensed a wound beneath the shell. She seemed oblivious to the parallels, but the comparison put a lump in my throat.

Then, she was gone.

THERE'S PROBABLY A FINE LINE between being smitten and becoming a stalker. For the next week, I walked that line.

I noticed where Rebecca liked to sit in each of our classrooms, and I started arriving early, positioning myself so I could observe her without her easily observing me. Every time she tugged her lower lip and it plopped back against her upper lip, I fell a little more madly in love with her.

I changed my evening running route so it took me by her first-floor apartment right at that moment when dusk had descended and lamps had been turned on, but no one had thought to close the curtains yet. Several nights in a row I caught a glimpse of her sitting on her new-used couch with her roommate, laughing at some syndicated sitcom or another.

I even went out of my way to shop at the supermarket near her apartment in the hopes of running into her. And it worked. Sort of. On Thursday afternoon I was tossing a package of hot dogs into my cart when I looked up and saw her debating heads of lettuce. I was so embarrassed by my purchase of mystery meat that I made a beeline for the checkout aisle and got out of the store as fast as I could.

I felt like I should file a restraining order against *myself*, and I wasn't proud of it.

More importantly, I didn't understand it. Before Rebecca put her leg on my lap, I would have told you I was just fine, thank you very much. A little bored with life, perhaps, but basically okay. For the last week, though, every time I'd thought of Rebecca's turtle—that shell, that lost leg—the same lump had returned to my throat.

In a way, I was familiar with that lump. It was the lump I felt whenever I was faced with another person's pain. An undergraduate adviser had called it compassion and said it was the superpower of the helping professions. I'd listened to him, declared psychology as my major, and my first month in graduate school had validated the decision. Every client I'd seen so far had put that lump in my throat, and I was more convinced than ever that most of our suffering is unnecessary: our hurts beget hurts and our flaws beget flaws because no one has taken the time to talk to us about them, to look at them, to turn them over and study them, to become familiar enough with them that we might actually come to have a choice about them.

This lack of examination goes back to the beginning, to the Garden of Eden, I think. What if God had kept us in the Garden and talked with us about our flaws so we might not have remained so ignorant about them and thus so doomed to repeat them? What if, instead of casting us *out*, he'd gathered us *in* to figure out the why of our mistakes—the who, what, where, and when? Throwing us out of the Garden. It never made much sense to me. I suspect that's why Jesus made so much sense to so many people. He invited people back into the Garden, through holes in the roof, through moments at a well, through loaves of bread and baskets of fish. As a therapist, I wanted to be part of inviting people back into the

Garden for a good conversation about what went wrong in their story.

But I'd never felt the lump toward *myself* before, and it was disconcerting. In it, I could feel an unfamiliar longing to be seen, to be known. However, I liked to think of myself as a "private person." Not evasive. Not scared. Just . . . private. I'd worn that word with pride. Then, Rebecca. And Geppetto. And the image of a hard shell hiding a missing limb. All week it had been difficult to look in the mirror without seeing a turtle staring back.

Eighteen hours after I'd absconded from the supermarket with a ten-pack of Oscar Mayer wieners, I sat on my patio on another fall Friday afternoon, though this one had more winter than summer in it. The sky was an overcast gray, the canopy of the maple next to the patio more sparse, the patio itself covered completely with leaves that had already fallen. A wind from the north made fifty degrees feel like forty.

Sitting in the dirty white chair, I stuffed my hands into the pockets of my coat. I'd forgone a hot dog in the hopes of taking Rebecca to lunch if she appeared, and my stomach was beginning to rumble. I checked my watch. One o'clock. Thirty minutes later than last week. I felt a tug of disappointment. I felt a tug of relief. I noted the disappointment was the stronger of the two tugs, and the lump returned to my throat. I stood and stepped toward the sliding doors but stopped short when I heard a rustle of leaves along the side of the house. I turned around. And there she was, standing beneath the maple.

"Hi," I said, with poorly pretended nonchalance.

She just stood there, doing that thing again with those hazel eyes of hers, looking me over, taking inventory. Her smile said she knew I'd been waiting for her, and that she knew I knew she knew, and that we didn't have to talk about it. The gifts just kept on coming.

"Want to get some lunch?" we asked simultaneously.

"Jinx!" we shouted at the same time, followed by synchronous laughter. I suppose if you're not becoming like kids again as you fall in love, you're probably falling into something other than love.

"I'm buying," I said quickly, trying to avoid another jinx.

"You're on, Campbell. I'm dying for a Big Mac."

I breathed an inner sigh of relief. McDonald's was relatively cheap, and my student loan money had been dwindling quickly.

She shivered. I walked toward her, shedding my coat and throwing it around her. She pulled it close, saying, "I don't usually go for such chivalry, but thank you. This weather caught me off guard. Do you need to get another coat for yourself?"

"No, no, I'm fine," I replied, trying to sound casual.

I wasn't fine. I was freezing. However, I didn't have another coat.

"All right," she said, taking me at my word and turning with her arm crooked so I could link mine through it. "Shall we?"

Thankfully, the nearest McDonald's was just a few breezy blocks away. I learned along the way that she'd gotten the egret tattoo because it was the city symbol of Seaside, Maryland, the beach town where her parents lived. I told her tattoos were counterintuitive to me—there's enough pain in life without seeking out more of it voluntarily. She told me that was part of what she loved about tattoos—they hurt while they're happening, but you love them in the long run, and she was planning to turn as much hurt as possible into something that could be loved in the long run.

I thought of her turtle and the lump returned.

We supersized our meals and chose a table where the cloudy residue of someone's halfhearted swipes at sanitizing could still be seen. By the time she'd polished off her Big Mac, Rebecca knew I was an only child, and I knew she had two younger sisters, who she adored. I knew she loved her mother without caveat, but she was without question a daddy's girl, even though I could already sense she'd bristle at the label. Her father was an attorney. Mine had been a lawyer, too, before his death. I was relieved at finding some common ground again.

The conversation was clipping along nicely until I saw him.

He sat alone at a table for two, directly facing me over Rebecca's shoulder. He was probably forty years old and wore a short-sleeved button-down shirt with a bland brown tie. It was poorly knotted and sagged away from the collar, not intentionally but obliviously. A head of strawberry-red hair about a month past due for a cut was overly combed to the side and slicked down in a way meant to blend him into the world, but it advertised effort and had the opposite effect. A weak chin beneath thin lips that were topped by a scraggly mustache. A face so boyish it would never be respected in any setting requiring him to wear a tie. Big, gentle, puddly eyes, creased by sadness at the corners and framed by glasses left over from a previous generation. He ate french fries one at a time and stared straight ahead. Straight at me, actually, but really through me. The kind of stare that is always looking into a past it can't seem to escape.

The lump in my throat was so big I could barely breathe, let alone eat.

I tried to bring my attention back to what Rebecca was saying. Apparently her father was not just an attorney but a very successful one. The kind of success that allows you to buy one of those houses at the shore that tourists drive by every summer, gawking, wondering what *those* people do for a living, assuming it must be something exceedingly evil. His vocation was the opposite of evil. He was in environmental law and sued really wealthy companies for doing really terrible things to the planet. The Earth had thanked him for his service by rewarding him with one of its finer views.

"Eli? Are you okay?" I got the feeling she'd asked me a question to which I hadn't responded. She sounded worried.

"Yeah," I said, bringing my attention fully back to her. "It's just this guy over there. He's . . . I don't know, there's something about him. It's sort of messing me up."

She responded to the huskiness in my voice by briefly placing her hand over mine. Then she brushed a napkin to the floor, bending over casually to retrieve it while turning her head slightly to see the man. By the time our eyes met again, there was understanding in hers.

"Oh my goodness, Eli, he's so lonely looking."

At the word *lonely*, something in me unraveled, something that had been wound up tight for a very long time, wound so tight I hadn't consciously known it was there, though the lump in my throat had probably known it all along.

Rebecca was asking again if I was okay. I sort of heard her and sort of didn't as I got up and walked to the table where he sat. I exchanged words with him, the puddles in his eyes growing a little larger, different creases appearing at the corners of them as his lips formed a rusty little smile. I wished him a good day and turned back to our table, where Rebecca was watching me, her mouth slightly ajar.

"I'm sorry," I said, taking my seat again. Her mouth was still ajar. I felt prickly hot with self-consciousness again. "That was rude of me to leave you sitting here like that." Still ajar. The forehead sheen was about to make its return. "I don't know what came over me. I hope you can forgive me."

Her teeth clicked together as she closed her mouth. "What did you say to him?"

"Well, I, the guy, you know, you said it, he's lonely, it's oozing from his pores. I just wanted to let him know he'd been seen by somebody." I corrected myself. "I guess I *needed* to let him know that. So I apologized for interrupting his lunch and told him he has the kind of eyes that make the world feel like a safer place to me."

I was too embarrassed to look her in the eye, so I looked past her once again at the man who was still staring off into the distance. The stare looked different to me now, though. It seemed possible his past was forgotten for a moment. It seemed possible he was staring into his future.

Rebecca was silent. I forced myself to return my gaze to her face, cringing slightly at what I might find there. What I found was a trail of tears running down each of her cheeks. She looked at me that way for a long time. It didn't make me uncomfortable though. In fact, I was feeling something exceptionally pleasant, something I hadn't felt in a long time: hope disentangled from fear.

It seemed possible that Rebecca Miller, too, was staring into her future, and I was a part of it.

REBECCA AND I NEVER REALLY made anything official. One week she was putting her leg in my lap, the next we were eating at McDonald's, and by the following week I was having a hard time focusing on much of anything else. The rest of that autumn was a blur, the kind of blur you must see when you're falling from a high cliff into the ocean below. Rebecca was my ocean and I was falling fast. Everything else was just the world I happened to be falling through.

By the time winter break rolled around, going our separate directions already felt unnatural. Nevertheless, she planned to return to Maryland for the holidays, and I had no plans at all. I'd considered returning to Bradford's Ferry for a day or two. There would be old friends gathering at the Draughty Den—a cozy, dimly lit pub on Main Street—including my best childhood friend, Benjamin, a burgeoning literary agent. Everyone would be sipping beer, watching the snow fall past wreaths hanging from the streetlamps outside, retelling old stories. But that reward just wasn't worth the investment to me: the long bus ride home, the stilted conversations with my mother, the otherwise deafening silence of my childhood home, the long bus ride back. Rebecca left campus the Friday before Christmas.

She was very nearly killed three days later, on the shortest day of the year.

The phone call from her mother woke me up just before noon. Rebecca had been driving home shortly after midnight, returning from a night out with old friends. She was sober. The other driver was not. She glanced left, saw his failure to slow down for his red light, and tried to hit the brakes. A rare Maryland dusting of snow on untreated roads added up to a slippery surface. She skidded into the intersection, and he collided with her side of the car at thirty-five miles an hour. By the time she awoke eight hours later, the doctors were describing her survival as a miracle, side-impact airbag or not. She had some minor cuts, some bad bruises, and two cracked ribs, but the worst of it was a severe concussion. Upon waking, she'd asked her mother to call me. It was the first they were hearing of me. She'd planned to tell them about me on Christmas morning.

I asked Mrs. Miller if I could come see Rebecca. I heard some hesitation in her yes but pretended I didn't. I threw some clothes in a bag, purchased a ticket for the earliest train out of Philadelphia, and was in Seaside, Maryland, by dinnertime. I met her parents in the hospital waiting room. I was unshaven and pretty sure I hadn't brushed my teeth on the way out the door, but of course they weren't really focused on me.

Rebecca was heavily sedated, buying time for her brain to recover from the closed head injury. However, she was conscious enough for the corners of her lips to curl upward on seeing me, and for a tear to roll down her cheek when visiting hours for everyone but family were over. I took that tear to mean she wished I was family. I wished I was too.

Over the next several days, I found myself in a strange situation: I was living in the home of people who barely knew me, wanting nothing more than to care for their daughter but knowing my name fell way below theirs on the list of candidates for primary caregiver. So I made myself useful by offering to pick up the slack in their home instead. They cautiously accepted my offer. I bought groceries. I waited at the house to sign for some last-minute FedEx Christmas shipments. I even wrapped a pile of presents.

By the time Rebecca was released from the hospital on Christmas morning, I'd been gladly added to the Miller guest list for the rest of our winter break. They were courteous enough to ask if my mother might be offended by me spending the holiday with another family. I told them my mother was perfectly pleased by the size of her holiday gathering. It was true. It was also true she spent the holiday completely alone.

Their home was beautiful, but the beauty of those two weeks went far deeper than tasteful decor, warm lighting, and ocean sunrises filtering through my bedroom blinds. It was beautiful for its lack of pretense, for the sincere affection shown among the Millers, for how different they were from each other and how much they celebrated those differences, for the sense that nothing was being withheld. By the time the break was over, I was reluctant to leave.

In the days before we departed, Rebecca's father offered to buy her a new car. She declined for the same reason she'd made her way home from Italy on her own: she liked to know she was strong enough to stand on her own two feet. So she rented a car instead, and we drove back to Philadelphia.

The next day, before we returned the rental, I went car shopping with her. Rebecca had only enough money to look at used car lots. I suggested that together we had enough money to split the cost of a new car in a responsible price range. She mulled it over for about two seconds and agreed. Our first purchase together was a Ford, but I think it was more than a car—it was Rebecca's acknowledgment that I'd become a part of her independence, not a threat to it.

For Rebecca, the purchase tapped out her automotive budget for the rest of the academic year. For me, it tapped out my entire savings. I didn't tell her that, though. There were credit cards for situations like these. Also, I didn't feel like I'd just spent thousands of dollars I couldn't afford. I felt like I'd just found my calling, and it was priceless: I was going to give Rebecca Miller the life she deserved.

～

The following Christmas, I used a credit card to purchase Rebecca's engagement ring. At the time, the debt didn't bother me, because over the previous year credit cards had become both a necessity and a habit of mine. I just kept telling myself that only a few years and a couple of doctoral degrees stood between us and financial freedom.

However, it did bother me a little more the year after *that*, when in January we were married along the ocean in the Millers' backyard. It bothered me because our marriage meant we would soon mingle our finances and start paying bills from a joint account; therefore, in a way, she was about to pay for half of her own engagement ring.

It was a shameful thought, in direct contradiction to the purpose I'd identified for my life. So I ignored it, just as I'd ignored the hesitation in her mother's voice when she'd agreed I could join them at Rebecca's bedside. In other words, at first I knew it was there, but I simply looked the other way until I eventually forgot it had been there at all. I'd gotten so good at keeping secrets, I could even keep them from myself.

ᴖᴗ

Our honeymoon was a humble one, much like our car, and for much the same reason. Mr. Miller—he'd asked me to call him "Dad," but I couldn't bring myself to do so, for reasons I didn't understand—had offered to send us somewhere sunny and sandy, but Rebecca had again insisted we pay for it ourselves. So we spent a long weekend in the wine country of upper New York State. Peak tourism in the region is late summer and early fall. By January, hotel rates are rock bottom, and the wineries are so glad to see you they become very generous with their free pours. Beyond the occasional wine tasting, there wasn't much to do that weekend. That was fine with us. We weren't terribly motivated to leave our hotel room.

Which is probably why Rebecca found my journal.

I'd been journaling daily since our first date at McDonald's, but until Rebecca discovered the journal, there wasn't another soul in the world who knew about it. I was in the shower and she was bored, rooting through the stack of books I'd shoved into our suitcase, when she came across something smaller and leather bound. You can't really blame her for opening it, though I tried to when I walked out of the foggy bathroom and saw her holding it. She brushed aside my anger like you'd brush away a gnat distracting you from a glorious sunset. She was in awe, which really is the best reaction you can hope for when someone sees you turned inside out.

Holding it up, she delivered my first review. "Eli, this is exquisite. It's like you're speaking to all the clients you've worked with. It's like . . ." She left from behind her eyes and traveled backward through time, then returned. " . . . it's like you're speaking to that man at McDonald's again. It's like God is speaking through you to *all* of us, letting us know we matter to him, no matter how overlooked or ashamed we might feel. Where . . . where did this *come* from?"

It came from the voices within me, which had grown more graceful since I met Rebecca.

As a kid, the God who'd spoken to me through my church had been distant, disappointed, and dangerous. He hung out up in the heavens somewhere, mostly out of reach, and was more like Santa than like Jesus, keeping a list and checking it twice. You always seemed to come out naughty in his final tally, and he seemed a little trigger happy about casting you into hell for eternity. I'd watched my parents in the pews, nodding at all of it, as if it made complete sense to them, as if a love like that was one in which they could gladly participate. I'd figured it explained a lot about my parents and decided I wanted nothing to do with any of it. So when I'd gone off to the University of Illinois and met a bunch of atheists who were mostly happy, kind, and good, I tried to be one of them. No matter how hard I tried, though, I just couldn't get rid of my parents' God. However, he no longer felt so distant—rather, he lived on in the form of a disappointed and dangerous voice *within* me.

Then another voice had entered my life: Rebecca.

It seemed clear to me that any God worth believing in must look on me with at least as much affection as she did. So I decided to believe in that kind of God by listening for a more loving voice and, gradually, in our first year together, I'd begun to hear it everywhere. I heard it in Rebecca, in the books I was reading, in the wind through the top of that big maple in the back of my duplex. Eventually, I even began to hear it within me—a still, small voice, whispering of my worthiness and the worthiness of all things. I'd begun to record what I was hearing in a journal, and I'd told no one about it. In that honeymoon hotel room, Rebecca told me I needed to tell *everyone* about it.

Everybody in my life had always underestimated me; Rebecca always rounded up.

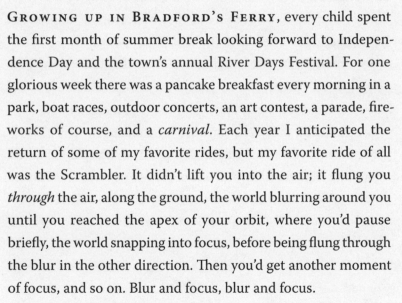

4

Growing up in Bradford's Ferry, every child spent the first month of summer break looking forward to Independence Day and the town's annual River Days Festival. For one glorious week there was a pancake breakfast every morning in a park, boat races, outdoor concerts, an art contest, a parade, fireworks of course, and a *carnival*. Each year I anticipated the return of some of my favorite rides, but my favorite ride of all was the Scrambler. It didn't lift you into the air; it flung you *through* the air, along the ground, the world blurring around you until you reached the apex of your orbit, where you'd pause briefly, the world snapping into focus, before being flung through the blur in the other direction. Then you'd get another moment of focus, and so on. Blur and focus, blur and focus.

The first decade of our marriage was a blur, with moments here and there that came into focus.

The morning after we returned from our honeymoon, I sat down at my computer in the modest apartment we'd rented off campus, searched Yahoo for how to join the blogging craze, set up a WordPress website, and published the first of more than five hundred entries from my journals. I called them "reflections" and was certain they wouldn't attract any kind of digital spotlight. Rebecca, on the other hand, insisted on calling them "inspirations" and predicted they would strike a chord in the blogosphere. It turns out she was right to round up about my writings. They went viral, over and over again. The ride was underway.

That first year of blogging was all blur.

Then, almost a year to the day after we returned from our honeymoon, Sarah arrived. The ride reached an apex and the world came into crystal-clear focus. Rebecca in labor for forty-eight hours, pushing for the last twelve, exhausted and scared but fighting to bring our little girl into the world. My first glimpse of Sarah's bald head. Her first howl. The rubbery resistance of her umbilical cord against scissors. The look on Rebecca's face when she first took Sarah into her arms, the look you might give your beloved on their return from a long journey.

Sarah's first year of life was more blur. My online platform was expanding exponentially, and one of my readers was an editor at a major publishing house. She reached out to me, asking if I had an agent. I said yes. It was almost true. By then, Benjamin had established himself as an influential literary agent, so I asked him if he'd like to represent me with the publishing house. We pinched ourselves—a couple kids from Bradford's Ferry publishing books together!—and within a month I had my first book contract. The first half of my advance arrived a week before our second anniversary. Theoretically, I put it in the bank. Actually, I put it toward credit card debt.

A week later, I had my first panic attack.

I was already stretched exceedingly thin by my various responsibilities: coursework, clinical training, dissertation research, figuring out how to be a husband and father, and writing my first book. So when it came time to travel the country to interview for our clinical residencies—the final hurdle before receiving our doctorates—it was the straw that broke Geppetto's shell, if you will. I'd been reading about panic attacks in my textbooks, but you can't really comprehend them until you've had one. Heart hammering wildly, sweating like a midsummer heat wave, certain you're on the verge of dying. I was afraid Rebecca would see me at my weakest and lose all faith in me.

Instead, she showed *more*.

She said the second half of my advance would be enough to get us through the next year. She said no marriage needs two doctors in it anyway. She said I'd be an amazing work-from-home father. She said I should drop out of graduate school and finish my book. She beamed as she said it. I momentarily considered correcting her assumptions about the advance—which I'd mostly already spent—but I didn't. I wanted to become the man she was imagining as her smile stretched from ear to ear. So I stayed quiet. I let the truth float briefly at the edge of my awareness, until it drifted away. And I became a full-time writer.

Most of what came after was especially blurry, though once in a while life would come into focus long enough for me to really see it.

For instance, the morning Rebecca found out her clinical residency would be in Chicago, just a couple hours east of Bradford's Ferry. The day we moved into a second-story flat in the Lincoln Park neighborhood of the city, within walking distance of the hospital where Rebecca would be a resident for a year. Later that day, when newly-walking Sarah tripped and skinned her knee on a sidewalk and reached for me instead of Rebecca.

The release of my first book—*The Whisper in the Wind*—about listening for the voice of God within us. The early sales reports suggesting it wouldn't be bothering any bestseller lists, but it would probably earn out its advance and eventually produce a little more income for our family.

Rebecca's graduation from UPenn. Her interview for her dream job in a western suburb of Chicago: a low-paying, full-time therapist position at a nonprofit community mental health center. The conversation about whether my writing career could compensate for her meager salary. My continued clarity of purpose: to give Rebecca Miller the life she deserved. Rebecca's butterflies upon leaving for her first day of work. Her joy upon returning.

A contract for a second book—*A Manifesto for Marriage*—about how the Beatitudes might shape our vision for marriage. Rebecca's mother teasing me about the temerity of writing such a book only four years into my own marriage. Benjamin telling me about the size of the advance, bigger than the first but not big enough to solve some monetary problems that were growing faster than their solutions. The week it was released and flirted with some bestseller lists. Finding out it would remain only a flirtation.

The afternoon Benjamin called to tell me *Manifesto* had sold well enough that my publisher had invited a third book proposal, blending the genres of my first two books. The week of our seventh wedding anniversary and Sarah's sixth birthday coinciding with the publication of *The Contemplative Couple*. A big party celebrating all three milestones. Sarah standing on her chair at the dining room table, blowing a kazoo, singing the praises of my new book, "The Competitive Couple."

Benjamin telling me the community forming around my books was beginning to see me as a guru of sorts, and my publisher wanted to capitalize on it. The word *guru* feeling like a very hot spotlight. Telling him I didn't understand why people thought I had it all figured out. Telling him I didn't write because I'd "arrived," I wrote because I was still struggling toward the place where all my readers were also hoping to arrive. Benjamin telling me to get over it because I had an offer for a fourth book, a sequel of sorts to my first one—working title: *The Voice in the Void.*

Sarah falling from a playground slide and breaking her wrist. Several weeks later, breaking my own wrist playing basketball at the gym. Typing with only one hand. Opening the hospital bills for both fractured appendages. Kicking myself for telling Rebecca to choose a high deductible plan. Stuffing the bills in a drawer and trying to focus on my manuscript.

On that Scrambler in Bradford's Ferry, it was blur and focus, blur and focus, until suddenly you sensed the ride was slowing down, and your time was up. It had never occurred to me the same thing could happen to my life. To my faith. To the words within me. To the purpose that had guided me. It had never occurred to me that my ride with Rebecca might come to an end.

It didn't occur to me until, on an otherwise ordinary Friday morning in August—just a few months short of our tenth anniversary—I was awakened by some rustling in our closet.

5

THE DAY BEFORE REBECCA LEFT ME began like any other, with one exception. There was an unnecessary rapidity in her morning routine, as if she couldn't get out the door soon enough.

It was a Thursday morning, and my cruise control was set to the speed we'd gradually established over Sarah's nine years of life. Wake up. Lie there. Grab for a phone and check email. Get up. Start the coffee. Stand and wait for it while checking the news. Wake Sarah and walk with her through her morning ritual: get dressed, get breakfast, banter, brush teeth, pack her lunchbox, pack her bookbag, kisses all around as my ladies rush out the door for work and school five minutes later than planned. All of it had a well-worn rhythm to it. A cadence. A pace.

Rebecca's pace was off.

She didn't stand by the coffeemaker with me, trading news stories. She went right from waking to the shower. She poured her coffee into a travel mug rather than the ceramic mug that I'd already prepared for her with cream and sugar. She ate a banana standing at the counter rather than a bowl of cereal at the table. It wasn't until I went to the fridge to prepare Sarah's lunch and discovered Rebecca had already packed it that I realized how eager she was to get out the door.

I watched her more closely as she quickly finished checking Sarah's bookbag for folders and homework, a pit threatening to form in my stomach. There was an urgency and an absence to her. Even as she gave Sarah's hair one final brushing she was, for all intents and purposes, already out the door. Sarah kissed me on the cheek as she said goodbye, but Rebecca didn't, and they left for work and school five minutes *early*.

Rebecca, it seemed, had finally run out of patience.

*So, how close *are* you?"

Benjamin's smile was warm and relaxed, but I'd known him long enough to know it was a reflection not of what he felt but of what he wanted me to feel. Behind that smile was the understandable tension of a literary agent whose client was already six months past the deadline for delivering a first draft of his next book. I heard the tension not so much in what he said but in how quickly he said it. No catching up about our kids first. No reminiscing about old times in Bradford's Ferry. No sports talk. It was August, and the Cubs held the best record in baseball after having swept the Marlins at Wrigley. Benjamin didn't even mention it. My old friend was wound *tight*.

I reflexively mirrored the warmth of his smile. "B, it's almost there. I'm about to let Rebecca read it, and she's going to weep." I made a lame joke about buying stock in Kleenex. "I'm sure she'll have a few suggestions, though. I'll make a couple of tweaks and then it will be good to go. It's close. Really close."

Despite his best effort, Benjamin's smile cooled a degree or two. Most people wouldn't have noticed it.

"Eli, I'd be happy to take a look at it too, if that would be helpful. In fact, Jill is so eager to get something on her desk, I'm sure she'd be happy to take a look at it right now, even if it's a little rougher than usual. Get the ball rolling on editorial ideas, you know?"

It was a nice offer, but embedded in it was the subtle suggestion that one of the most patient editors on the planet was beginning to lose her patience.

"That's really nice of you both." I played it off as if I hadn't noticed any pressure in the offer of support. "You know me, though. Rebecca has been my first reader for every blog post and book manuscript since she found that journal of mine on our honeymoon, and I'm superstitious. It would be bad luck to change things up now."

His smile cooled more noticeably, and he sat back, glancing around the Starbucks. Located on Michigan Avenue directly across from Millennium Park, it had become one of our preferred rendezvous spots during Rebecca's residency. I still enjoyed meeting him there in the anonymity of the city, where there weren't enough spotlights to go around. I gazed over his shoulder and out the window. The reflective gleam of the famous Bean could be glimpsed through the dense summertime foliage of the tree-lined park.

He leaned in again. "Eli, Jill told me in confidence that if she doesn't have a complete manuscript on her desk by Labor Day, the publisher is going to cancel your contract and recoup the first half of the advance."

I responded so confidently and calmly that even I believed it. "B, I've got this. Have I ever let you down?"

He sighed. "When have you ever let anybody down, Eli? But there's a first time for everything, especially ordinary things, like disappointing people."

"Now there's a book title for you: *There's a First Time for Every Ordinary Thing*. When are you finally going to join us pathetic scribes and write a book of your own?" I asked jovially.

With that, I steered the conversation toward more comfortable topics, like raising daughters, warming oceans, the demise of the Western church. Benjamin was unable to resist. An hour quickly passed before he had to leave for his next meeting. As we walked out of the Starbucks into the kind of liquid heat you can only find in two places—the equator and Chicago in August—we exchanged a hug, patting each other's back the way men do, inserting just a hint of aggression into the intimacy. This time, though, it seemed Benjamin's pats were on the verge of becoming smacks.

We were turning to go our separate ways when I said, "Hey, how about those Cubs." Half question, half statement, a whole invitation to end our meeting on a lighter note.

Benjamin paused. Then that smile again, too warm and too relaxed. "Just make sure you have it to us by the end of the month, Eli."

He turned and walked away, as rapidly as Rebecca had walked out the door that morning.

~~

Just hours after meeting with Benjamin, my therapist's patience seemed to be failing too.

I'd begun meeting with Jeff six months earlier, the week of my manuscript deadline. I'd left everyone with the impression

I would meet the deadline, but I knew I couldn't, and one morning while I was alone at home my heart started slamming, the room started spinning, and I lost the ability to breathe. My first panic attack since the one that had turned me into a career author.

That evening, when Rebecca arrived home, I explained to her casually that this next book was going to be a huge success, and success attracts critics, and I needed to get better at handling the haters. So could she recommend a good therapist?

She studied me with those hazel eyes of hers—the way she'd once done under a big maple on a broken patio in Pennsylvania— though there was none of the old affection in her attention. She'd been asking me to go to couples counseling for a year. I'd always found an excuse to delay it. And here I was, wanting to talk to someone without her. I named her frustration before she could show it and reassured her I'd keep her in the loop about my conversations with my counselor. The offer softened her, and she recommended a colleague of a colleague.

I'd met with Jeff for the first time on a Thursday afternoon. Within the first few minutes of our first session, I experienced firsthand what we'd been taught at UPenn about therapeutic ambivalence. Our clinical director's favorite adage was, "Remember, no matter what your clients say, they are deeply ambivalent about being in therapy." Most clients simply want to patch their old life back together. They want to return to the best of what has been, not go on to discover the rest of what might be, because deep down they know that real change costs something. An old identity might have to die so a new one can grow up in its place. Cherished relationships might have to be relinquished. Life callings may be called into question.

Growth sounds great, in theory. In reality it's often a bloodbath.

Jeff and I had met almost every Thursday afternoon for six months. I'd been ambivalent about attending every session, but he had been unfailingly patient with me. However, in the same way I could feel the tension in Benjamin's back slaps, I could hear a seriousness in Jeff's voice I'd never heard before.

"Do you want to know my secret to being a decent therapist, Elijah?" he asked. Without waiting for an answer, he went on. "I can practically smell the emotions coming off people. Happiness has a scent. So does sadness. Anxiety. Anger. Peacefulness. They each have their own scent. It's not something I have to think about. I just sense it. Then instead of talking about what my clients want to discuss, I invite them to talk about the aroma that fills the room." He paused, looking at me with an expression of the same tender seriousness that was in his voice. "But you, Elijah, you are odorless. Six months into therapy, and I've barely caught a whiff of you."

I felt like I'd been slapped as kindly as possible. I didn't know what to say. So, I summoned the smile that had saved me on so many occasions, and I made a joke. I told him I'd create some odor by eating beans before our next session.

Jeff was an impeccable listener, but he continued as if he hadn't heard me. "I really care about you, Elijah. I like who you are and I love who you might become. So I'm going to be more transparent with you than I usually am with my clients. Before we began today, I decided this would either be our first real session or our final fake one."

He allowed some space for his words to sink in. I opened my mouth to respond, then closed it. I ignored the knot in my stomach.

"So," he continued, "are you ready to start talking about what matters? Are you ready to talk about why six months ago, at our first appointment, you admitted to me that you were stressed about your book deadline and now—six months beyond that very same deadline—it doesn't seem to be bothering you at all? Are you ready to talk about why you and Rebecca have quit going out on your monthly dates? Are you ready to talk about the circles that keep getting darker under your eyes? Are you ready to start talking about the burdens you're carrying?"

I responded indignantly. It wasn't a decision. It was an instinct. "I don't know what you're talking about, Jeff. I come in here every week to work on myself, and I feel like you're telling me that work has meant nothing. I tell you more than I tell anyone else in my life. I'm not sure what more you want from me."

"I don't want you to tell me *more*, Elijah, I want you to tell me the *truth*."

He relaxed backward into his chair, placing his elbows on the armrests, making it clear he was done speaking and was ready to wait for a different response.

The space behind my eyeballs began to pulse steadily, and the sensation brought to mind an actual spotlight from long, long ago: my seventh grade spelling bee, in front of the entire school, the moderator asking me to spell *supercilious*. I was pretty sure I couldn't spell it, and I'd felt hot tears threatening to form. Then, I'd smiled widely and spelled *three* words: "S-U-P-E-R. S-I-L-L-Y. U-S." The auditorium erupted in laughter, and I'd been a middle school hero for the rest of the week.

"Super silly us," I said to Jeff, smiling broadly and hopefully.

He didn't find it as funny as my seventh grade peers had. Instead, he just waited on me while I waited on him. I figured if I waited long enough, he'd say something. After all, I was *paying* him for this. As if he'd read my thoughts, he did speak.

"Let's end this session early, Elijah. I won't charge you for it. And when you are ready to open up, you can give me a call. I'll be eager to resume our sessions."

I was stunned. "You can't do that. You can't fire me. Ethically, I mean. I never finished my degree, but I was in grad school long enough to learn the ethical code."

"Actually Elijah, not only am I ethically permitted to end our therapy, but you could argue I'm required to do so. If you were coming in here legitimately struggling with something, suffering emotionally, then I would be ethically required to see you or to refer you to someone who could. But in six months, you've never given me any indication that you're really struggling with anything. When I sign your notes, I check a box that says your services are medically necessary, but by all appearances yours are not."

He stood and waited for me to follow suit. Slowly, I did. The pressure behind my eyes was back. *Supersillyus*, I said to myself. *Supersillyus. Supersillyus. Supersillyus.* Over and over again, the word repeated in my mind. As always, Jeff opened his door and stood aside to let me walk ahead of him out of the office. This time, though, he followed me down the long narrow hall to the suite's exit. "I wish you well, Elijah. I will think of you often. And for a long time, I will hope the next phone call I receive is from you."

He turned and walked back down the long hallway, disappearing out of sight around a corner. His pace was quite a bit slower than Rebecca's and Benjamin's, yet the message was even clearer. I'd worn out everyone's patience. Even the patience of those who practiced it for a living.

$\mathcal{uu}$

I didn't go straight home. I found excuses to delay in the form of errands I told myself needed to be done. I got gas; spent ten minutes cleaning big, unfortunate, Midwestern mosquitoes from my windshield; vacuumed a year's worth of debris from my floor mats; picked up bananas at the grocery store, ate one, and then decided I needed a second one, this time in the form of a banana split. By the time it was finished, one more dog day of summer was finished as well, the sun having put itself to rest beyond the horizon, only remnants of its lavender light still lingering in the western sky. Six months earlier, Rebecca would have texted me several times, wanting to be sure I was okay. Not tonight.

My phone was silent.

As I walked in the door, I could feel the hush that permeates a house with young children who have finally gone to bed. Sarah was asleep. I could hear the sounds of Rebecca in the kitchen, sink running, glasses clinking, finishing the day's chores. She would have heard the door, but there was no disruption to the clinking and cleaning.

I walked down the hall, past a series of framed photos on the wall documenting our development as a family. I entered the kitchen and eased up behind her, placing my hands on her hips. She didn't brush them away, but she didn't lean back into me, either. Those days were apparently behind us. Finally, she turned around and looked at me, and the look in her eyes quickly shifted from something hard to something concerned.

"Your eyes are red," she observed, "and you look like you've been crying. What happened? Are you okay?"

I opened my mouth to tell her what had happened, to tell her that my eyes were red because my therapist had fired me and I'd walked out of his office and gotten into my car and laid my head on the steering wheel and cried so hard it felt like something important had torn somewhere deep in my abdomen. Instead, what I heard coming out of my mouth was, "Have I ever told you the story about my seventh grade spelling bee?"

Rebecca stared at me, her lips slightly parted. To most observers, it would have seemed like a blank look. I knew it was her stunned look. She blinked hard, shaking it off, and shook her head emphatically from side to side. "No," she said.

I smiled that big, broad smile again and opened my mouth to tell the story, but before I could get a word out, she threw up her hand, palm out, fingers splayed, the skin made white with tautness.

"No, Elijah." She hadn't called me anything but Eli in years. "I don't mean, 'No, you haven't told me so lay it on me.'" She said it with an exasperation that made her sound more tired than I'd ever heard her. "I mean 'No,' as in, 'No more stories, Elijah. No more smiles. No more nonsense.' No. No. No. *No!*"

Each no had more jagged edges on it than the previous one. And with the final no still echoing in the air, she turned on her heels, walked into our bedroom, and slammed the door behind her.

It was a long while before I moved. I waited for the sounds in our bedroom to cease and for the light beneath the door to be extinguished. Then I slunk in, conducting my bedtime routine by the glow of my cellphone home screen, before climbing beneath the covers with Rebecca. I placed my hand on her hip. She rolled over so my hand slid off. Six inches separated us. It felt like six miles.

I fell asleep on my side of the chasm, telling myself none of this could be as final as it felt.

6

CLUNK. THUNK. Rustle, rustle, scritch, scratch. Bump. Another *clunk.*

I was accustomed to Rebecca waking up before me. The sounds of her day getting underway had been my alarm clock on countless mornings. Usually, though, those sounds came from the bathroom—a sink running, a toothbrush plunking back into its holder, the shower starting—and they usually started sometime after the sun was up, especially during the elongated days of summer. The sounds I was hearing, however, were coming from the closet, and my phone showed 5:05 above an image of Sarah holding her finger to her ice-cream-smeared lips in the universal sign of secret keeping.

"Rebecca," I croaked, "what's going on? Are you okay? What are you doing?" The rustling stopped. Rebecca emerged from the closet holding the largest suitcase from the set we'd received as a wedding gift. It was banged up, like us, but it still worked fine, like us. Or so I assumed.

"I'm leaving," Rebecca said as she walked to her dresser and began removing clothes with her back to me. "I've left a message at work. They've been telling me to take time off for years, so I think they'll understand, but if they don't, I don't care. I'm going to Maryland. Sarah still has a month of summer break left. She'll love spending it with my parents."

"You're leaving for a *month*?" I asked, my voice tight with incredulity, my disorientation deepening.

She stopped shoving clothes into the suitcase. I saw her shoulders slump. She turned slowly to face me. Her jaw was set resolutely, but moisture pooled on her lower eyelids.

"Eli, I'm not leaving for a month, I'm leaving for good. Obviously, we can't stay in Maryland forever. Sarah starts school the day after Labor Day. We'll come back. But I'm not coming back to this house. I told you a long time ago I was going to show up with my whole self, and I expected you to do the same. I've waited for the rest of you for years and I'm *done* waiting."

"Rebecca . . ." I began, but she held up the same hand she'd held up the night before. This time she didn't say anything, but I could still hear the echo of the *noes* that had accompanied it hours earlier. I stayed silent. She turned and resumed her packing, moving quickly again, like the morning before. As I lay there watching her, it hit me: both mornings looked less like a departure than an escape.

I'd quit drinking several years earlier, after an anniversary celebration during which I'd drunk way too much and had to lie awake in bed for several hours, waiting for the room to stop spinning. As I lay there listening to the sounds of Rebecca finishing the packing, rousing Sarah from her sleep, and pouring cereal for them both, the room seemed to be spinning again.

I closed my eyes and gathered myself. Formulated my appeal. Crafted it quickly in my head. Edited it. Polished it into a passable final draft. I got up, rehearsing my lines, and walked to the kitchen where my ladies were putting their bowls in the sink.

Sarah turned to me. I expected to see my dismay mirrored on her face, but of course she was all smiles.

"Daddy!" she chirped. "Mom planned a surprise trip to see Mom-mom and Pop-pop. We're leaving now and we get to stay for a whole month and Mom-mom's going to make pancakes every morning and Pop-pop's going to build sandcastles with me every day." She glowed while she said it, then grew more somber. "I wish you could go with us too, Daddy, but I know you have to stay here to finish your book. I'm going to miss you *so* much." She leaned into me and wrapped her arms around my waist. "I love you, Daddy."

I managed to clear my throat in order to play our game.

"I love you more, sweetie."

"I love you most, Daddy."

"I love you to infinity, sweetie."

"I love you to infinity and beyond, Daddy!" she said with her hands on her hips, like Buzz Lightyear.

I followed them to the door, opened it for them, and flashed back to Jeff opening the door for me just twelve hours earlier, back in a different lifetime. Sarah was beyond earshot when Rebecca turned to me one last time. This was my chance. I summoned my soliloquy.

However, I wasn't the author of this morning. Rebecca was.

She held up her hand again, silencing me before I began. "You've always tried so hard to give me everything I've wanted, but all I've ever really wanted is you, and when it comes to you, Eli, you're a total cheapskate. I'm done feeling like I don't know what's going on in my own life. I'm done reading your stuff to find out what's been going on in your head. I'm done sleeping next to a man I don't really know. I can be alone all by myself."

I opened my mouth to tell her she was right, to tell her I was tired of me too, to tell her secrets are the heaviest things to carry, to tell her I was ready to put them all down, to tell her I'd trade the safety of every secret I've ever kept for one more day with her and one more chance to make it right. I opened my mouth to say all of that and more, but like the previous night, I heard something else come out.

"I'm sorry I haven't lived up to your standards, Rebecca."

The fire in her eyes was her only reply. Then, they were gone.

7

In the February of my fifteenth year, I walked home from school in the midst of a winter day that was breaking records. The forecast had called for temperatures in the mid-fifties, but by the time the bell rang, the mercury was in the midsixties. We lived on a street without curbs and gutters, so water drained into gullies that ran alongside the road, and they were rushing with melting snow trying to find its way to lower places. In those racing waters, I'd seen the promise of springtime and warmth and light and leaves and short sleeves. I walked the final block home with a bounce in my step, changed into shorts and a T-shirt, and spent the remaining daylight shooting baskets alone in my driveway, visions of summertime dancing in my head.

The next day the temperature plunged, and the water in those gullies froze and stayed frozen until the real arrival of springtime. But for one afternoon I let the weather untether me from the reality of the winter still ahead.

More than a decade later, in graduate school, I'd recalled that afternoon while listening to a lecture about *depressive realism*. For decades, psychologists had assumed people become depressed because they view the world pessimistically. However, a group of researchers proved this wrong. When they brought depressed people and happy people into a laboratory to watch social scenes and then asked them to report on what had happened, the depressed people were actually *more accurate* reporters of reality. It turns out that depressed people see the world accurately, and happy people view the world with an optimism slightly removed from reality. That had been my preferred method for staying happy since I was fifteen years old.

On the day Rebecca left, I didn't think about that melting afternoon in my adolescence, nor did I even really attend to the reality of the moment. Instead, I did what I'd been doing for a quarter of a century: whatever it took to keep a smile on my face.

~~~

I had no memory of pouring the cereal nor of eating it. After Rebecca's car pulled away, I must have walked into the kitchen, opened the pantry, chosen Sarah's cocoa-infused cereal reserved for special occasions, decided this was a special occasion, and poured myself a bowl.

The metallic clack of our mailbox lid brought me back to attention.

I blinked. Looked down. Noticed one lone, brownish sphere floating in a puddle of muddy milk. I tilted the bowl to my lips and finished it off before setting the bowl in the sink and retrieving the mail. I shuffled through it on the way to my study. A flier from a realtor we'd almost worked with a number of years ago. An opportunity to upgrade our internet speeds. And a stack of bills.

I dropped the junk mail into a recycling bin by the door and tugged on the knob to the topmost drawer of my desk, where I stored bills I didn't want to think about. It didn't budge. I tugged harder, heard a ripping sound from within it, and almost fell backward as the drawer released. Several envelopes—including the one that had just ripped, a thick one from the insurance company explaining how much I owed the hospital—sprang from the drawer and fell to the floor. I picked them up, added them to the clutch of bills in my hand, closed the top drawer, opened the one beneath it, and created a second drawer for unpaid bills.

The silence of the home I could handle; after all, nine months of the year I worked alone while Sarah was in school. It was easy enough to imagine that school had simply started a little earlier this year. Rebecca was at work. Sarah was at her first day of fourth grade. Soon I'd pick her up and receive the first reports about her new teacher. You can pretend those sorts of things for a little while, if you need to. What I couldn't handle was the thunderous sound of that envelope ripping and echoing within the silence. It sounded too much like a life being torn in two—a before and an after.

I grabbed my house keys, donned running shoes and a baseball cap, and went for a walk.

Walking usually centered me. When I was a boy, I'd walk through the woods at my grandmother's house in the country, feeling a little less alone among its sounds—the muted crunch of the forest floor underfoot, the wind-whispered chorus of the canopy above, the uneven babbling of the creek I'd follow into the deep forest where little light could penetrate. Then in high school, there were two years' worth of those walks to and from school; by the time I got my license, I was almost sorry to see them go.

After Sarah was born, I would put her in a stroller on weekend mornings, and we'd go for long walks, giving Rebecca a couple more hours of sleep. For several years, I'd practiced the discipline of prayer by walking the streets of our neighborhood late at night, pausing outside the home of any household with a light on, praying for the souls within. And until six months earlier, whenever I'd been stumped by a creative problem, I could go for a walk and the solution would magically surface within me, usually within a block or two. With Rebecca gone, I was hoping some of that old magic would return.

I needed solutions, and I needed them fast.

Ours was a suburb of young, mostly churchgoing families. You could stand just about anywhere in town and, if you had a decent arm, throw a tennis ball and hit either a church or a park. When I walked out the door, my insides were filled with some mixture of hurt, defensiveness, numbness, and cocoa cereal. However, I hadn't reached a park nor a church by the time that old magic was producing some new ideas.

For one thing, I needed to apologize to Rebecca. She had been angry and she'd said some things she probably didn't mean; however, that didn't give me an excuse to respond defensively and passive-aggressively. For crying out loud, I'd written an entire book about how to handle those moments in a relationship. I could do better, and I'd tell her so. It was an idea with some light in it. However, I'd barely had time to think it before another thought passed over it, like a dark cloud over the sun: *she looked like she meant exactly what she said.* I felt the pressure behind my eyes again.

Supersillyus.

The cloud within me passed and my inner sunshine returned.

I began crafting my apology as I walked, oblivious to my course and surroundings. When it felt like I'd found words humble enough to begin repairing our rift, I stopped on the sidewalk to tap it out on my phone. When I had it recorded, I looked up and, sure enough, I was standing at the edge of Sarah's favorite park. A girl about her age was being pushed on a swing by her father, who was about my age. He looked up from his daughter, smiled, and waved.

Supersillyus.

I out-smiled him in return.

I walked on, and more possibilities emerged. For instance, I had to admit, there was some truth to what Rebecca had said. I had not been as forthcoming as I could have been with anyone about my struggle to write this next book. I'd come to think of it as my curse. My tormentor. My demon. In my mind's eye, I saw an image of the book, alive and animated somehow, staring at me with a dangerously mischievous grin, horns growing out of its upper corners, a deep red goatee hanging from the bottom edge of the cover.

Suddenly, I felt like Bruce Willis at the end of that movie about the kid who sees dead people, reviewing all the recent scenes in my life from a new angle. In every scene there was this book, chipping away at my life. Its stubbornness explained my struggles with Rebecca. It explained the growing rift between Benjamin and me too. Not to mention the drawer—drawers *plural*, now—full of bills in my desk.

It was the eureka moment I'd been hoping for.

If the biggest problems in my life could all be traced back to this book project, then the solution was clear: I needed to write the damned book. I could turn all of it around by getting down to work. And that was very good news, because there was just a handful of problems in my life I had not been able to out-smile, and even fewer I had not been able to outsmart, but I still hadn't encountered the problem I couldn't *outwork*. Then some more good news dawned on me—to outwork a problem you need two things: time and space. And my ladies had just given me more time and space than I'd had since the day Rebecca lifted her leg onto my lap.

By the time I got back to our house, I felt like I was out in the driveway shooting hoops on a warmer-than-possible February afternoon, the winter gone for good, nothing but springtime to come.

I began preparing my heart and my mind for a prolific Saturday of writing. I went for a long bike ride. I made myself a salad for lunch. I took a hot shower. I brewed some herbal tea and listened to the kind of music that gives me the feels. I prayed. I meditated. I cleared the top of my desk of everything but my laptop and the monitor to which it was attached. I ignored the drawers beneath the surface.

I called Rebecca and, when she failed to pick up, I left her a message expressing my happiness that our family tracking app showed they were making good time. I let her know I was thinking of them constantly. I told her I'd taken a long walk and I had more clarity and I was hopeful about what the future held. I asked her to call me back when they arrived at their hotel. I told her I'd look forward to talking to her then. It never occurred to me she might not call back.

I found my Bible beneath a stack of books next to our bed, opening it to where the tassel marked a passage that had

anchored everything I'd believed about God and life and creativity for the last decade. The highlighter had aged from a neon
yellow to a dirty mustard, but 1 Kings 19:11-13 was ancient
and unchanged:

> The Lord said, "Go out and stand on the mountain in the
> presence of the Lord, for the Lord is about to pass by."
>
> Then a great and powerful wind tore the mountains
> apart and shattered the rocks before the LORD, but the
> LORD was not in the wind. After the wind there was an
> earthquake, but the LORD was not in the earthquake. After
> the earthquake came a fire, but the LORD was not in the fire.
> And after the fire came a gentle whisper. When Elijah heard
> it, he pulled his cloak over his face and went out and stood
> at the mouth of the cave.

In the morning, I would pull the cloak over my face, stand at
the mouth of the cave, and write down what I heard in the whisper.

I made myself an early dinner and ate it while watching one
of my favorite movies, about aliens who reveal to us the true
nature of time and existence. When the credits rolled, I decided
to turn in early. I changed into pajamas and brushed my teeth,
noticing Rebecca's empty space in the toothbrush holder.

Supersillyus.

I took a long slug of Zzzquil to ensure a good night's sleep.
I got into bed and checked my phone. No call from Rebecca.
I checked the app—they were still driving. I placed the phone
on my chest so I wouldn't miss her call, and I waited. Somewhere in the middle of my waiting, I drifted off into a deep
and dreamless sleep, unaware of the surprises that awaited
me on Saturday.

8

THE FIRST SURPRISE was announced by birdsong.

I hadn't woken without an alarm in years, and I'd planned to set my phone to wake me around sunrise as always. However, by the time my eyelids parted, the birds had been singing for hours and the sun was well above the horizon, coming through our bedroom windows at an angle I was accustomed to seeing well after breakfast.

I patted my chest. No phone. I moved my hand in concentric circles outward until I found the device hidden in the bedcovers, where it had come to rest sometime in the night. The screen showed it was a few minutes after ten. I hadn't slept in so late since sometime before Sarah was born. The second surprise of the day was announced by the absence of anything else on my lock screen.

No text notification from Rebecca. No voicemail.

My pulse quickened. I couldn't imagine a noncatastrophic reason for her failure to let me know they'd arrived at their hotel. I quickly tapped the family tracking app, and my surprise became complete. Her blue dot was hovering directly over her parents' house. She'd done the whole drive in a single day, something I always voted for on our road trips east, but something Rebecca always vetoed. Too much sitting, she always said. Apparently, the sitting had been worth it this time. It had the feel of someone trying to get far away from something as quickly as they could.

Supersillyus.

I pushed the feeling aside. My ladies were safe and sound, probably already enjoying Mom-mom's beloved pancakes. And without having to worry about their safety while traveling, I had a surplus of both the physical and emotional margin I needed in order to write. The thought energized me, and the energy announced the third surprise of the morning—I was exceptionally well-rested. I felt like a young man again. My eyes were wide. My mind was clear. I was completely prepared to write.

I got out of bed, did some gentle stretches, and made myself a smoothie, tossing in the frozen kale I usually skipped. I got dressed in my most comfortable clothes, brewed myself an unnecessary but habitual cup of coffee, and sat down at the computer. I opened the most recent version of my manuscript and stared at the monitor. The fourth surprise of my morning was not so much announced as triggered. It was a panic attack that hit me like a truck, caused by what was staring back at me from the monitor, which was nothing. The screen was blank. I was at square one, and I had no idea how to get off it.

Extreme writer's block is a little like watching a horrific traffic accident.

When I was thirteen years old, my father had been driving me to an eighth-grade graduation party when I witnessed an accident. It was a gorgeous evening, I was wearing a new outfit marked with the trendiest brand, and all my friends were going to be there. Life was predictable and dependable. Then, just ahead of us, a car pulled out in front of the motorcycle we'd been trailing, and before I had a chance to register what was happening, there was blood and glass everywhere. We pulled over and remained there until the paramedics arrived; then my father drove me the rest of the way to the party. In many ways, the evening was unchanged—the weather was still warm, my outfit was still trendy, and my friends were still my friends—but the predictability of life had died in that accident. I was at the party, and all was well, yet I could only imagine what other cars might be waiting to pull out into the middle of my life. I could only picture the blood and the glass.

Likewise, the morning was unchanged—my wife and daughter were still safely in Maryland, I was still well-rested, and I still had all the time and space I needed to craft my next book. I was "at the party," so to speak. And yet my creativity felt like blood and glass scattered across hot pavement.

For months, I'd been scouring the internet for the cure to writer's block. Most of the advice boiled down to this: there's no cure for it because there's no such thing as writer's block. It's all in your head, the experts proclaimed. Every time I read one of those articles, I wanted to scream, "Of course it's in your head! Unfortunately, that's where my creativity is too!"

On a Saturday morning in a house all alone, I thought about those articles and I thought about a year's worth of failure to write and I pictured writer's block pulling out in front of the career that had been motoring along so nicely and all I could see was blood and glass all over the hot pavement of my life and my panic swelled like a mushroom cloud within me and I tried to say *supersillyus* but it was pulverized by the shock wave. I didn't know what to do. I only knew what I *couldn't* do: I couldn't write.

I couldn't sit for another moment in front of that blank screen.

a

In our first appointment, Jeff had taught me several skills for coping with panic. Ways to breathe. Ways to think. Ways to ride it out if it happened again. He'd also recommended me to a psychiatrist for a prescription of Xanax—a little extra help when I needed it. The orange bottle was stuffed in my sock drawer because Rebecca didn't need another thing to worry about. Anyway, I'd never taken a pill.

At the end of that first session, Jeff had also casually mentioned that you can't feel anxiety and anger at the same time. He said, sort of laughingly, "So, if you're ever having difficulty shaking a panic attack, just get yourself really pissed, and you'll be good to go."

I was standing in front of Sarah's favorite park again, the panic unabated, when I recalled that advice. Miraculously, the playground was vacant on a late Saturday morning. Or perhaps not miraculously. Summer vacations to Europe. Travel soccer. College orientations. Lawns to mow. Grocery shopping to do. Suburbia to conquer.

I took a seat on Sarah's favorite swing, in the very space in which she usually sat, and my presence within her absence brought with it an upwelling of sorrow that overflowed in the form of more panic. My heart skipped a beat as it kicked in to overdrive. Fresh sweat broke out on my brow. I tried to breathe, but it felt like someone was giving me the Heimlich and forgetting to let up. So, with no other alternative, I followed Jeff's advice—I closed my eyes and let my rage surface.

What surfaced with it was the fifth surprise of my Saturday. A memory. The dining room in my childhood home.

It's dinnertime. My dad sits at the head of the table, my mother to his left and me to his right, facing each other. I'm in high school. My father is serving himself asparagus from a platter and then passing it to my mother. He's saying something about his day at his law office, but even if I cared to understand it, it would be incomprehensible to me. Something about mortgages and titles and attorneys' fees. The only thing I understand for sure is that I want to leap across the table, insert my forefinger and middle finger into his eyes, my thumb underneath his upper teeth, and rip his head from his neck, rolling it like a bowling ball out of the dining room and into the kitchen, where I picture it stopping, *thunk*, against the side door of the house.

A searing pain in my palms called me back to the present.

The strength of my grip on the swing chains was carving painful grooves in my flesh. I relaxed my hands quickly and let my arms drop to my sides. I tried to take a deep breath. It came easily. I scanned my body—heart rate returning to normal, no sweating, no tingling. Jeff had been right; the panic was gone. In its place, though, was a cauldron of something scalding and bubbling, not located in my chest like the panic but located in my gut. I took a few more deep breaths. The boiling thing within me gradually cooled into something simmering and manageable. And in the quiet that followed, I felt only one thing—utter exhaustion, every molecule of my being a burden to carry, atomic weight transformed into actual weight. I sat in that swing for a long time, unable to get up.

A couple of kids materialized out of nowhere. One of them stood in front of me and stared at me, locking eyes with me, and I knew him to be the alpha and I knew myself to be the beta. I got up and relinquished the swing to its rightful ruler.

As I walked home, I dialed Rebecca's number, listened to it ring, and heard her voicemail greeting and the beep telling me it was my turn.

"Rebecca, it's Eli." Duh. "I see you're at your parents' house. That's good." At some point, facts would have to give way to feelings. "Rebecca, I miss you. I miss you both." Pause. "I'm really sorry about the last thing I said to you. I know you don't do standards. I know that's not the reason you left. I know there's more to it. Anyway, I just wanted to let you know I'm trying really hard, trying my best. You deserve the best, and I'm determined to give it to you." Another pause. "Um, I'd love to hear your voice. Could you give me a call back and let me know you got this? And tell Sarah I love her to infinity and beyond. Okay, talk to you soon. Bye."

The final surprise of my Saturday was once again triggered by the absence of something. Rebecca never called back.

9

I HADN'T BEEN TO CHURCH in over a year.

I'm not really sure how it happened, but at some point the Sunday morning routine we'd practiced for most of Sarah's life—wake up a little too late, bowl of cereal, quick showers and hair dryers, our Sunday best, Sarah to Sunday school, Rebecca and me to our adult programming, and back home for an early lunch—had been replaced by the liturgy of waking up whenever, the sacrament of Dad's banana pancakes, and the holy scripture of digital news.

I woke up on Sunday more rested than expected, after having stayed up late waiting for the call that never came. My sleep had been helped along by an extra gulp of Zzzquil and the first Xanax I'd ever taken, retrieved from my sock drawer as the clock ticked past Rebecca's bedtime on the East Coast. Before drifting off, I'd made the decision to set my alarm and go to church. Maybe I was trying to avoid banana pancakes for a party of one.

Or maybe I was simply throwing a Hail Mary.

When Sarah was seven, she'd come home from school one day crying. It appeared one of her best friends had excluded her from a birthday party invitation. While coaching her through it, I told her that when things seem to be going wrong you have two choices: either start fixing it or start praying about it. She decided to try fixing it first by calling her friend and asking why she had not been invited to the party. Her friend told her Sarah *was* invited and she was sad Sarah had not RSVPed. Sarah went to the party and, several weeks later, her friend found the invitation at the bottom of her bookbag.

Since then, whenever something went wrong, Sarah and I would look at each other and ask, "Fix it or pray about it?" Once, upon spilling her milk at the dinner table, she looked at me and, with a clever smile in her eyes, bowed her head in prayer. In moments like that, the magnitude of my gratitude for her was a transcendent thing. It made me feel closer to God.

Having said that, for about the last year, God and I had not been on speaking terms.

My first book—*The Whisper in the Wind: Hearing God in Unexpected Places*—was about how, once you clear away all the painful and unhelpful thoughts most of us have hollering in our heads all the time, you can begin to hear the graceful voice of God within you, like a whisper that has been drowned out by the raging winds of shame and self-doubt. According to my email inbox, it had brought many people closer to God.

Scattered among those emails, though, was a substantial number of messages from people lamenting that they'd silenced most of their inner noise and still, inside of themselves, they heard no whisper, only a void. Over and over again, reading those emails put that familiar lump in my throat. So, despite the success of my two books about marriage and some pressure to establish myself as a relationship expert by writing another one, I'd pitched a sequel to my first book. *The Voice in the Void: How*

to Speak with God When God Seems Silent was about how to dialogue with God even when God has gone quiet.

At the time I signed the contract, it had never occurred to me
that I might develop something even worse than writer's block—
believer's block. It had been a year since I'd heard the whisper in
the wind, let alone the voice in the void. So just before drifting
off into my medication-assisted sleep, I'd decided I had a problem
I couldn't fix, and I might as well start praying about it. Church
was as good a place to start as any.

When the alarm went off on Sunday morning, I swiped it into
silence and checked my lock screen. Still no message from
Rebecca. I got out of bed and picked up our Sunday morning
routine where we'd left off a year ago: I ate the rest of the chocolate cereal, took a quick shower, brushed some dust off the
shoulders of a polo shirt hanging in the closet, and left for
church. The routine itself had aroused some old hope.

Unfortunately, stepping into the church aroused some
new panic.

It was triggered by the radiant expressions on the faces of the
greeters and everyone else milling about in the lobby. You
weren't supposed to stare into the sun, and yet you were expected
to look at these solar smiles, so bright they were blinding. Wondering how many times I'd blinded some poor soul with my own
solar smile, I lowered my chin to my chest—where I could already feel something tightening—and made a beeline for the
back row of the sanctuary. There I sat, apparently unnoticed, for
fifteen minutes, my lack of exuberance an invisibility cloak to
hide me from the festivities. As the seats began to fill, a rock
band took the stage, turning up the happiness and celebration

to eleven. It was a place for people overflowing with joy, not someone with a big, silent void at the center of himself.

I could feel the cold prickle of sweat coming out on my forehead.

Eventually the music gave way to announcements that assumed you were familiar with everything, and a sermon that assumed your faith was already strong but could get a little stronger. I couldn't listen to a word of it. Instead, I found myself gazing around at the young families scattered about. Husbands extending an arm along the back of their wife's chair and wives leaning into that sanitized Sunday morning embrace. My eyes settled on the back of one woman's head, indistinguishable from Rebecca's, and that's when the panic really blossomed. I tried to take a deep breath, but it seemed there was no air left in the room.

And I couldn't bring myself to decapitate my dead father in a house of God.

By the time I reached the exit, I was fumbling for my phone. By the time I got to the car, I was dialing Rebecca's number. I just needed to talk to my wife. I needed her to tell me that we would find our way home from Italy. I needed her to tell me this was just the painful part of the tattoo. I needed her to round *up*.

By the time I got into the car, my call had already gone directly to voicemail. No rings. Her phone was turned off. By the time an automated voice announced her voicemail was full, I felt like I was having the mother of all heart attacks.

By the time dinner rolled around, my third Xanax of the afternoon was taking the edge off everything. By the time the sun went down, I'd found a bottle of old red wine tucked away in a kitchen cabinet, and half of it was gone. And by the time I decided to take my first bath in three decades, I'd come to the conclusion my pain was something that could be neither fixed nor prayed about.

However, a third option was beginning to present itself.

While the rest of our house was modest by suburban standards, the previous owner had spared no expense on the main bathroom. It featured an intricately tiled walk-in shower cove with two rainfall shower heads. Between the entryway and the shower, though, was something that had sold Rebecca on the house—an oversized and deeper-than-it-needed-to-be jetted tub. She'd fallen in love with it instantly during the showing, both for the relaxation it would afford her and for its convenience—it was situated so you could lie against the headrest and reach one of the vanity drawers. Rebecca and the realtor had imagined together everything Rebecca could put in that drawer, from bath salts to candles to her razor and blades. I had just signed the contract for *Manifesto*, so it felt like the kind of house we could afford. It wasn't. But it *was* the kind of house you bought when your purpose was to give Rebecca Miller the life she deserved.

I stood at the toilet, the half-empty wine bottle in one hand, trying my best not to miss the bowl with the other. The floor tipped from side to side. The bowl in front of me was a blur. My eyes drooped and I lost sight of it momentarily. I finished. I thought of my bed off yonder and how much effort it would take to reach it. I glanced at the bathtub. I decided I could manage a journey of that length. I set the bottle of wine down on the edge of the tub and disrobed. I turned on the tap, quite a bit hotter than my skin would be comfortable with under normal conditions, and got in.

A part of me—let's call him Eli—was simply planning to wait out the worst of the sedation until the bed felt more reachable. He wanted nothing more than for this episode to be behind him. However, another part of me—let's call him Jah—a part with which I was completely unfamiliar, had a different plan. That part of me picked up the wine bottle, took another large swallow, and pictured the razor blades in Rebecca's drawer. Jah wanted nothing more than to open the drawer, retrieve a blade, and put an end to all the suffering. Even in my condition, I could remember enough of my graduate training to recognize what was happening: the self-destructive part of me that normally hibernates in my depths had awakened to compete with the self-protective part of me from which I lived most of my life.

For the next ten minutes, they dueled.

At UPenn we'd been taught to have empathy for the suffering of a suicidal client while also pointing out the part of them that does *not* want to die—the part of them that came to therapy and told a therapist, in a plea for protection from the dangerous part. As therapists, we were instructed to ask the client if we could speak exclusively with the part of them that wanted to live. So, with the image of Rebecca's razor blades filling the movie screen behind my eyelids, I tried to do just that. I tried to focus on Eli, who was horrified at the idea of opening the drawer.

Jah, however, pictured the razor blades and took another slug of wine.

Fortunately, the other thing I'd learned in that graduate lecture actually happened to me. It turns out, life is designed to keep itself alive. If you try to choke yourself to death, you'll pass out before you are able to do so, and your hands will release. If you try to drown yourself, the water will do its best to push you back up to the air on the surface. If you cut yourself, the body will clot its blood as quickly as possible. And if you are in the process of slowly sedating yourself to death, you may put yourself to sleep before you put yourself in the grave.

In a bathtub full of water cooling to a more tolerable temperature, I passed out.

10

I'M STANDING AT THE RIVER'S EDGE *once again.*

The water before me is murderous. The land beyond it is mysterious. Nevertheless, I begin. I lift my right foot, in its dirty shoe with its protruding toe. As I look downward, searching for the least rotten slat to place it on, I see with my thirty-nine-year-old eyes this footwear of my five-year-old self. In the timelessness of the dreamworld, I am both ages, and I don't even think to question it.

I place my foot on a plank that—unlike the dark gray boards around it—has retained some of its original yellowish hue and still features two rusty nail heads in each of its ends, suggesting it may still be anchored to the supporting structure. These will be my criteria: color and placement. The darker and more angled boards I will do anything I can to avoid.

I look down past the slat on which my foot has come to rest, and I see solid ground beneath it. I'm not over the water yet. The sight of the grass below steadies me—if something goes wrong now, all is not lost. I shift all my weight to this foot and bring my left foot ahead to join it. Even this relatively healthy-looking board sags beneath my weight, the nails at its ends giving a little and squeaking as they do. I repeat this process several times, with each step finding a relatively strong board on which to land. Finally, though, I'm forced to choose a darker board, lying at an angle, pockmarked by rot and decay. As soon as I bring my full weight to it, I hear it crack dully, and I leap to another board ahead of me just as the board I've left behind splits in two and falls away.

My leap has carried me out over the water.

I look downward for my next foothold. There is more driftwood rushing past in the water below than solid wood left on this bridge above. The speed of the water startles me. Its roar terrifies me.

I scan the boards ahead of me. Beyond a two-foot gap is a darkened plank nearly disintegrated in the middle. Then two more feet of empty space, followed by an inexplicably pristine board anchored solidly to the bridge in its original position, with nails barely rusted at all. However it, too, has several feet of space beyond it. It's my only choice. I spring for it, just as terrified as every other time I've made this particular leap, because there's no guarantee I'll stick the landing like I have before—my momentum might carry me forward into the gap on the other side of the good slat. And even if I make it without falling, I know what's going to happen next. It's happened every time.

Like flipping a switch, landing on that bright board will trigger the water to rise.

My feet land solidly on the fresh-looking plank, and I lean backward, neutralizing my momentum. I've made it. But the moment of relief is quickly washed away by the noticeable reduction in distance between the walkway and the water. Once again, the current is quickening and the river is rising. It's three yards from the bottom of the bridge. Then it's three feet. The thunderous sound of the swollen waters all around me becomes one with the thunder of blood pulsing in my ears; the shaking of the bridge syncs with the pounding in my chest. I look up toward the distant shore. Somehow it is farther away than ever, and the fog is thicker than when I began. I look down and the water is now three inches from the bottom of the bridge. Its churning sends a wave crashing up onto the walkway, and the next reachable plank bursts free in an explosion of frigid water that drenches me from head to toe.

I try to scream, but the loudest sound I can make is the chattering of my teeth.

The water is at my ankles now, and the walkway has completely disappeared beneath the muddy surface. I turn frantically in every direction, searching for some way out, some way across. The ground from which I've come has now been swallowed whole by the river. There is no going back. The water rises and I begin to lose my footing on the board beneath the waves, the force of the water advertising where it is about to take me.

And finally, somewhere within me, I find my scream.

I bellow it, the one word I've unleashed over and over in countless nightmares exactly like this one. The word that haunts me every time, long after I return to the waking world, because no matter how hard I try, by the light of day, I can never recall what that word was. In the dream, the scream is so loud it tears at the tissues of my throat and creates a constellation of black spots in my vision.

In the real world I'm screaming too, but the scream is caught somewhere in the depths of my heart, and it is as silent as the space into which I awake.

11

"I'LL BE HONEST—I hadn't expected to see you so soon."

Jeff's smile told me the surprise was a pleasant one. He wasn't accustomed to being wrong, but he was clearly happy to have miscalculated in this case.

I'd awoken, thrashing, in a bathtub full of water cooled to room temperature, drenched from head to toe, teeth chattering, with that one word echoing somewhere inside of me. Twenty-eight years, almost three decades since I'd last dreamed that dream. At least a quarter of a century since I'd last *thought* about it. And yet there I was, an almost forty-year-old man, dreaming it again, in conditions that approximated the dream world much more closely than my childhood bedcovers ever had.

Several other differences: As a kid I never woke with a hangover that felt like one of those rotted planks cracking in half. Also, as a kid I always woke in the middle of the night, never at dawn as I'd done on that Monday morning. And last but certainly not least, as a kid I always went back to sleep and never, not once, on waking did I remember the word screamed during the dream.

I had toweled myself off, poured out the wine, taken twice as much Tylenol as the bottle suggested, and dug a pair of sweatpants and a hoodie out of my dresser. I'd called Jeff and left a message with his answering service requesting an emergency session. Then, as soon as my hands were warm enough and steady enough to type, I'd sat down at my computer to record every detail of the dream. By the time Jeff's answering service called me back, I'd written more words than I'd written in the last year.

Jeff had no openings, but he'd been willing to come in an hour early to meet with me.

"You said in your voicemail you'd dreamed a recurring nightmare from your childhood. I'm guessing that was terrifying at worst and disturbing at best."

His smile had morphed into a creased brow. The sincere concern in his voice assured me that when he'd fired me, he hadn't quit caring about me. He was ready for me to be shaken badly, and he wanted to create a space where I could shake safely. I figured that would make me the most pleasant surprise of his day. I *was* shaking a little, but it was with hope that my writer's block might finally be behind me.

"Thank you for seeing me on such short notice, Jeff. I know you didn't have to do this. I really appreciate it. Especially after the way things ended last week." I said this last part with a sheepish smile, and then I drew a deep breath. "And you were right, it's time that I finally come clean with you. I'm sorry it took me so long, but I want to be completely honest with you."

Then I came as clean as I could possibly imagine as quickly as I possibly could. I told him I'd been in financial trouble pretty much since the day I met Rebecca. I couldn't really afford that first meal at McDonald's, and I certainly couldn't afford the car we'd purchased together several months later. The engagement ring I'd bought her. The decision to give up a guaranteed salary as a psychologist in favor of an author's fickle royalties. The meager salary of Rebecca's dream job. Our house. The recent medical bills.

I told him Rebecca was under the impression every book advance and royalty check was new financial margin when, in fact, they simply chipped away at old debt. I'd paid off back taxes with the first half of my advance for this next book, and I needed the second half to keep the debt collectors at bay. That was six months ago, though. Now the publisher was on the verge of canceling the contract and joining the ranks of my debt collectors.

I told him Rebecca had begun to sense all was not as it seemed. She'd accused me of hiding something. I'd denied it. She'd ventured guesses anyway. Drug problem. Mistress. And her most painful guess—you don't love me anymore. Finally, I told Jeff that on Friday morning Rebecca had taken Sarah and left for Maryland and ignored all my attempts to reach her. I told him about my rising anxiety, my attempt to manage it with anger like he'd advised, the image of my father.

I expected him to be shocked. He wasn't. What he'd say over the next few minutes, though, would shock *me*.

"Elijah, thank you for trusting me with some of your truth." I flinched a little at the word *some*. "You've been carrying a great burden all by yourself for a very long time. I'm so glad you've laid some of it down here, and I will be more than glad to carry the rest of it with you. However, I have to say, more than anything, I'm *confused*. You just described to me a life on the brink of ruin, and you described it lightly, almost . . . excitedly?"

"Yes," I said, smiling broadly, "that brings me to last night's dream."

I told him about my experience at church and what I'd done when I got home, though I told him it was two Xanax, and the bottle of wine didn't seem important enough to mention. I described passing out in the tub, and I narrated almost every detail of the dream—I told him about the scream at the end of it, but I didn't tell him the word. And I told him I'd written something that morning for the first time in almost a year.

"This is why I reached out to you, Jeff. I think the dream might be the key to turning all of this around. I need you to help me interpret it. What does it mean? The fact that I dreamed it again after so many years must be a gift of some sort, right? Is it the anchoring metaphor for this book I've been trying to write?"

A thought landed and brought even more hope.

"Think about it. A bridge. A passage. Maybe it could be turned into an online curriculum. I don't know. I just think there's a lot of possibility here. I think it could be the answer to my problems. I . . ." I trailed off. Jeff usually tried to mirror my emotions, but this time, I could read none of my excitement on his face. "What is it? Why are you looking at me like that?"

Jeff started slowly. "Elijah, when you were in graduate school, did you ever come across the phrase *flight into health*"?

Suddenly, I felt very, very cautious. "No, I think I must have missed that one."

"Well, the idea is that oftentimes, when people come to therapy with big problems, they seek a quick and complete conclusion to those problems. When they feel just a little bit of relief and thus just a little bit of optimism, they throw themselves into the positive feeling and tell themselves everything is going to be okay. What *looks* like health is actually a way to avoid the hard work of genuine healing."

I stared at him. No need for *supersillyus*. The cauldron within me was beginning to bubble again. "You think I'm trying to use this dream as a shortcut solution."

Jeff smiled slightly. "You said it even better than I did."

"Okay," I said, trying to humor him as my anger grew. "Why do *you* think I dreamed the dream? What do *you* think it means?"

He didn't hesitate. "I think it means you need to go home, Elijah."

I was too stunned to speak. Jeff was too wise to speak. We sat there like that, staring at each other for three minutes that felt like three hours. As soon as I trusted myself to speak without saying something I'd regret, I opened my mouth. "Go on." Despite my best efforts, it sounded more like a dare than an invitation.

"Elijah, you started dreaming that dream as a child, when you lived in Bradford's Ferry. I can't help but wonder if the river you're trying to cross in the dream is the river that runs through your hometown. You describe hiding so much of yourself from Rebecca, but surely your habit of hiding was well established by the time you met her, by the time you left home for good. Clearly, you have anger toward your father that began there but didn't end there. You rarely talk about your mother, rarely visit her. You speak so fondly of Bradford's Ferry itself, but when was the last time you went there? I know you said Rebecca and Sarah have given you the space to write, but I think they've given you the space to go home."

I stood up. Jeff stayed seated.

"Coming here was a mistake, I'm sorry." Apologizing out of habit, not because I felt it. "I came here this morning to get your insight into a problem I'm on the verge of solving. Instead of helping me, you're creating an even bigger problem for me."

There was a lecture-y tone to my voice, as if I were chiding Sarah for speaking rudely to her mother. I looked at him. Waited for his apology. He looked back at me, plenty of sympathy on his face but not a trace of apology. The sympathy snapped something within me.

"Well, thanks but no thanks," I spat, before choking off the next word that almost came out of my mouth. I'd almost called him Dad.

The textbook psychobabble of the near Freudian slip was a fresh humiliation and, apparently, one humiliation too many. It felt like the walls were closing in. My head hurt. My heart hammered. I took a deep breath, seeking something calm within me, and instead discovered the cauldron bubbling over. I moved past him, trying to save him from the full force of it, opening the door for myself this time. I was halfway through it when Jeff said my name.

I turned around.

"You've remembered this time, haven't you?"

"Remembered *what*?" Pretending I didn't know what he was talking about.

"The word. The one you screamed at the end of that dream every time as a child. Do you want to tell me what it is?"

The cauldron finally overflowed in strange, hot tears that blurred my vision.

"I don't know what you're talking about," I lied. "I can't remember anything more than I've ever remembered. Perhaps you're not as a smart as you think you are." Then, with a fire in my eyes far more malevolent than the fire in Rebecca's eyes during her departure, I told Jeff exactly where he could put the help he was trying to give me. On Thursday evening, Jeff had fired me.

On Monday morning, I fired him.

12

I COULD BARELY DISCERN THE OUTLINE of the swing set through the darkness.

It must have been sometime after ten o'clock because the late summer sunset had completely faded from the western sky. I'd been walking for hours. How many, I couldn't be sure. I hadn't looked at my phone since a few minutes after walking out of Jeff's office, when it vibrated and the caller ID showed it was him. I'd thrown it into the back seat, where it bounced off the cushion, ricocheted into the passenger-side armrest, and came to rest on the floor, the screen a spiderweb of cracks. The metaphor for my life had been too heavy to pick up. It was still lying there.

The first time I'd felt rage like I'd felt toward Jeff, I'd been in the seventh grade. A kid named Toby Gazinski had come up behind me and poured a thirty-two-ounce cup of orange soda over my head while I was waiting to deposit my lunch tray at the cafeteria's kitchen window. I looked down and saw my white T-shirt clinging to the baby fat on my stubbornly prepubescent body. Then I looked up and made accidental eye contact with Samantha Stiller. I'd been stumble-over-your-words in love with her since sometime in the sixth grade. She was a grade ahead of me, though, and she'd already hit her "growth spurt," so my plan had been to stay under her radar until I caught up. It didn't matter that I saw sympathy there when our eyes locked. I was now on her radar, and I wanted to hurt the kid who had put me there.

I turned around and went after his eyes.

Toby Gazinski was bigger than me. I could barely *reach* his eyes, let alone harm them. By the end of the day, I was humiliated to the core, suspended from school, and nursing a swollen lip where he'd fended me off with his knuckles. The rage bubbled for several hours, but by dinnertime it had simmered back down, replaced by an exhaustion so complete it was difficult to sit up straight, let alone eat a meal.

The second time I'd felt rage like that was several years later, at the very same dinner table, when I'd pictured decapitating my dad. In the midst of lecturing Jeff, the memory of that scene had returned in even more vivid detail. I wasn't outside of myself observing it. I was behind my sixteen-year-old eyes, looking out. I could see the image I was trying to scrub from my mind during that dinner. I remembered the certainty that I couldn't tell anyone about it. I recalled that pulling my dad's head free of his neck felt like the only way to get free of him and our unspoken pact. I'd been only half right about that. I got free of *him* three years later, when a heavy snowfall and his stubborn refusal to buy a snowblower added up to his fatal heart attack.

However, my rage and our unspoken pact had lived on.

In contrast, my anger toward Jeff had subsided by the time I pulled into the garage. In its place, once again, was an exhaustion that seemed to double the force of gravity. I felt weighed down by Rebecca's absence and silence, by a night spent dreaming in a bathtub rather than sleeping in a bed, by a hangover that was beginning to reassert itself, and most of all by the millstone of an idea Jeff had hung around my neck. I sat in the car for two or three hours before finally surrendering to the midday heat of the garage. I dragged myself to the bedroom, where I expected to sleep the day away, but it can be difficult to fall asleep when you *need* to fall asleep. Neediness often pushes the object of its desire beyond reach. Sleep is no different, no matter how tired your mind and body are.

So, sometime in the late afternoon, I went for a walk. I assumed it would be a short one, but its conclusion was sort of like the park out there in the dark—still not in sight. I continued walking. Eventually, the pain in my feet began to outweigh every other kind of pain I was feeling, and I turned for home.

On our block, one house was still lit dimly by a lamp behind curtains. I stopped and stared at it and began the practice of an old ritual. I prayed for the people inside. For their rest. For their peace. I prayed that no matter what trials this day had brought, tomorrow would be a fresh start. I think it's okay to admit when you say a prayer like that for someone else, you are also, almost always, saying it for yourself.

By the time I arrived home, I was thinking of Rebecca's favorite movie, *Groundhog Day*, in which Bill Murray wakes up every morning with another chance to do the same day over again. I was hanging my hopes on a good's night sleep, waking up refreshed, pretending I had never reached out to Jeff, and building on what I'd written down about my dream. A tidy little reset.

I should have known it wouldn't work. The man paid to cure my disease had infected me with a new one, a viral idea that, even as I walked, was multiplying and spreading everywhere within me.

I'm standing at the river's edge once again.

Rather than taking my first step onto the bridge, I take a moment to look around. Sure enough, upriver I see a dam and hydroelectric plant, identical to the one in Bradford's Ferry. I turn around and look up the street I've presumably just traveled. It is, without a doubt, Main Street in Bradford's Ferry, though it seems to be an amalgamation of time and space. Shops that once existed there when I was a child, and shops that only exist there now, and shops that have never existed there at all, are all standing next to each other in the here and now of the dreamworld.

I turn back to the river and, as always, I begin.

This time, as the water reaches my ankles and I scream my scream, I know at least that I'll be dying in Bradford's Ferry.

I woke up with that silent scream once again caught in my throat, waiting out that disorienting moment between dream and reality, becoming aware of the mattress beneath me, the sheet on top of me, the darkness all around me. It felt like I'd been asleep for hours. I reached for my phone, which I'd retrieved from the car after returning from my walk, and the disorientation returned ever so slightly. I'd probably drifted off somewhere around midnight. The splintered screen read 12:55.

My mind had returned to the nightmare at its first opportunity.

The water is above my ankles and I begin to scream.

~~~

I woke again, thrashing about, with the scream halfway out. My phone, which had been resting on my chest when I drifted off again, had fallen to the floor. I retrieved it to discover its screen cracked a little more. Something in *me* cracked a little more when I saw the time. It was 1:12. I'd fallen back to sleep and the dream had resumed immediately, not from the beginning, but at the end. At the terror. At the scream.

It went like that for the rest of the night.

Every time I drifted off, the dream resumed again with the water rising above my ankles—my five-year-old self standing in that vast horizon of rushing river—and each time I woke up again, screaming. Around three o'clock I took my last two Xanax. They might as well have been aspirin. The dreaming continued. By the time the birds began to sing outside the bedroom window, my choice seemed clear. I couldn't tell if Jeff had caused it or predicted it, but it didn't really matter. I could drive home to Bradford's Ferry and try to turn this dream into a book, or let this dream drive me into madness.

Exactly four days after I awoke to Rebecca retrieving her suitcase from our closet, I was in the closet myself, packing a smaller suitcase in preparation for my departure. I added enough clothing to get me through the week—I wasn't planning to stay long. I went to the bathroom to grab my toothbrush. I couldn't bring myself to pick it up, though. One toothbrush in the holder looked like a lonely interlude in my life. *No* toothbrushes looked like the end of a story whose conclusion I couldn't bring myself to consider. I'd buy myself a new one in Bradford's Ferry.

We assert control in senseless ways when it's the only kind of control we can still assert.

By the time I pulled out of the driveway, the sun was up. Out of habit, I set the GPS destination for Bradford's Ferry. An hour and thirty-eight minutes to get home. Staring at the preview screen, with its blue line tracing a path from my house to my mother's house, a new image came to mind. In this image, my dream was like a sheepdog, Jeff was the shepherd, and I was the beleaguered creature being driven in a predetermined direction.

Sheep may not have a choice in their destination, but they do have a choice about what to do when they arrive, I thought. *I'm going to get some sleep, I'm going to write my book, and then I'm going to get the hell out of there.*

Nevertheless, the sound of my nighttime scream, bellowed a dozen times over the last six hours, still echoed in my head. That word, hollered in both horror and desperation. That word which was also a name. That name which was also the whole world to a five-year-old boy. That whole world which was also one person. That word.

Mom.

13

JOHN MARCUS BRADFORD was an entrepreneur before the word existed.

Growing up in Bradford's Ferry, what we were told about the man was almost certainly a mixture of history and myth. He was born sometime in the last decade of the eighteenth century and orphaned during a Native American raid on his hometown. When we were taught the story as children, the Native Americans were called Indians, there was a lot of talk about the scalping of people, and there was the implicit but clear suggestion the raid had been unprovoked. I have my doubts.

At any rate, Bradford managed to do more than survive the life of an orphan in a newborn country. He thrived. Since the opening of the Broadway musical *Hamilton*, the schoolteachers in Bradford's Ferry have been comparing him to the orphan Alexander Hamilton. It's a little like comparing an ordinary chair to a princely throne, I think, but I suppose there's something to be learned in the juxtaposition. Apparently, like Hamilton, by the time Bradford reached adulthood, he'd achieved a level of respect and prominence—albeit in his small but growing burg outside of New York City—mostly owing to the fact he could fix anything and was happy to do so for anyone who asked.

His singular passion in life, though, was the distillation of liquor. His wife, Ruth, was known to be jealous of the attention and affection he gave to his liquor, not because he drank it— indeed, he was a teetotaler who taste tested only one swallow from every batch—but simply because he seemed to enjoy the making of *it* even more than he enjoyed the making of love to her. Fortunately, they left that detail out of the grade school curriculum. His crowning achievement, if you asked him, was something he called Bradford Bourbon. Not a soul who ever sampled that spirit thought it tasted anything like bourbon, but fortunately, almost all of them also said two other things: it tasted better than bourbon and it did the same trick.

Despite the bourbon's quality, Bradford had a hard time finding a market for it out East. He was known to curse the fact—always under his breath—that there was subpar liquor being distilled in every house on his street, not to mention the taverns at the four corners of the town. He was a savvy enough businessperson to recognize the uphill climb a startup faces in an already saturated marketplace, though he didn't put it that way. He just said, "These people will settle for any ole swill, and there's far too much crummy swill around here!" Every night he dreamed of the open spaces he kept hearing about out West.

Really, he was dreaming of the open *markets*.

As winter began to thaw into the spring of 1831, he packed up everything he possessed—which mostly included Ruth, their two children, and his midlife crisis—and set out for parts un- known. Bradford wasn't one to meander. They traveled away from the sun in the morning and chased it every afternoon through wild lands, around growing cities, and across the prairie, eventually arriving in the Saukenuk River Valley on a midsummer day.

He stopped in part because it was the kind of immaculate Midwestern day in which the royal blue sky stretching to the horizon is packed with white-as-snow cumulus clouds that somehow never seem to obscure the sun. He also stopped because they'd come to the edge of the Saukenuk River, and he wasn't immediately sure how they were going to cross it. But most of all, he stopped because he was wise enough to have had one word repeating in his mind for most of their travels: location, location, location.

They'd caught their first glimpse of the river from a rise several miles away. They'd also caught a glimpse of a small US Army fort built along the edges of it. He'd aimed for a spot about a half mile to the south of that fort, and they made camp there that night along the river. Ruth and the kids retired early, and he sat by the fireside watching the surface of the flowing water smooth out until it looked like glass, reflecting the light of the full moon. For the first time in years, his heart felt smoothed out like that river, peaceful and in the flow of things. Also, there were soldiers just a stroll upriver who might appreciate a little bit of Bradford Bourbon. He thought he might have found his market.

He was more right than he realized.

Thanks to the army presence, the region was already being peppered by freshly cut log cabins, a number of less permanent encampments here and there, and a steady flow of people to and from the valley, not to mention the flow of commerce up and down the Saukenuk River itself, which eventually emptied into the Mississippi. Ruth was a hard worker and a faithful companion, and Bradford was grateful for her grit as they quickly built the largest structure other than the fort in a fifty-mile radius. It needed to be large to house both the family and their distillery. By the time winter arrived, Bradford Bourbon was keeping soldiers and settlers warm throughout the Saukenuk Valley. Bradford, on the other hand, kept himself warm throughout the long, bitter winter by developing another market niche—the local native people made up mostly of the Sauk tribe.

Bradford couldn't remember the raid that had killed his parents in New York, and he'd never held a grudge about it, so he encountered the native people simply as people, and he found them to be as generally likable as anyone he'd ever met. Sure, there was a language barrier, but liquor is a universal language unto itself. He traded it to them for the supplies he and his family needed to survive the winter. It was strictly business at first, but by the time spring began to advertise itself in the rushing, snow-melted waters of the Saukenuk, he had been embraced as a sort of elder among their tribe. Even their chief, Black Hawk, who was known to be a fierce warrior, welcomed him among their people.

Later that year, when the US Army insisted Black Hawk leave his home village of Saukenuk per the conditions of an 1804 treaty, he refused and the Black Hawk War ensued. As usual, the war was bloodier for the region's native inhabitants, and Black Hawk's band of warriors was eventually annihilated on August 2 while attempting to retreat west across the Mississippi River. It is said that Bradford grieved for a little while, but business was booming and there was bourbon to distill.

The winter that turned into 1833 was even colder and more snow blown than the Bradfords' first one in the valley, and the

Saukenuk River froze over so thoroughly that for the entire month of January, no one thought twice about crossing it on foot. During that month, Bradford's profits doubled and he almost ran out of Bradford Bourbon twice. He scratched his head for an evening until he realized his customer base had doubled because settlers from the other side of the Saukenuk could easily access his distillery. In the spring, he poured the profits from January into a new log structure set apart from the home—a tavern—and the region's first ever ferry for taxiing folks back and forth across the river.

Thus, Bradford's Ferry was born.

He platted the town a year later, and it quickly became a hub of travel in the Saukenuk Valley region. A decade later, it was named the county seat. In Bradford's later years, he served a stint as mayor, but his real contribution to the town was bigger than its name or a few years in office or the spirits he distilled there. His real contribution was the spirit of the town itself. It reflected his openhearted generosity, industrious attitude, ceaseless ambition, wise leadership, and enjoyment of life's simple pleasures.

For almost two hundred years, people from the Ferry—as locals have been calling it for over a century, since a movement to drop Ferry from the town name and rename it simply Bradford, Illinois, engendered such a resistance that many townspeople dropped the name Bradford in everyday conversation altogether—were generally kind, charitable, inventive, and playful. In the Ferry you worked hard and played hard.

Of course, like most rural towns across the United States, Bradford's Ferry had been challenged by the notion that if you had ambition, you were meant to live somewhere else, somewhere like a suburb or a city. However, thanks to its founder's ethos, that notion hadn't taken root in the Ferry as deeply as in many other towns, and there continued to be plenty of ambition and plenty of celebration happening in it. Bradford's Ferry was still small, but by modern standards it was still thriving too.

In spite of myself, as I crossed into its city limits, I felt what John Marcus Bradford must have felt on that first night by the Saukenuk in the summer of 1831. Something in my center settled down, its surface becoming as peacefully smooth as glass. Unfortunately, as was always the case on my return home, the peacefulness was short-lived.

14

I HAD INTENDED TO TEXT my mother before I left the house. I didn't. I knew I needed to text her from the road. I didn't. I planned to pull off at the first gas station in Bradford's Ferry to grab a granola bar for breakfast, and I told myself I could text her then. I didn't.

Instead, I drove past the gas station, skirted the edges of town—avoiding the main roads and passing only two other cars along the way—and pulled into the back parking lot of a hole-in-the-wall breakfast nook called Joey's. Upon entering, I was greeted by the familiar clatter and chatter of early morning dining, a sign that said, "Don't just stand there, seat yourself," and an aroma of grease and cheese and syrup that made my stomach rumble for the first time in days.

Despite the sign's command, I stood there, feeling a little insecure. I felt it every time I returned to Bradford's Ferry. I came back to the town so infrequently that I imagined its people were secretly rejecting me for first rejecting *them*. I'd once confessed this neurotic fear to Rebecca, and she'd responded by telling me about how middle school kids often experience a psychological phenomenon called "the imaginary audience," in which they assume everyone they encounter is watching them and following their every move. "They're not thinking badly of you, Eli; in fact, they're not thinking of you at all." She'd given me a hug and said affectionately, "It's like going home brings out the middle schooler in you." At the time, it felt like she was trivializing my insecurity, but she was probably right.

The past is always behind us, but it is also, always, within us.

Thinking about Rebecca triggered another kind of pang within me, but as I took my seat, I tried to stay focused on my hunger. A server spotted me and made a beeline for my table. Her name tag read "Jennifer," and though she was about my age, we were unfamiliar faces to each other. Nevertheless, she called me "sweetheart" with a platonic jingle to it, and by the time my omelet order was placed I knew more about her two kids than I knew about any of the kids in our suburban neighborhood.

I sat back, sipped my coffee, and looked around. At the counter, a man in a crisp suit and tie sat next to a man in construction gear, chatting like they'd been friends for life. They probably had. This mingling of socioeconomic status could be seen throughout the restaurant. In Bradford's Ferry, you weren't defined by your bank account, you were defined by your birth certificate: if two people were born in the Ferry, they were kin. The whole town was haunted by the spirit of John Marcus Bradford, who welcomed the soldiers and the settlers and the Sauk, not because of who they were but because of *where* they were—with him.

It was a good haunting.

Before the coffee had a chance to cool, my omelet was sitting in front of me. It was twice the size of any omelet I could order in the city at half the price, and I didn't leave a trace of it on the plate. I waited five minutes for Jennifer to return with my check, but she was nowhere in sight, so I left cash on the table and stood to leave.

As I moved toward the exit, I heard a boisterous exclamation over my shoulder, "Eli-Cam!" and recognized the voice of Joey Jr. himself. Junior and I had been classmates throughout our childhood. His father had started the restaurant, but I could remember Junior outlining his plans for running it as early as the fourth grade. Sure enough, he'd taken it over as soon as Senior had passed. We weren't close in high school, but in the Ferry if someone wasn't your enemy, they were your friend.

He greeted me with a bear hug.

"Eli-Cam, it's great to see you, buddy! What are you doing around these parts? Home for long? What do you think of the changes I've made to the restaurant? How was your meal? I hope we took good care of you. Hey, man, the tab's on me." I tried to remember all the questions I was supposed to answer.

"Junior, it's great to see you!" I tried to match his energy. "Man, the place looks great, my omelet was excellent, and Jennifer took great care of me, but I insist on paying."

He walked over to the table, picked up the cash I'd laid down, and pushed it into my hands. "No way, buddy. This one's on me. I tell you what, are you still going to be around tonight?" Once again, he didn't wait for an answer. "Swing by the Draughty Den. We close here at 8:00, and I'll be there by 8:01!" He laughed heartily and slapped me on the back.

I couldn't refuse him, but I couldn't bring myself to commit to him either. I told him my plans were still up in the air, but if I could get free, I'd buy him a drink. Another bear hug from him and he was gone. He'd always been the kind of whirlwind that could drive a teacher into early retirement.

I walked out of the restaurant, knowing it was time to text my mom. I didn't. I got into the car planning to drive in her general direction. I didn't. Instead, I found myself turning toward a place that had flashed in my mind along with my near Freudian slip in Jeff's office. I drove to the site of my greatest secret.

Campbell & Cooper, Attorneys at Law.

When they opened their law practice together, my father, Steven Campbell, and his best friend, Samuel Cooper, had the choice of almost any location in town. Most of the other law offices in Bradford's Ferry were clustered together on Main Street, as close as possible to the courthouse up on the highest hill in town. However, with the kind of optimism that is present at the birth of almost anything, they had imagined themselves to be different from the average law office. Like John Marcus Bradford himself, they wanted to make a buck, but they wanted to do so by honoring all the people of the Saukenuk River Valley. So they'd chosen an office space with a small brick façade on the outskirts of downtown and on the side of town that was struggling. The neighborhoods there had boomed right after the Second World War before slipping into the same state of dilapidated promise that had beset much of rural America in the late twentieth century.

The law partners were men of the people, or at least they tried to be. And though my dad had died years ago, rumor had it Mr. Cooper was still plugging along. I wondered if he'd be in the office this early. I hoped he wouldn't be. I wasn't going there to talk. I was going there to remember.

It was a short drive from Joey's to the office, and there was no shortage of parking spaces along the curb when I arrived. Large rolling blinds were lowered over the east-facing windows that looked out on the crumbling street, but I couldn't tell if they were down because no one was in or because someone was trying to keep the morning sun out.

I crossed the street and stood in front of the office with its large green-and-gold sign over the doorway, now faded into grays and browns by decades of weather and sunlight. Though it wasn't yet nine o'clock, the morning was already growing hot, and beads of sweat were forming at my temples. Maybe it was the heat, so similar to the day I'd come there to remember, or maybe it was the old wrought iron doorknob that seemed to have not aged at all in the intervening years—or maybe it was simply the fact that the past is behind us but it is also, always, within us—but when I reached for that knob, it didn't feel like remembering.

It felt like *returning*.

15

IT'S A THURSDAY AFTERNOON in mid-May. I'm sixteen years old—near the conclusion of my sophomore year—but due to the unfortunate timing of my birthday and Bradford High's driver's ed schedule, I still don't have my license. So I've walked the mile or so from school to my father's office, a blurry walk, head down, hiding tears from passersby, my sorrow carrying me in the direction of my best friend—my dad.

I'd spent much of my boyhood tucked beneath one of his arms in his La-Z-Boy recliner, watching every kind of sport we could find on television, wrestling on the living room floor during commercial breaks, and sharing ice cream sundaes at any time of day despite my mother's protestations. As I got older, I came to understand he was a respected figure around town, and I was proud to be his son. Gradually, I grew out of the recliner, but I hadn't grown out of our friendship. We were best buddies, so when my heart got crushed, I instinctively sought him out.

The day had begun with all the potential and promise of springtime. The magnolia trees all over town were in full bloom. The precocious red maples were already leafed out. Even the white oaks and pin oaks were showing some early yellow signs of their summer foliage. The grass was as green as it would be all year. The sky as blue as it can ever be. I was seeing the world in high definition. Everything had crisp edges to it.

Because I was on the verge of going to prom with Samantha Stiller.

It turns out, it isn't such a bad thing when bullying puts you on someone's radar if that someone is full of compassion. By the time I arrived as a freshman at Bradford High, I'd hit my growth spurt, Samantha Stiller still remembered me tenderly, and in a fit of magic only adolescence can conjure, we found ourselves sitting next to each other at the first varsity football game of the season. By the end of the weekend we were dating, and two years later I was just days away from accompanying her to her junior prom. At least, at the beginning of the day I had been.

Samantha broke up with me at lunch, with an explanation that didn't really explain anything at all. I barely endured the rest of the afternoon and, when the bell rang, I rushed out of the building knowing I couldn't go through it alone, but the wound was too fresh and it was oozing too much shame to share with Benjamin or my other friends. I'd been repeating one mantra, over and over again, all afternoon: Dad will know what to do.

By midafternoon, the day had turned into one of those exceptionally hot late-spring days that feels more like midsummer. As I walked past magnolia trees with flowers prematurely browning and dropping from their limbs, I felt a sort of kinship with them, well aware of how quickly beauty could wither, how easily potential could simply become the past, how transient it all really is. It was enough to make a kid feel very, very old.

However, standing in front of my father's office, backpack slung over my shoulder, I'm a kid who feels more than old. I feel confused.

The rolling blinds are lowered, and I've never seen them that way in the afternoon. I see the sign in the window flipped to "Come on in!" and my confusion deepens further. Drying tears are tightening up the skin on my cheeks, but my vision and my mind are clear again. I realize I've been chewing a disintegrating piece of Winterfresh gum since the morning, straight through the lunch I'd lost interest in eating. As I spit it into the storm sewer, I decide my dad must have left early for the day, already lowering the blinds in preparation for tomorrow morning's sunrise, forgetting to flip the sign to "Sorry, we're out!" Nevertheless, I've come this far, so I try the door handle anyway. My confusion deepens even more as the handle gives and turns.

My dad had been talking for years about installing a bell that would tinkle upon entry. For the rest of that afternoon, that's what I will spend my time wishing—not that Samantha Stiller would change her mind and take me back but that my dad had heard me coming. It's remarkable, really, how much time we spend denying the present by wishing for a past that might have prevented it from happening.

16

TWENTY-THREE YEARS LATER, my hand was hovering over the doorknob.

But I couldn't do it. I couldn't bring myself to think about what I'd heard that afternoon upon pushing the door inward, or what I'd seen after walking into the waiting area. If the past is a long-lost land within us, and memory the highway that can take us there, I no longer wanted to travel it. I didn't want to travel it in my dreams. I didn't want to travel it at my dad's old office. And I certainly didn't want to travel it with my mother in the house I used to call home.

So I got back in my car and drove to Benjamin's childhood home instead.

It was the site of my first sleepover as a grade schooler, where we'd taken homecoming photos in high school, where we'd celebrated our college graduations, and the house in which his parents had lived together until the passing of his father the year before. Mr. Bruce's memorial service was the first time I'd felt grief at the loss of a father figure, and it was the last time I'd returned to Bradford's Ferry. Mrs. Bruce had always welcomed me into their family as if I were her very own son. I'd always been drawn to her warmth, like a moth to a flame, and so I was again.

I took Main Street through the heart of the Ferry's little downtown, passing the darkened windows of the Draughty Den, and approaching the only bridge spanning the Saukenuk River for miles in either direction, in the very location where Bradford had operated his ferry centuries before. As it came into sight, my heart quickened, and I found myself noting the presence of concrete and the absence of rotted wood slats. The dam upriver, on the other hand, appeared exactly as it had in my dream. I was embarrassingly relieved to cross the river without a sudden rise in the water level.

On the other side of the bridge, I took the second left and found myself passing humble homes, some being valiantly maintained despite meager resources, others looking sadly surrendered to the elements—time and weather and economic downturns. Turning onto the Bruces' block, I noticed the size of the homes increased dramatically. Mr. Bruce had been one of the few therapists in town, and a good one. The principles of supply and demand had made for a successful business and a comfortable small-town life.

As I pulled into the Bruces' driveway, though, the long grass and overgrown flower beds were like a vacancy sign hanging on the property. I remembered Benjamin telling me that, since his father's death, his mother had been spending more and more time at their winter home in Scottsdale. I'd assumed she had returned to Bradford's Ferry for the summer months, but it appeared she hadn't. I decided to make sure.

When my knock at the front door went unanswered, I walked around the side of the house to peer through a living room window. The interior was dark and had the kind of orderly look that only a house prepared for seasonal neglect can have. I made my way back to my car, crouching near a flower bed to pull several particularly long weeds that were choking out a struggling rose bush. I pulled another one, and another one.

I pulled weeds for the next six hours.

The afternoon sun was tilting well toward the horizon when a text notification buzzed in my pocket, disrupting my trance. My chest tightened as it had when the bridge had come into sight. *Rebecca.* I wiped my hands on my now-grimy shorts and tugged the phone from my pocket, looking at the notification on the lock screen. My chest tightened the *rest* of the way. It wasn't from Rebecca. It was from my mom.

I hear you're in town. Are you planning to swing by before you leave?

I stuffed the phone back in my pocket and proceeded to pull weeds for another two hours, until every last flower bed was immaculate. Tired, dirty, wrung out, and beginning to get hungry again, I pulled the phone from my pocket once more and responded. *Hey, yeah, sort of a spontaneous visit, who told you? I was actually thinking of staying for a night or two, if it wouldn't be too much trouble.*

I hit send. The little dots that immediately appeared suggested she'd been waiting for my response, though the tone of her next message communicated something less than eager anticipation. *Someone thought they saw you at Joey's this morning, and Joleen Jarrett says you've been weeding Marjorie Bruce's flower beds all afternoon. You are welcome to stay overnight. If you want.*

Great. I'm done here. I'll head over now, I replied.

Will you be hungry for dinner?

Don't worry about it.

Okay.

Two people doing their best to avoid hurting each other and succeeding only at inflicting the most exquisite of wounds—the feeling that you don't matter very much to each other at all.

My childhood home was located less than a mile away, in one of those humbler neighborhoods. As I drove past homes with siding more than a generation overdue for replacement and lawns burned brown by the August sun, I noted the gullies lining both sides of the road. They were a little deeper than they'd been thirty years ago on that warm February afternoon, but their destinations were unchanged. The gullies seemed like a metaphor for the past, and water a metaphor for the self. You could try to force yourself to flow on other courses, but the gully of your history is insistent—always drawing you back in, deepening over time as a meager concession to you, but channeling you in a direction of its choosing, and never changing the destination at which it deposits you. The writer in me noted I was thinking in metaphors again. This was a good sign. It gave me hope.

That hope was quickly dashed by guilt as I pulled into my mother's driveway.

To say the house lacked curb appeal would be an understatement. It didn't even have *gully* appeal. It was originally a tiny, two-bedroom ranch dwelling with a rectangular façade adorned only by a barren door and one large window, but my father had expanded the home twice with additions that couldn't be seen from the road, extending behind the original structure. So, from the street, it looked like something you survived in, not something you lived in. However, my guilt wasn't triggered by the appearance of the house; it was triggered by the appearance of the landscaping.

My mom's flower beds were almost as overgrown as Mrs. Bruce's.

I'd spent the day coming to the aid of my surrogate mother instead of my biological mother. I imagined what that must feel like for her, and I disliked myself for doing it to her. Apparently, though, the lid of that cauldron within me had been lifted for good, and the feeling of guilt was quickly swept aside by a thought hotter than the August sun: "You've always kept your warmth to yourself, Mother, so you can keep your weeds to yourself too." Warmth and weeds. An alliteration. The writer in me was waking up, and with that awakening came another wave of hope.

I coasted down the driveway, which wrapped around the back of the house, to where my father had attached a garage to the second addition. The garage door was open, and his old spot was sitting empty next to my mother's car. Out of habit, I parked next to the garage, where I'd been parking since I was sixteen years old. Getting out, I examined the old hoop hanging from the garage, the same hoop at which I'd shot baskets on that warm February afternoon so many years ago. Back then, the acrylic backboard was as clear as glass, with a net as white as the driven snow hanging from a glossy, pumpkin-orange rim. Now, the backboard was foggy and cracked across the top left corner. The rim was rusty brown and tilted at an angle. The net was long gone. Time had done to the hoop what it had done to my hope.

Hoop and hope. The wordplay was music to my ears. It sounded like writer's block coming to an end. The decision to return to the Ferry was starting to feel like the right one, old memories and old law offices notwithstanding. I added "apologize to Jeff" to my relational to-do list, gathered my bag from the back seat, and entered the home through the garage.

The aroma of sizzling beef filled the space. Good, I thought, she'd heeded my text and had not planned dinner for me. I hadn't eaten meat in more than ten years, not because I was principled in any particular way but because my stomach had quit getting along with it sometime shortly after I met Rebecca. My mother's responsiveness to my request opened my heart to her a little. You had to seize opportunities like that with my mom. They were few and far between.

I followed a long, narrow hallway past her bedroom, where it opened up into a family room with high ceilings and a dramatic stone fireplace. From there, a large arched doorway connected this second addition to the first addition, which was comprised almost entirely of a sprawling kitchen. My mother was standing at the stove with her back to me, monitoring a skillet with two beef patties on it, and she turned as I entered.

Her appearance never ceased to take me off guard. In my mind's eye, she was always the mother of my adolescent years. This woman standing in front of me, though, was in her seventies. She had finally allowed her hair to go white and, though she was healthy, frailty was lapping at the edges of her aging body. She was skinnier than I remembered her too. I couldn't picture someone in her condition getting down on her knees to weed anything, and the pang of guilt returned. Hope. Guilt. Hope. Guilt.

I was swinging on a pendulum without a steady center.

She didn't come toward me to embrace me, nor did I move toward her. Hugging her had always been an awkward experience. You could sense she felt obligated to do it—you could sense it in the space she left between the two of you, the awkward pats on the back, the brevity of it—and its obligatory nature nullified anything meaningful a son might receive from it. Instead of embracing me, she smiled a vague sort of smile and then exclaimed—with a gaiety that matched nothing about the situation—that she'd made burgers for both of us. My head spun. It had taken us exactly ten seconds to re-create yet another precarious moment in our relationship.

I had a couple of options. I could show up authentically, graciously thank her for the gesture, and remind her that I don't eat meat anymore. Or I could eat the burger. If I did the latter, I'd wake up in the night with excruciating stomach cramps. If I was honest with her, however, that merest wisp of transparency would set off a chain reaction of *relational* cramps, which were just as painful, and in some ways more so. I'd feel all the energy with which she'd mustered her happy hello suddenly evaporate, like a vortex of light gravitationally drawn back into the black hole at the center of her. In its place, I'd be left either with silence or a sequence of passive-aggressive comments, likely to culminate in something more venomous after a glass of wine or two. Then, I'd leave.

We'd done this dance countless times over the years, and I'd concluded long ago she was too emotionally fragile to handle the weight of my honesty. In other words, I'd eaten a lot of burgers—made both of meat and metaphor—in the hopes of avoiding the worst of being loved by my mom. So I opened my mouth, planning to tell her that burgers were fine, and I was shocked to hear myself showing up honestly instead.

"I can't eat burgers, Mom. My stomach can't handle them for some reason."

She stared at me, her chin raising almost imperceptibly. *Here we go*, I thought.

"What are you talking about, you ate burgers the last time you were here." Not a question nor a statement, but a challenge.

I still had an opportunity to put this evening back into its disingenuous box, and I tried, but I couldn't get it all the way back in. "Yeah, it's been getting worse. Thanks, though. I can grab something from the fridge or order a pizza. I'm not really hungry anyway." I was ravenous.

"This is prime grade beef from Paisley's Meat Market," she said in a clipped tone. "I'm sure it won't be a problem for you." She turned her back to me and flipped the burgers. They sizzled as she pressed them into the skillet. "Do you want the works on it?" I saw next to the stove two plates, each with an open bun already layered with the works.

"Mom, seriously. I'm good. It's no big deal. I'll run out and grab a sandwich from Subway." Then, in a moment of desperate inspiration, "I'll swing by the grocery store and pick up some ice cream. We'll split it." I hoped I'd made a successful plea, but when she turned around, I saw it hadn't done anything to ease the blow to her complicated matrix of maternal self-image. She decided to defend that self-image with a non sequitur.

"Is this one of those environmental things, Eli? The libs are always ranting about cow farts destroying the world. Meanwhile, the dead babies are piling up and they seem to have no problem with that. This meat was fed on grass and killed before it had any chance to stink up the skies. You can eat a burger and get your priorities straight."

I looked at her, hoping to see the same kind of fire in her eyes Rebecca had shown me on her departure. After all, you can relate to fire—it gives you something to put out. But there was none there. In fact, she was completely gone from behind her eyes. It had taken all of about a minute and a half.

"Mom, I don't want to talk about burgers or politics."

Her chin was jutting now. "Where are Rebecca and the kids, are they okay?" Then, apparently deeming that question too soft, she lobbed another one at me. "You know, I've been getting calls from people looking for you. They sound like creditors. Are you in some kind of trouble, Eli?" It wasn't concern, it was an accusation. Answering her wouldn't give her clarification; it would give her ammunition.

"Would it be okay if I took a quick shower?" Already I'd been reduced to a little boy asking for the most basic of permissions from his mother. The past is always behind us, but it is also, always, within us.

She turned back to the stovetop. "Yes, but make it quick," she ordered in a singsong voice, as if we'd just had the most pleasant of chats. "This burger won't take long to get cold!"

17

WHETHER IT WAS THE WARMTH of the water or the pressure of the past pushing its way into the present, by the time I got out of the shower, my hunger had been replaced by fatigue. I wanted only to go into that great alone which we call sleep, and become oblivious to everything. However, I couldn't, because long ago my dad had bought me a waterbed.

My bedroom was preserved like a fossil in the sediment of childhood. Medals draped over trophies on a slightly dusty dresser. Posters still gummed to the walls with putty. Memorabilia from every Chicago sports team, including a Bulls wristband perched at an angle against a framed and autographed photo of William "The Refrigerator" Perry on my desk. My old waterbed was still pushed against the far wall, partially obscuring the room's only window. When I was twelve, I'd asked my parents for that waterbed; my mom had said no, and my father had overridden her veto.

My hope for sleep quickly evaporated as I put my hand on its yielding surface, confirming it would need to be warmed up for several hours before sleeping on it. I turned the knob on the headboard to eighty-five degrees and resigned myself to going back downstairs. I'm not sure why I did what I did next—perhaps

I was too tired to pretend, or perhaps there was a part of me still hoping for some nurturance—but as I sat down to a hamburger I had no intention of eating, I decided to answer my mother's original question, and to answer it honestly. I told her Rebecca had left me and taken Sarah with her.

Her face went blank and, in that moment, I had a chance to wonder if my mother might have changed. Then her chin tilted higher than I'd ever seen it, her lips pursed, and God help me, I saw victory in her eyes as if to say, "See, the hamburger isn't *my* fault. You're difficult to live with. *So* difficult in fact that no one wants to live with you at all."

Her lips unpursed into a question. "Why, Eli, what did you do?"

Before she could see the tears in my eyes, I got up and left.

I drove around aimlessly for a while before remembering Joey's invitation to join him at the Draughty Den around eight. I decided to beat him there by a couple hours and get a head start. I parked in the small lot behind the Den and entered through its back door. The single room was dimly lit as always, despite the evening sun filtering through the tall windows looking out onto Main Street at the far end of the space. A bar with a copper counter extended the length of the left side of the room, backed by an exposed brick wall and adorned by a dozen taps. The wall to my right was dark oak paneling and lined with booths. Down the center, there was a smattering of raised bar tables and stools.

I chose a seat at the near end of the bar and got a nod but no recognition from the handful of men sitting together at the other end of it. I didn't recognize them either. Bradford's Ferry was small, but not so small you couldn't remain a stranger to people. The bartender was no stranger to me, however. She'd been a year or two behind me in high school, and we'd had a passing acquaintance but not much more. I must have looked like fresh meat to her though, because when I ordered a beer, she poured herself the same kind, drank it at the same pace, and started flirting with me. I didn't return the flirtation, but I didn't discourage it either. Along with the beer, it took the edge off the loneliness.

I was already two drinks in at eight when Joey arrived as promised. His obvious delight at seeing me was more emotional sustenance than I'd received in days. I bought us a round. Then he bought us a round. And so on. The beer was light, tasting more like water than barley, but I hadn't eaten anything except the omelet all day. So several hours later, after bidding Joey and the bartender farewell, and trying to insert my key into the ignition several times without even coming close, I decided to walk the mile back to my mother's house.

Crossing the Saukenuk in the buzzing light of the streetlamps that lined both sides of the bridge, I leaned, woozy, over the railing and stared down into the calm, not rushing, not rising waters well below me. A sensation of tipping came over me, and though my feet were firmly on the ground, Jah wished they weren't. Jah wished to fall into those peaceful waters and be swept away to parts unknown.

Eli walked on.

Leaving the bridge behind me, I passed the Bruce home with its tidy flower beds and arrived at my mother's house with its abundance of weeds and scarcity of warmth. I tiptoed past her room and into the kitchen, where I was greeted by a hamburger with the works still sitting on the table, spotlighted by the chandelier over it, which had been left on for me. I ignored it, proceeding to my bedroom, where I dropped onto my warm waterbed without changing out of my clothes.

As the ripples died down beneath me, I decided coming home had been a mistake after all, and I planned to leave first thing in the morning. Then came one final, foreboding thought before I sank into the kind of deep-shallow sleep only too much booze can produce: *When was the last time anything went as planned, Eli?*

18

THE NEXT MORNING, my resolve to leave—like my guilt and hope the day before—swung back and forth on a pendulum.

At first, it was weakened by the way I was awakened—the vibration of my cellphone in my pocket. The in-between-sleeping-and-waking sense it had been vibrating for a while. Jerking upright. Something detonating somewhere behind my eyeballs. Hands shaking. Fumbling to extricate it from the clinging fabric of my blue jeans pocket. Failing to do so quickly enough. The vibrations ceasing. Raising the screen to my squinting eyes. Three missed calls from Rebecca. Heart racing. Trying to call her back. No answer. Dropping back onto my pillow, waiting, the bed undulating beneath me, triggering a wave of seasickness. The buzzing of a voicemail notification.

Sarah's voice.

"Good morning, Daddy!" Bright, oblivious, and unaffected by the realities of her life. I was glad for that. It also made my loneliness complete.

"Mom and I are having *so* much fun with Mom-mom and Pop-pop. Mom-mom has made us pancakes *every* day and Pop-pop and me built a *huge* sandcastle, even bigger than the one I built with you last summer!" Going on, updating me about what sounded like an ideal summer vacation, concluding with, "I hope your book is going good, Daddy, love you, bye!"

No mention of her mom. No indication of returning. No request to call back. Somehow, the whole thing made the prospect of returning to our empty house even more unpalatable than my mother's hamburger with the works. Staying in Bradford's Ferry felt like an option again.

I ventured into the kitchen, hoping to find a cup of coffee. Instead I found another "message" from my mother on the table. It was a note, friendly enough at first glance if you didn't know my mom and if you didn't know what had transpired the evening before. It read, "I'm out to breakfast with a bunch of friends! Help yourself to anything!" The word *bunch* was underlined twice, and a smiley face had been drawn above it. It was her way of telling me that, if I wasn't perfectly pleased with her, it clearly had nothing to do with her because just *look* at all the people who loved her. The pendulum swung back toward leaving. Being alone forever was better than being hurt over and over again.

My bag was half packed when the pendulum swung back toward staying, as it occurred to me that my sleep had been uninterrupted by my childhood nightmare. "I think it means you need to go home," Jeff had said, and once again he'd been right. Like a dream whose mission had been accomplished, it had ceased, at least for a night. The part of me that was desperate for a decent, sober night's sleep worried the dream would return if I left Bradford's Ferry. That part of me wanted to stay.

Another part of me, however, would have rather died a thousand deaths from which I could awake than to have my hope for a mom die one more time in the inalterable light of day.

That part of me wanted to get out of town as fast as possible. My pendulum was suspended in a kind of center that felt anything but centered. I concluded nothing definitive was going to happen until I got a cup of coffee into me.

And the little bit of love that would come with it couldn't hurt either.

$$\sim\!\!\sim$$

The folks of Bradford's Ferry were proud of a lot of things about their little town, and Books on Main was near the top of the list. Founded by my high school English teacher Gus Dempsey—shortly after the school district made room on their payroll for two recent college graduates by offering him a big bonus to retire early—the local bookstore was stewarded by him through the rise of Amazon and the demise of brick-and-mortar bookstores. He'd done so by mimicking what worked for both models. For instance, he'd always insisted on paying his employees a little more than whatever the going wage was at Amazon, and his customer service rivaled that of the online behemoth. Meanwhile, as the big chains began to close their stores, he'd recognized the loss of gathering spaces and added a café, where anyone from the Ferry could get the best cup of coffee and the liveliest conversation in town.

Books on Main was just up the street from the Draughty Den, where my car was already warming in the morning sun. As I set out on foot for Main Street, I was planning to kill three birds with one stone: a good cup of coffee, some conversation with the man who took a fatherly kind of pride in me, and the retrieval of my car. The pride came first.

"Elijah Campbell well I'll be damned!"

Gus greeted me exactly the same way every time I appeared in the store, a flowing sentence as if the whole thing were my whole name. I smiled widely despite my situation. It wasn't a social smile either. It came from a deep and sincere place. It was the smile of the prodigal son beneath all his guilt. It was a quantum smile, recalling every other time Gus had exclaimed those words, grateful for every one of those moments in this particular moment, reveling a little in this ritual of recognition and homecoming that was threaded throughout my story over the last two-plus decades.

I held out my hand and it hit him somewhere in the solar plexus as he wrapped me in a big bear hug. This, too, was part of the ritual. He drew back, holding me by my shoulders at arm's length. His head was wild with salt-and-pepper curls hanging low over eyebrows that were still as bushy and as black as the day I'd first met him in freshman English.

"Gus, I don't know how you do it—you look younger every time I see you."

His smile finally dimmed a little. "Well, young man, I wish I could say the same thing about you, but you're looking a little rough around the edges, aren't you? What you need is a good cup of coffee, and then we're going to do some catching up."

He turned and circled around the counter, transforming himself in a flourish from bookseller into barista. "Now, if I remember correctly, you prefer a light roast with one teaspoon of sugar and a dash of heavy cream?" He didn't stop to confirm. He knew he remembered correctly, and I was so grateful for being so specifically known that the caffeine began to seem duplicative—my energy was already expanding by the moment. "We have an Ethiopian blend this morning that you're going to love," he declared.

From under the counter, he pulled the same mug he reserved for me every time I visited, and within a minute I had my cup of coffee. I sipped it and started to tell him how good it was, but Gus was on to other things. He didn't have to watch and wonder if I liked the coffee. He knew he'd taken good care of me.

He came out from behind the counter and put his arm around me, leading me toward a cluster of tables in the middle of the seating area where five retired gentlemen were gathered, trading jokes and barbs and gossip in what was clearly a daily ritual at Books on Main. We passed the front endcap in the store, where all my books were featured prominently. Gus snagged a copy of each on the way before introducing me to the group as his former student and a published author. He didn't recite my résumé, he just beamed. The men greeted me and then teased Gus about the miracle of his teaching producing anything that could be published. Gus was prepared. He slapped the books down on the center of the table and declared, "The proof is in the pudding, fellas!"

He put his arm around me again and led me beyond them to a table in the far corner of the café where we could have some privacy. "So, young man, I hear you have another book in the works. How goes it?"

"It's going," I said vaguely, looking down at my coffee and sipping on it intently. Gus must have felt the shift in my energy because he graciously shifted his attention away from his favorite subject: writing.

"How long has it been since we last saw you, Elijah? A year? More? What brings you back to the Ferry?"

I was tempted to lead with the truth but couldn't find it in me. How much disappointment could fatherly pride withstand?

A little writer's block, probably. But a broken marriage? Spiritual decay? Financial ruin? This time, I drew on my social smile. "You know, it was sort of a spontaneous thing. Got here yesterday morning, had dinner with my mom last night, some drinks with Joey Junior down at the Den. Just making sure nothing has changed around here, and sure enough, nothing has changed, so I'm headed back home within the hour. Wanted to stop in and make sure you're not starting any trouble before I leave."

His face had grown more serious as I'd remarked on the lack of changes around town. "Well, now, there is one change happening around here, and I bet you'd like to know about it. Father Lou is retiring. At the end of the summer, he'll be heading to Arizona. He says all he wants is to stay warm until the good Lord comes for him!" Gus laughed aloud at the gallows humor.

I sat back in my chair, a little stunned. One of the blessed illusions of Bradford's Ferry was its sense of timelessness. The Saukenuk still ran the same course as it had in the days of John Marcus Bradford. The pub that had reopened as the Draughty Den predated Prohibition. The barber shops still featured the same spinning red-white-and-blue poles as they had when I was a kid. People didn't come and go with the changing of a job. Sure, moments of tragedy shook the illusion, but the Ferry's steady way of life restored it quickly, until the next loss or leaving.

Father Lou was leaving.

He had been the rector at St. Mark's Episcopal Church my entire life, arriving in Bradford's Ferry as a young priest right out of seminary and, over the years, becoming more than just a priest to the Episcopalians at St. Mark's, becoming indeed a spiritual father to anyone in town who needed or wanted one. Though our family had attended the Baptist church across town, Father Lou had been a savior to me on a number of occasions, always appearing at just the right moment. For instance, when I'd skinned my knee on Main Street after hitting a curb with my bike on a summer afternoon in my elementary school years, Father Lou had appeared, helping me to the corner convenience store where he'd purchased a bottle of peroxide and a box of Band-Aids, carefully applying both to my wound. Or the morning of my high school graduation when I'd been sitting at a picnic table in a local park, distraught at my inability to finish my valedictory speech, Father Lou had appeared, and his wise words had inspired what I said later at the ceremony. Or a couple years later, when my dad passed, Father Lou had been the one I turned to for some simple solace in the midst of my complicated grief. I had walked away from that conversation wishing that, on the afternoon Samantha Stiller broke up with me, I'd walked to St. Mark's instead of my dad's office.

Now Father Lou was leaving, and I couldn't let him get away without saying goodbye.

Gus must have read my thoughts because, while I'd been sitting in speechless reflection, he'd picked up his phone and tapped something into it. "I just texted him," he said with a reassuring smile. "I don't know what he's up to this morning, but I do know it won't matter. I'm sure he'll be here within five minutes to say goodbye to you."

Less than three minutes later, Father Lou walked through the door.

~~

"Son, your shoulders are rounded with a heavy burden. Why don't you put some of it down, right here? Gus and I wouldn't mind carrying some of it for a little while, would we, Gus?"

Dressed in his favorite clerical garb—faded blue jeans and a Grateful Dead T-shirt—and with a shock of white hair on his head that made the line between bald and not-bald seem fairly random, Father Lou had joined us at our corner table. After asking Gus for "a cup of whatever Elijah is having," and after Gus returned to the table with a steaming mug marked "Lou," he extended the invitation to unburden myself.

I could feel the strength of my façade beginning to give.

Perhaps it was the gracefulness of his spirit—perhaps he really had allowed himself over the course of his life to be formed into the likeness of Jesus, and I was yet another woman at yet another well. Perhaps he had perfected the art of coaxing confessions from crumbling souls. Or perhaps it was simply the fact that both Gus Dempsey and Father Lou had gotten into my heart in childhood, before I had hidden it away from the rest of the world. Whatever it was, I decided to reveal a little more of the truth than I'd shown to anyone besides Jeff.

"The truth is, Father Lou, I'm struggling to hear my muse." I looked sheepishly at Gus. "I didn't exactly lie to you, Gus. The book is going, it's just not going very well at all." The softening around Gus's eyes told me he had already discerned as much from my tepid response.

I turned back to Father Lou. "I'm supposed to be writing a sort of sequel to *The Whisper in the Wind*. I'm calling it *The Voice in the Void*. It's about hearing the voice of God within us during our dark night of the soul, so to speak. The thing is, I proposed the book when I was feeling spiritually alive, and now I'm having to write it in this spiritual wasteland, and it never occurred to me that there wouldn't *be* any voice in the void. God is gone. The voice of grace within me is silent. Everything I write feels fraudulent. It's like I'm a prisoner sitting in his cell writing a book about how to make a jailbreak. I don't know where to begin."

I stopped there. Short of Rebecca's departure. Short of the creditors calling. It was enough confession for one day.

I looked at Gus, who looked from me to Father Lou as if to say, "Hey, I just sell books, I don't save souls. You're in Lou's neighborhood now."

Father Lou simply sat there quietly, thoroughly present to us while also thoroughly attentive to something going on within himself. We waited until, eventually, he said carefully, "Elijah, I don't have all the answers here. You cannot rush this season you are passing through. The dark night of the soul knows no deadline." He paused, having laid this foundation, then went on. "What I do know is this: When you can't hear God anymore, it's not because God is gone. It's usually because God's waiting for you to have a different kind of conversation." He paused again, then added, "Maybe a more honest conversation."

I laughed a laugh that sounded more like a bark. "Honest conversations have not been my strong suit."

His face softened with compassion. It was the same gentle countenance with which he'd attended to my skinned knee, with which he'd discussed my valedictory speech, with which he'd made space for me to talk about how hard it is to love someone and hate them and lose them all at once. "You know, sometimes it *is* too hard to have those kinds of conversations with those around us. Too much baggage, you know? Sometimes, though, it's a little easier to have those conversations with those who are within us."

"That's the thing, though," I said, confused, "I can't hear the voice of God within me. I can't get the conversation off the ground."

"Oh, I don't mean God, so to speak." He sat back in his chair and gazed out the front window of the shop at Main Street. "You grew up here in this place, Elijah. The ghosts of your loved ones are everywhere in this town. They are also everywhere within *you*. I think it's possible to have honest conversations with them, somewhere on the inside, and I think when you do, the Lord may just speak to you in some mysterious ways."

I laughed again, but this time there was some levity in it. "The Baptists would be freaked out by that idea, Father Lou. Sounds a little New-Agey, if you know what I mean."

He smiled too. He was no stranger to freaking out the Baptists. "That's the funny thing, Elijah. The practice I'm suggesting is as ancient as the Christian faith itself. In our tradition, for instance, we have a way of reading Holy Scripture called *lectio divina*. It's been around for thousands of years. It involves harnessing all your God-given imagination to read the Scriptures in new and trans-formative ways. I guess I'm just suggesting you might draw on that same imagination to start a different kind of conversation within you, and then wait to see who shows up for the discussion."

I thought about how the past had pushed its way into the present at my dad's old law office twenty-four hours earlier, and I wondered if Father Lou might have come to my rescue once again. Thirty minutes later, when I walked out of Books on Main to retrieve my car, I didn't say goodbye to Father Lou for good, because my pendulum had swung decidedly in the direction of staying in Bradford's Ferry for a little while longer.

19

FROM THE ROAD ABOVE IT, the house looked exactly as I remembered, and that sense of the timelessness of things in Bradford's Ferry was fully restored.

Its restoration had begun about an hour after I left Books on Main. Father Lou's words had awakened something within me, something I knew to be true but had always allowed to orbit the outer rings of my consciousness, like yet another secret I was keeping from myself. This town of mine seemed to have thin places in it, places where the distinction between past and present was erased, and all moments that had passed through that particular space somehow congregated in this moment, in the fullness of time so to speak.

I don't think Bradford's Ferry is unusual in this way. I think whenever we root ourselves in any space for any length of time—could be a town, could be a relationship, could be a bar in Boston where everybody knows your name—it becomes a thin place in which time travel is not only possible but probable, assuming your soul is the traveler. They are liminal spaces, bridges, cross-roads, thresholds between everything that has happened to us and everything that is yet to come.

For the first hour, I'd driven around Bradford's Ferry a little aimlessly, awakening, searching for such a space with nothing to show for it. Then, with my awakening waning a little, and contemplating a drive into the countryside, I came to the local bowling alley near the city limits. I'd almost passed it when suddenly I flashed upon Benjamin and me during the winter break of our senior year of high school, opening the place and closing the place every day, on a hopeless quest to bowl the perfect game, both of us knowing it was hopeless but trying anyway because the real goal was to be together as much as possible in those final precious months before adulthood pulled us apart.

I jerked the wheel and pulled into the bowling alley's old unpaved parking lot. The grinding of gravel beneath my tires was slowly silenced as I found a parking spot. Meanwhile, the sound of the gravel transported me to another moment within this very space.

It's a morning in my freshman year of high school. We've gone to the bowling alley for gym class and we're getting back on the bus when, just a few feet from the bus door, one of my classmates exclaims that her earring just fell out. Most of my peers get down on their hands and knees to scour the gravel for it, but I seek a different vantage point. I get on the bus, push one of the windows all the way down, and scan the gritty ground for something sparkling. The springtime sun glints off something, and there it is. I shout directions to my classmates below. I'm a hero, but the adulation matters little to me. I'm marveling instead at my discovery—what you can see when you find a new angle from which to look at the world.

Time fully collapsed in on itself: I was both fourteen and thirty-nine, all at once. It was springtime and summertime, all at once. I was looking for a new angle, then and now, all at once. My mind's eye climbed above the gravelly ground of Bradford's

Ferry and looked down on it, scanning the town for the glint of sunlight off one sparkling place. And I saw it. My instinct to drive into the countryside had been correct—if there was one place in Bradford's Ferry outside my own home where I'd spent most of my youth, it was my grandmother's house. Nestled in a wooded subdivision just outside the city limits, it was the place where my heart had always felt most free, and perhaps the place where it could be freed once again.

Five minutes later, I was there. And looking down the steep driveway to a colonial-style home whose backyard ran the rest of the way down the hill to a creek separating the lawn from the wild, I could feel the thinness of things.

I'm riding on a tractor with my grandpa, mowing the empty lot next to the home. I'm burrowing caverns for my Star Wars action figures in the large dirt pile that sits at the far edge of the lot. I'm rooting around in the musty shed down by the creek, discovering my uncle's boyhood baseball bat, half-rotted but somehow more valuable than ever to a boy like me. I'm indoors with my putter, knocking golf balls around their living room on a rainy day, eating freshly sliced peaches sprinkled with sugar, napping beneath the warm country breeze rustling the curtains on the guest room windows.

Indoors. I sensed that's where I would find an even thinner space.

However, I had no idea who lived there. My grandfather had sold it shortly after my grandmother's death—unable to live within his thinnest of spaces without her—and he had passed shortly thereafter. The idea of knocking on a stranger's door and begging entrance to their home seemed impolite and absurd, at first. Then again, I thought, my life had become absurd. Everything I loved was dying right in front of my eyes. My heart was in hospice, and in hospice everyone is a little less particular about social niceties. I got out of the car.

Whoever answered the door would have to be either dangerously naive or completely kind to let me in.

I rang the doorbell and heard the frail voice of a woman call back from inside. It took her almost a minute to reach the door, and she opened it slowly, though not cautiously. She said hello with a question mark at the end of it. I spoke to her through the screen door.

"Hi, ma'am. My name is Elijah Campbell. I'm not sure if you know my mother, Annette Campbell?" There was no recognition on her face. "Anyway, I, uh, I grew up here in Bradford's Ferry and I'm an author," as if writing books precluded you from being completely unhinged, "and well, uh, I know this is a strange thing to ask, but my grandparents built this house and it's a very special place to me and I was, uh, just sort of wondering if I could come in and have a look around. I'll totally understand if you're uncomfortable with that and need to say no, but . . . I just had to ask."

Her tiny smile looked like the sparkling of something in the gravel.

She introduced herself as Mabel and walked ahead of me into the living room, where a door to our left revealed a kitchen adorned with the same wallpaper as in my youth. The living room decor, too, was almost completely unaltered. On the wall to my right, a brick fireplace was surrounded by dark wood paneling. Ahead of me, sliding glass doors opened onto a small patio and steps leading down to the back lawn, the creek, and the forest. However, the thinnest of all things was the La-Z-Boy recliner sitting at an angle, partially blocking the sliding doors, and the sofa facing it, a coffee table between them. The furniture was different, of course, but its placement was a re-creation of the conversational space I'd enjoyed most with my grandmother.

"Can I get you a glass of lemonade?" Mabel asked with concern in her voice.

I got the sense she'd already asked me this at least once. I tried to explain myself. "I'm sorry, this is all just so familiar. My grandmother's chair used to sit in that very spot. I used to sit right there on the couch and talk to her. The last time was the spring of my junior year of college. She died later that spring before I got a chance to come home and say goodbye." My voice was husky with the past.

Mabel noticed. "I have a few things to tend to in the kitchen. Why don't I take care of those, give you a minute or two in here, and then I'll bring you that lemonade." She shuffled off without waiting for an answer, and I was alone, or at least as alone as you can be in a space as thin as that one.

I sat down on the couch, remembering Father Lou's words, his description of the ancient practice of harnessing our imagination to start a dialogue with Holy Scripture, and his encouragement to draw upon that same imagination to start a new kind of conversation within me. It was the strangest step of faith I'd ever taken, to close my eyes, to open that door within me that holds the past apart from the rest of me, to insert the key of imagination into its lock, and to allow whoever showed up to speak up. I closed my eyes.

I turned the key.

20

MY MEMORY BRINGS US TOGETHER on a Saturday morning sometime in the autumn of my freshman year of college. It's homecoming weekend in Bradford's Ferry and the first time Benjamin and I have seen each other since we left for college two months earlier. I'm making my favorite stop of the weekend—Grandma and Grandpa's house, where I'll sit on the couch while she listens quietly to stories about my adventures on campus. In actuality, I remember nothing specific about that visit, which is perhaps why I can imagine whatever I want about it.

In my mind's eye, it's just her and me. My grandfather has left the room because the smell of the grape soda she poured for me has quickly made him nauseous. She sits in her turquoise recliner, leg rest down, feet on the floor, hands in her lap, her right thumb and forefinger rubbing endlessly together. Dried leaves skitter across the patio outside the sliding glass door next to her. A white, lidded bowl sits at the center of the coffee table between us, containing candy—a chalky mint with a jelly center—that I never really liked but could never really resist.

Some things are different, though. I may be eighteen in this memory, but I'm also every other age I've ever been. I suspect she's every age she's ever been, too, and then some. Also, there's something clearly different about her. I tell her about my courses and my roommate and how the cafeteria food is already making me a little thicker, and she's listening attentively as always, but she's not as quiet as she used to be. She's talking more. Somehow, though, in the talking, I feel more heard than ever. I decide to ask her about it.

"You were so quiet then, Grandma, when you were alive. You would listen to me for as long as I was willing to talk. You just went along for the ride. Right now, though, you're more talkative. It's like you're steering the ride. Why?"

She smiles, then responds in a way that makes me feel like she's scratching my back before a nap on one of those summer afternoons. "Well, I suppose it's because back then you needed me to listen. You needed my interest. Now you need me to talk. You need my direction."

The way she is showing up differently makes me want to show up differently, too. "There's something I never told you, Grandma. I told you about all the good things that were happening at college, but I never told you how terribly alone I felt most of the time there. It wasn't just homesickness. It was heartsickness."

She considers this. "No, you're right, you never did tell me. But I could sense it in you. The unhappiness in me could see the unhappiness in you."

She says this mildly, almost pleasantly, as if we're chatting about a forecast for passing showers in the afternoon, and I feel something unfamiliar to my relationship with her: I'm frustrated. I don't like her nonchalance about my unhappiness, about *our* unhappiness.

"You say that so matter-of-factly, Grandma. You say that as if unhappiness is something you're okay with."

"Not only am I okay with it, I'm grateful for it." Though she's speaking more, her speaking is as simple and sincere as her listening once was.

"You don't think we should be happy?" I ask, though it doesn't sound like much of a question at all. It sounds like a challenge.

"Oh no, I want you to be happy." She pauses. The far-off look in her eyes suggests she's searching for a memory of her own. She appears to find it. "Do you remember your first day of kindergarten?"

Suddenly, I'm five years old again and I'm not sitting in her living room; I'm playing in her yard. The day had begun like it begins for many kindergarteners on their first foray into the world—new and lonely and scary. Walking into that cavernous school had felt like walking into a strange land where I neither know the language nor another soul.

That changed at recess when I spotted a kid named Benjamin sitting apart from the other kids on the playground, thumbing through some baseball cards. Baseball cards were a language I could speak. He'd had a Lee Smith Donruss rookie card and I'd had a Jody Davis Fleer All-Star card, and by the time my grandmother picked me up at noon, I was as relieved and as happy as a five-year-old can be. Upon arriving at their house, I discovered my grandpa had attached an old apple bushel basket, with the bottom cut out, to one of his trees. He handed me a ball, and I spent the afternoon shooting baskets and basking in my happiness.

Now, the smile on my face shows I've remembered that happiness. She goes on. "You see, happiness is good. Very good." She pauses momentarily. "It's just not reliable. It comes and goes as quickly as our good luck and our bad luck."

Speaking more to herself than to me, she says, "Of course, that's not really a problem, either." She pauses again, brow furrowed. Then her brow unfurrows and she looks me in the eye. "The problem is, happiness is sticky. And it's sweet. Like the caramel on the apples we bring you every fall from the orchard up north. It feels so good you want more and more of it. The truth is, though, it's really just the surface of your deepest want. There's fruit underneath it. But if you never run out of caramel, you'll never get to the fruit." She pauses again, looking for a way out of the metaphor. "If you never run out of happiness, you'll never taste anything deeper than it."

This time, she seems to hear my question without me even asking it: What's deeper? And with the most unassuming of smiles, she says it.

"Joy."

I'm silent for a while. Then I repeat it. "Joy," I say, though the word doesn't come out sounding joyful. It sounds dull, and I sound dissatisfied. Her patience with me, though, apparently knows no end. The joy hasn't left her voice as she invites me into more memory.

"Do you remember what you did later that afternoon when you got tired of shooting baskets in the yard? I do, because I called you for dinner and you didn't respond and you scared the living daylights out of me." She chuckles to herself, recalling her alarm.

At first I shake my head no, but already a memory is surfacing within me. I picture that big pile of dirt at the edge of their property and an opening in the trees beyond it. A path.

"I went for a walk in the woods, didn't I?" There's awe in my voice, the kind of awe you might feel if you had hidden a little childhood treasure—the horror novel that awakened you to the wonders of reading, say, or the only photograph of you with your first dog—beneath a loose floorboard, forgotten you'd done so, and stumbled upon it a quarter century later while putting in new floors.

"Yes, you did," she says, chuckling again. "And do you remember what you told me about that walk when you finally got back, long after all the hamburgers were cold?"

It's starting to come back to me, though I'm not totally sure I can trust its veracity after so many years. Then I, too, chuckle because I'm starting to wonder if, in this place of memory and imagination, with the ghost of my grandmother, there's a Truth that is truer than eyewitness reports.

"Did I tell you that I found the stream, deep in the woods, even though the path ended way before it?"

She smiles. "Yes, that's exactly what you told me. You started out on the path, and you followed it as far as it would take you. By then, though, you could hear ever so faintly the babbling of the brook somewhere off in the distance. So, given that you couldn't depend on the path anymore, you wandered into the wilderness and, every once in a while, you'd stop and listen . . ."

"And I'd turn in the direction of the sound," I say, completing her thought.

"That's right," she confirms. "And you know what? When you told me about starting out on the path, I could hear happiness in your voice. But when you told me about winding your way through the woods with only two things to guide you—the sound of the stream and your faith that it was worth walking toward—you had something else in your voice entirely."

"Joy," I say, but this time the dissatisfaction is replaced with a kind of awe.

"That's right," she says, now beaming at me like a proud teacher toward her prized pupil. "Happiness is had on the well-worn paths of our lives, when our plans are working out and our direction seems clear. But you have to leave that kind of happiness behind in order to venture into the wild, to fine-tune your ability to listen for love, and to enjoy the journey toward it, despite all its uncertainty and hardship."

She says the word *enjoy* as if it has a hyphen between the *n* and the *j*. En-joy. To enter into the joy of.

"Your cancer, that was your journey into the wild, wasn't it?"

"Yes, it was." She ponders for a moment. "Of course, there were others. That's just life. You leave the path, then you feel like you find the path again, for a while. But it never lasts very long. Not if you're growing, at least. Not if you're listening to that beautiful babbling far off and trying to find your way to it. Cancer was my wild, but I had a lot of wilds in my life." I watch her travel through her own memories for a moment or two before she returns to me. "Lymphoma was certainly my longest, though, and my last."

I pick up a mint and eat it to distract myself from the sadness I'm feeling, but it doesn't work. I think of how sweet it is, like the caramel of an apple, like happiness, and I think about the deeper thing—the fruit, the joy—that waits for us beyond our happiness. My eyes begin to fill. "I always thought you were so peaceful at the end, Grandma. But you were more than peaceful, weren't you? You were . . . joyful."

She smiles, and for the first time I see a twinkle in her eye. My grandma's eyes had been soft and kind, but they never twinkled.

I begin to realize there's more going on here than meets the eye. There's more going on here than even mere memory can muster.

"Right now, you're more than joyful, aren't you?" I ask. "Right now, you're . . ." and I hesitate here because what I'm about to say sounds bizarre, even to my own imaginative ears, "you're even more than my grandma, aren't you? That's why you're talking more than usual. You're *more* than you used to be."

The size of her smile doesn't change, but the tenderness of it grows. "Yes," she says.

I wait, and once again she can hear my unasked question.

"I am Joy itself, right here inside of you." The way she says it, it feels less like an answer to my unasked question and more like a finger wagging, beckoning me forward.

"Are you even more than *Joy*?" I ask, with more than a little incredulity.

She smiles that tenderest of smiles once again and reveals to me the rest of the good news. "Yes. I am all of it. I am the happiness you have felt. I am the joy for which you yearn. I am the poorness of spirit—the unhappiness—by which you travel from happiness into joy. I am the path and the babbling brook and all the getting lost in between. I am the whole journey and the destination and the grace that holds all of it together. I'm here within you, putting a face to all of it. You have left the path, Eli. You are in the wild. Keep going. There is something beautiful waiting for you, beyond all of this, beneath all of this."

"Underneath the caramel," I murmur.

"Underneath the caramel," she agrees.

And her thumb rubs against her forefinger, endlessly, eternally.

21

WHEN I OPENED MY EYES, Mabel was standing over me with
the lemonade in her hand. The look on her face was that of a
woman about to call 911.

Opening my eyes didn't help the situation. There was a light
in them that hadn't been there just a few minutes earlier, like the
sun dawning over the ocean at precisely the moment a nighttime
of clouds begins to part, a sliver of radiance on the horizon, all
the more dazzling for the grayness surrounding it. I looked at
Mabel and she took a small step backward. To her, I'm guessing,
the light in my eyes looked a little maniacal.

I considered telling her the truth—I'd been enduring a long,
dark night of the soul and something had just happened that I
believed was the beginning of its ending. I considered telling her
my imagination had unlocked the magic of this thin space, and I'd
had a conversation with my deceased grandmother that felt as real
as any conversation I'd had with her while she was alive. I considered telling her my imagination had mingled with my history
and my faith to transform this living room of hers into a holy place.

I considered telling her all these things, but then I pictured
the look that would come over her face—the look of somebody
who is pretending they don't know the person in front of them

is crazy in the hopes of not provoking them into deeper madness. And *that* image made me laugh out loud—a sudden "Ha!" that echoed in the stillness of the house—which did nothing to enhance the sense of sanity I was hoping to project. Mabel took another step backward.

It was clear if I wanted to reciprocate Mabel's kindness, the thing to do was to get out of her life as quickly as possible. So that's what I did. Thanking her for her hospitality, I showed myself out the front door with her trailing me at a safe distance, the deadbolt clicking behind me as soon as I'd cleared the front steps. As I got into my car—knowing Mabel thought I'd gone a little crazy when in fact I'd gotten a little liberated—I vowed to never again judge someone based on their outer appearances.

I managed to honor that vow for all of about three hours.

I spent most of those three hours driving around, snacking on drive-through food while reflecting on what had just happened in my grandparents' old living room. Eventually, with the gas gauge teasing the empty line—but my heart and stomach as full as they'd been in a long time—I headed for my mother's house, hopeful about what might happen there. Of course, it is silly to hope the world around you will change simply because the world *within* you has. Grace doesn't change *what* we see; it changes the *way* we see it. In that sense, I suppose, the work of grace is never done in us, and in me it had barely gotten started.

I pulled into the driveway, windows down, playing an old Tom Petty song about falling gracefully, when I smelled it. Coming from the grill on the back deck, wafting on the warm summer breeze, the smell of barbecuing chicken. My mother's specialty. And the source of our next conflict. I hit the brakes at the top of the driveway and anticipated the scene.

HER. I made your favorite—honey-barbecued chicken breasts!

ME. Oh, Mom, it smells great, but I just ate and, uh, remember . . . I don't eat meat?

HER. Chicken isn't meat! Besides, nobody ever blamed a chicken for ruining the ozone!

ME. Mom, I told you, it's not an environmental thing. It's a stomach thing.

HER. Nonsense, your stomach liked this recipe just fine as a kid. I made you two but you only have to eat one.

ME. Mom, I'm not a kid anymore. You can't make me sit at the table until my food is done.

The evening would grow gradually nastier as it wore on. She'd pick at me like she'd pick at her chicken breast, wordlessly implying that my refusal to eat my meal was going to, in a selfless act of solidarity, result in her own starvation. The wine would mix with her empty stomach, and she'd slip into a particular pattern of dialogue—questions about my life, reflection on the superiority of hers, questions about my life, reflection on the superiority of hers—until I'd express, in one form or another, how exhausting it was to be with her, and she'd finally have evoked a behavior of mine that she felt justified to attack more aggressively.

I killed the engine, left the car parked at the top of the driveway, and took a seat on the front stoop. The gap in my mental clouds through which I'd glimpsed that gorgeous light had been erased by a new storm front rolling in. My thoughts were cumulonimbus in nature—big, dark, and stacking up on each other, blocking out everything else. I shuffled through various doomed solutions to this predicament. I considered changing the script with my mother by walking into the house and preempting her aggression with some of my own. I considered another shower, another evening at the Den, another night of oblivion in my old waterbed. I considered getting back in the car and driving out of town—there was nothing in my duffel bag that couldn't be replaced at a price much lower than the cost of walking back into my mother's house—but I couldn't leave my laptop behind.

I looked up indecisively, taking in the neighborhood around me, and without warning I felt twelve years old, fourteen years old, and thirty-nine years old, all at once. Sometimes you go looking for thin places, and sometimes they come looking for you. This time, I didn't draw on my imagination to unlock the compartment within me that holds my past.

This time, that door seemed to open from the inside.

22

IT'S A SUMMER MORNING between my sixth- and seventh-grade years, and I'm sitting on the very same stoop, in the very same space, waiting for my grandfather's car to come into sight.

My father's father. A giant of a man, both physically and reputationally. Born in Pennsylvania to Scotch Irish farmers, he was drawn to the Midwest by his stationing during the Second World War. A decorated veteran and a natural leader, he left his mark on Bradford's Ferry. Police chief. School board president. Youth athletic coach extraordinaire. Handyman to all, in the tradition of the town's namesake. There was a decade during the heyday of Bradford's Ferry in which, if you asked anyone to name the most dependable person in town, Richard "Rich" Campbell would have been at the top of the list.

I only ever knew him as Grandpa. Mostly bald, beginning every day with an unambitious comb-over that by noontime was always in wispy disarray. Tiny potbelly protruding through ever-present suspenders. Skinny arms and legs. Quiet. Until you needed something from him. Then, a word or two, or a silent solution, or a little of both, like the time my mother's earrings were accidentally swept into her bathroom sink. My father had called Grandpa Rich, asking if there was any way to get them back. He'd arrived ten minutes later toting a toolbox, knowing my father didn't have one. Within minutes, he'd retrieved the earrings from the p-trap beneath the sink, saying with an unassuming smile, "You can find almost anything if you know where to look."

On this morning, he's taking me to play nine holes of golf, as he has almost every weekday morning for the last three summers, and we both know what's going to happen. After nine holes he's going to say, "Well, this ole mutt is whupped, ready to head home?" and I'm going to beg him to play another nine holes and he's going to tell me to go for it and I'm going to finish my round and then call him from the clubhouse to let him know I'm ready to be picked up.

Which is why I have his phone number memorized.

I'm also fourteen years old, sitting on this stoop. It's my first day of high school, and I'm enduring the greatest humiliation of my young life. I'm waiting for my ride: Wendy Valhalla. She's a junior and a varsity cheerleader and she spent the summer keeping an eye on me while my parents were at work. My parents called it "babysitting," but Wendy herself refused to use the term. We'd hit it off and, on her last day of "work," she'd offered me a daily ride to high school. "I'll pick you up at 7:30 sharp," she'd said. 7:30. Those digits had been emblazoned in my mind for a week. They were luminous inside me.

I'd gotten up earlier than necessary and parked myself on the front steps by 7:15. As the seconds ticked by, a kaleidoscope of butterflies collected in my stomach, their fluttering growing in intensity as the time on my wristwatch changed to 7:30. Then, as the minutes continued to tick by, the fluttering morphed into cramping.

It's 7:45 now and miles away the school bell is ringing, and I'm beginning to admit to myself that Wendy Valhalla has forgotten about me. The reality of my forgettability is so shameful it's almost debilitating. My brain won't work. My dad is in court all morning, unreachable. I could call my mom, but she'll pepper me with questions, each one suggesting I must have done *something* to alienate Wendy.

I'm paralyzed until the number 7:30 is replaced in my mind's eye by my grandfather's phone number.

I call him and sure enough, within ten minutes, he's pulling into the driveway, his car coming to rest in the same spot where my car sits now. I can't bring myself to move, so he gets out of the car, ambles across the lawn, and sits down beside me on the step with an exaggerated groan, reminding me what an ole mutt he considers himself to be. I have no idea what to say, but I don't need to, because Grandpa always knows what to say.

"Well, no matter how crappy your round of golf, it's better than this, isn't it?"

Just like that, knowing where to look, he's found my shame, but he's found it with the tools of grace. The dam of sorrow that has built up inside me lets go. Tears begin to flow. I'm fourteen years old, sitting on the front steps, crying with my grandfather.

And I'm thirty-nine years old, sitting on the front steps, crying once again. In the mystery of imagination, he's sitting next to me now, too, wispy hair swaying ever so slightly in the evening breeze. I look at him through my tears.

"I miss you so much, Grandpa." Then, because it's one thing to tell a person you miss them but another thing entirely to tell them why, I go on. "I could call you whenever I needed something. You were always just ten minutes away. It made the world feel safe. Problems had solutions. Pain had a cure. It seemed like you could fix anything, and you could fix it so simply." I pause to consider my disintegrating life. "I wish I could call you right now, Grandpa, because I've got a lot of problems to solve and a lot of pain to cure, and I don't know where to begin."

Just saying the words out loud is cathartic. I begin to sense a rich delta between us, where my meandering river of mourning may open into bigger and stiller waters.

"Ahhhh," he sighs, as if he's already found the solution to something. "You *did* call me, though, Eli. You dialed me up in your soul rather than on your phone, but I can assure you, it amounts to pretty much the same thing."

I'm a little surprised to hear him naming this strange thing that is happening here between us, and I'm even more surprised to hear the word *soul* come out of his mouth.

"You never struck me as the spiritual type, Grandpa. I mean, I know you went to Mass on Saturday nights, but I always figured Grandma was making you. You were such a practical guy. I didn't think you had much use for such things."

He nods in agreement. "You're right, you're right. I didn't. But everything is spiritual, Eli. It just takes some of us a little longer to figure that out than others. I have to admit, I was a slow learner in that regard."

There's not a trace of regret nor guilt nor self-condemnation in his voice. He's simply stating a fact, and he seems to be completely at peace with it. I can feel my soul rumble with hunger pangs. The fast food may have satisfied my stomach, but my heart is wanting more of whatever is nourishing my grandfather.

"You say that with such acceptance, Grandpa. As if you are totally okay with having spent your years here unaware of something so important. How is that possible? I can't let myself off the hook for a single day of regret, let alone a lifetime."

"Well, that's the thing, Eli. I don't regret it."

He pauses as he ponders what to say next, his breath whistling softly through his nostrils.

"You see, regret is really just a way of denying our ordinariness. It's a way of pretending we aren't, all of us, always growing and evolving and learning. It's a way of insisting we should be finished when, in reality, all of us are always in process."

He looks into the distance, and it's clear he's looking backward into his own life.

"I liked to solve problems because solutions felt like conclusions. I was always so eager to be done with things. And it took being *truly* done, if you know what I mean," he laughs at his own dark humor, "for me to learn that nothing is truly finished. We think death is an ending, but it's just one more step in the creative process. Now that I'm on this side of it, I'm no longer concerned with arriving at the end of the journey. I know I'm still traveling. Somewhere. Everywhere. The living have a hard time releasing their attachment to completion in this way. The few who do, they're the truly humble ones. I guess you could say, humility isn't modesty about having arrived; it's the acceptance that you never really will."

Again, the image of a river's delta comes to mind—that space where the river appears to end but really becomes a body of water more endless and boundless, more ebbing and flowing than it ever was as a mere river. Now I'm seeing my *grandfather* as a kind of delta as well—this once-comforting river of mine, previously bounded by banks of flesh and bone, now emptied out into something oceanic.

I can feel myself torn between my desire to be liberated from the tyranny of the finish line and a lifetime of habitually striving for it. My tears begin to flow again as I feel just a modicum of grace for myself, knowing in a solid-feeling way my release of the finish line will be a process, too, and being in process is okay. However, as in the conversation with my grandmother, I'm also feeling a frustrated resistance growing within me.

"Grandpa, I hear what you're saying. I really do. But my life is in *shambles*. Almost everywhere I look, something is broken right now. When everything is falling apart like this, you *have* to try to fix it, don't you? Are you telling me I should just stand by and let it happen?" I'm trying to keep the edge out of my voice, but I can hear it there anyway.

"Eli," he says, turning to look at me for the first time, a quiet compassion in his eyes, "when it feels like everything is broken, it means something is dying."

I'm watching him and holding my breath, both desperate to hear what he is going to say next and also dreading it. He goes on.

"What I'm hearing you say is that for years you depended on me for security and stability. Then, I think, once I was gone, you began to depend on something else for that security." Here, an apologetic look comes over his face, like someone admitting to having heard a rumor about you a long time ago. "I think you've been depending on your secrecy to maintain your security."

I exhale loudly, punched in the gut by my truth coming out of his trustworthy mouth.

"And Eli, there's nothing terribly wrong with keeping secrets. We keep them when we believe we can't handle the consequences of telling them. Of course we do. Who could blame us? No, the real problem here is your attempt to preserve your sense of security at all costs. And hear me clearly, son," he says, patting my arm reassuringly, "clinging to your security is not a problem because it's a *bad* thing. It's a problem because it's an *impossible* thing. Security cannot be preserved forever. It's a temporary condition. Not designed for the long haul, so to speak. It comes and it goes but it never stays. So our addiction to it can wreak a good deal of havoc. It may look like your life is breaking, Eli, but it's really just your attachment to your security finally dying, and that is a very good thing, indeed."

"It doesn't *feel* very good," I respond, sounding like a disgruntled little kid who's been denied some candy in the checkout aisle. This isn't the kind of fixing I've come to expect from my grandfather. Then again, this man sitting next to me is something more than the grandfather I used to know.

"No, you're right, it doesn't feel good. That's why we call it grief. Mourning. Loss. Death and dying. It feels like hell, but it ushers you into heaven."

This spiritual language catches me off guard again, and I realize I've twitched in response to it. "What do you mean by heaven?" I ask. "What's it like when we release our attachment to security? What happens?"

His smile now reminds me of the smile on his face when he held up my mother's grimy earrings all those years ago. "Resilience, Eli. Heaven is knowing you don't need safety and security—you don't need life to go right—because you've got what it takes to endure risk and danger and vulnerability and all those moments when everything goes wrong. Grief is the bridge we walk from security into resilience."

I feel the last of my resistance to him crumple within me.

He pats me on the back this time and then lumbers to his feet, groaning again in advertisement of his age, which is of course young and old and everything in between and everything beyond. He turns to me, waiting on me. I search for the words to thank him for this blessed palaver.

I open my mouth to do so.

The front door behind me opens instead.

And its opening closes the door on the past within me.

23

"ELI, WHAT ARE YOU DOING OUT HERE? Are you okay? I saw your car in the driveway and searched the house for you. I was about to call 911. Why didn't you let me know you were home?"

I stood quickly, pivoted away from her to prevent her from seeing the puddles in my eyes, and brushed past her into the house, declaring, "Sorry, Mom, I've got to go to the bathroom, almost waited too long!"

If there was one thing my mother never questioned, it was the need for the bathroom. In the fourth grade, I'd faked a sudden case of diarrhea with mysterious origins and discovered it could get me excused from school on a moment's notice. I'd always been careful not to overplay that hand, arousing her suspicion only once when, three months in a row, I'd spent the entirety of her garden club meeting—during which her friends liked to get in my face and pinch my cheeks— on the toilet. The next month, aware I had made her suspicious, I'd volunteered to serve the appetizers at the meeting, and she'd eyed me skeptically for a few minutes until her friends started gushing about what a great son she'd raised. And just like that, my sudden transition from gastric disaster to world-class waiter was forgotten.

The possibility of an accident in your pants had always transformed my mom from tormentor into cheerleader, and I was relieved to discover this had not changed with age. "Oh my!" she exclaimed. "Go, go! Hurry, hurry!"

I was happy to oblige.

Locking myself in the bathroom and turning on both the faucet and the exhaust fan to cover up the conspicuous absence of catastrophic sounds, I lowered the lid of the toilet and sat down. I had several reasons for keeping yet another secret from my mother. I had no idea how to explain to her the conversations I'd just had with my grandmother and grandfather, nor how my next book was finally taking shape in my mind. After all, my mother wasn't exactly my target audience. Also, I needed some space to write down every detail of the conversations before any of it faded from memory.

I sat there for about a minute—the nice thing about manufactured bathroom crises is everyone assumes they will be over quickly—flushed the toilet twice to make clear the magnitude of the ordeal I'd just survived, and scampered across the hallway into my bedroom, where I extricated my laptop from its travel bag. Before opening it, though, I did the one thing that felt more urgent than transcribing the conversations. I texted Rebecca.

Hey, it was great to hear Sarah's voice this morning. I know you're not eager to hear from me, though, and that's okay. I just wanted to give you an update about what's been happening to me. I'm at my mom's house. Got here last night. We haven't killed each other. Yet. Ha! Anyway, I've had some real breakthroughs. If I tried to explain it by text, you probably wouldn't believe it. I'm realizing how much I've been avoiding unhappiness and how that's been preventing joy in our lives. I've clung to safety instead of learning how to embrace whatever struggles may come our way. This image of a bridge keeps coming up, and I think it's the missing ingredient in my book. I guess what I'm saying is, I know you and I are on a bad bridge right now, but I'm learning how to walk that bridge so we can get to the other side together. I love you, Rebecca. I hope we can talk on the phone sometime soon.

Four screens' worth of heartfelt plea.

Thirty frenetic minutes later my fingers were aching. I'd recorded everything I could remember from my conversations with my grandparents, and I'd created a rough outline for my book. It was a book about life's bridges—those blessed passages from the life we all *want* to the life we all *need*. A three-part book: this side of the bridge, the bridge itself, the other side of it, and interwoven through it all the guiding voice from the void, speaking to us through the mystery of memory and imagination. It was all right there. My writer's block had ended in an explosion of inspiration, and I was dizzy with the euphoric aftershocks.

As I slapped my laptop closed, my mother called me for dinner and my phone simultaneously pinged with a text notification. I could feel the tumblers of my life clicking back into place as I eagerly grabbed for the device. I could imagine Rebecca's reply. I could see myself walking out of the bedroom, my bag packed, mustering some regrets for my mother, and then getting in the car. Destination: Seaside, Maryland.

I tapped on the notification, and her message appeared. *Oh baby, I love you so, so much. So much that I don't know how to say what needs to be said. I've written this and erased it multiple times already. I guess I just need to say it. I can't live another day with someone who insists on seeing the world the way he wants it rather than the way it is. This isn't a bridge we're on, Eli. The last ten years were the bridge. THIS is the other side of the bridge, and on this side of it our marriage is over. I'm going to block your number. Not because I don't want to hear from you but because it hurts too much when I do. Sarah will call you from one of my parents' phones. Write your book, Eli. Write your future. Just don't write me into it.*

She'd needed only three screens to erase my four.

For the next two hours, I became a spectator to myself, as if I were sitting in an empty theater watching a movie of my life on a screen. The guy in it was a dead man walking. He drifted into the kitchen. He sat down at the dinner table with his mother. He cut his chicken breast into bite-size pieces, pushing them around on his plate, tucking some beneath the salad he didn't eat, and mingling some with the diced potatoes he didn't touch. His mother didn't notice. He was docile, and as long as he didn't challenge her self-image, she didn't have to pay much attention to him.

He helped her wash the dishes. He sat down to watch television with her. One of the Avengers movies. Her choice. He tried to nod, grunt, and titter at all the right moments in the movie and all the right junctures in their conversation. There was a lot of margin for error there. He'd made himself invisible to her, and this was a son she could get along with, no matter how absent he might seem.

All the while, one phrase kept repeating in his head, to the rhythm of that Tom Petty song about falling: "A man who sees the world the way he wants it rather than the way it is." The way he wants it rather than the way it is. Over and over again.

As his mother droned on, he watched Captain America get pummeled repeatedly, and it reminded him that the perfect time to get punched is right after you've been sucker-punched, because the shock from the first blow numbs the second. In other words, he decided it was the perfect time to return to his father's office.

The next day, he would stare his greatest secret right in the eye.

24

I WAITED TO CALL SAMUEL COOPER until my mother finished her breakfast, based on two certainly false assumptions: all septuagenarians keep approximately the same schedule, and once a person has eaten their breakfast it's acceptable to disturb their day. Mr. Cooper wasn't bothered by the early call, though. Indeed, he was ebullient about hearing from the son of his deceased law partner.

Our banter about Campbell & Cooper made for an easy segue into my reason for calling—I wanted fifteen minutes alone in the office.

Mr. Cooper laughed heartily at my request, telling me I could have the whole day, because even though he called himself semi-retired, the semi part was mostly an excuse to get out of the house when "Ginny starts pining for the spaciousness of my working years." He also volunteered the location of a spare key beneath the potted plant outside the front door. "Everyone in town knows it's there, and in forty-plus years no one's ever used it without permission. I'll never leave the Ferry, son, these people are the salt of the earth."

Forty-eight hours earlier, on my first visit to the office, my past and present had collapsed into a pinpoint of experience, and I'd had no way to account for the vividness of it. *Twelve* hours earlier, however—right around the time Captain America and the Winter Soldier were duking it out—it had dawned on me Campbell & Cooper was the first thin place I visited on returning to Bradford's Ferry. There I could fall into the past with no effort at all, indeed perhaps even against my own will, and the falling was exquisitely painful.

The word for that kind of falling is trauma.

In a graduate course on psychopathology, we'd learned trauma is sometimes a secret we keep from ourselves. In extreme cases, the trauma is literally hidden from the self, as the individual develops multiple personalities, each tasked with keeping a part of the pain a secret from the other parts. It's called dissociative identity disorder, an exotic and tragic affliction.

The rest of us, however, keep our ordinary, everyday trauma a secret from ourselves in more pedestrian ways. We drink, drug, and distract, for instance. Or we tell ourselves we're remembering it incorrectly—overreacting to it, perhaps—and we criticize ourselves for being so soft. We compare our story to the Holocaust and minimize it into insignificance. We forgive and "forget" a little too expediently. We spend the rest of our lives making sure it will never happen again, the prevention becoming more prominent than the pain itself. Like a broken collarbone that never properly healed, we may not feel it at all, until one night we accidentally sleep on our bad side. Then, we're reminded.

Twelve hours earlier, I'd decided it was time to roll onto my bad side. It was time to talk to my dad.

The key was right where Mr. Cooper had said it would be, and the creaking door opened into a large foyer. Dim light penetrated the blinds. Dust motes danced between shadows. The musty air was redolent of mildew growing in secret places of its own. The light switch next to the door was the antiquated two-button type. I pushed the raised button, and the chandelier above me illuminated a hallway straight ahead. Twin doors on either side gave entry to matching, darkened conference rooms. The hallway opened into a large central waiting room, which was now ablaze with light as well. Through the opening, I could see a couple of chairs on the far wall of the waiting room. They were upholstered in the same woolly pea-green fabric in which they'd been clad when I was a kid.

And just like that I'm falling.

I'm sixteen again.

The taste of Winterfresh gum is still lingering on my tongue . . .

The confusion triggered by the lowered blinds in the middle of a weekday is deepening as I slowly step into the hallway, hearing sounds ahead of me. Voices. Sort of. The sounds are not phonetic. They're guttural. Groaning, but pleasurable. In the innocence of the preinternet age, I've never heard such sounds before, but I've heard about them. And in the innocence of my childhood—which is just moments from ending—I wonder to myself, *What is Mom doing here on a Thursday afternoon?*

I freeze midstep, as if someone has called out "Red light!" in the game of Red Light, Green Light we used to play as kids.

I consider retreating, leaving, pretending I was never there. Briefly, I imagine that a few hours later my parents will exchange knowing looks at the dinner table, and I'll act like I don't notice. Except my imagination can only go so far—my parents don't look at each other at all, let alone exchange clandestine glances about romantic weekday trysts. And why is my mom here on a

Thursday afternoon? The obvious answer is, she's not. Someone else is.

Green light.

Dread is a thread drawing me forward.

I turn the corner toward my dad's office, expecting the door to be closed. It is not, and the next few seconds are a shoebox full of old Polaroids, jumbled together in no particular order. Him standing at his desk, facing me. Royal blue Bradford's Ferry High gym shorts in a ball on the floor in front of the desk. His desk chair behind him at an angle. His pants folded neatly over the back of it. A picture taped to the wall behind him: Big Bird, colored in a child's scrawl—mine—the paper around Big Bird yellowing too, corners turning inward with age. A woman lying on the desk. The top of her head facing me. Unnaturally red hair. An inch of gray roots on either side of a center part. Then, an image of Mrs. Andrews, my gym teacher, demonstrating push-ups to us at the beginning of the school year, the top of her head facing us, too-red hair, gray roots.

The shoebox is life-altering, but it's not traumatizing. I can handle what it means. I can weather the divorce of my parents. The disruption to my life, bouncing back and forth between homes. Two Christmases. Switching gym classes. All of it a window through which my friends and everyone else will be able to see the humiliations of my family. It's a small town. People will talk. I can cope with the chatter. I can find my way through that particular future.

The trauma comes from what happens next.

My dad looks up. His eyes meet mine. They widen ever so slightly in surprise. But only for a fraction of a second before relaxing again into an expression of relief. Then my dad—my best friend, my hoped-for confidant and comforter—does the one thing I least expect and the one thing from which I'll never recover.

He winks at me.

And in that wink, I can imagine an entirely different shoebox full of snapshots. I see not the end of my family but the secret that will keep it together. I see how my confidant now expects me to become his. I see knowing glances at the dinner table, but they are not between my parents; they are between my father and me. I see how all of it flows naturally from the relationship we've always had. Sneaking ice cream together behind Mom's back. Snickering together at her admonitions. The waterbed she denied but he delivered. I see how I'd always thought I was my father's son, but really I was merely a pawn in my parents' game of marital chess—a pawn the king used, over and over again, to checkmate the queen.

I see all of this, and then I see a smile tug at the corner of his mouth as he tilts his chin upward, as if to say in a fatherly way, "All right, Son, I've got to get back to work. Run along now. I'll see you when I get home."

My sixteen-year-old self listens to my dad. The teenage boy beats the retreat he now wishes he'd made just a few seconds earlier, a whole childhood earlier. He walks home. In a terrible sort of way, his hopes have been fulfilled: he's forgotten entirely about Samantha Stiller.

My thirty-nine-year-old self stays, though. I hadn't returned to this thin place just to retreat. I'd come here to have a conversation with my dad. So I stood my ground in that waiting room, looking toward my father's office, the door once again open but the innards of it darkened. I drew on the imagination that had served me so well in the last twenty-four hours, trying to summon him from the past. The previous evening, I'd imagined he'd be sitting on the front of his desk, me standing in the doorway, and we'd finally talk about it after all these years. I figured it would be good practice for talking about it with Rebecca.

I'd figured wrong.

My memory was stuck in the on position, and my imagination was out of order. As I stood there, staring into his darkened office, all I could see was gray roots and that wink and that chin tilt. Wink. Tilt. Wink. Tilt. Over and over again. With each wink and tilt, my heart hammered harder in my chest. Sweat broke out on my brow. Wink. Tilt. Wink. Tilt. My plan had been to create a space where God could speak into the moment on which my life had hinged. It turns out trauma has a way of silencing the voice of God.

It creates a void, where only the voice of the past can be heard.

25

JUST OUTSIDE BRADFORD'S FERRY is a park nestled into a bend along the Saukenuk River. You enter the park through a rusted wrought iron gate, and the road disappears into a nondescript opening in the forest. Then it descends the bluffs that hug the river in a series of harrowing switchbacks. The Saukenuk carved the bluffs out of sandstone in a relationship that has lasted millennia. The exposed slabs of stone are reddish in hue due to the iron ore infused throughout them. It was the iron that made them more resilient against the weathering effects of the river than the softer earth around them.

As I wound my way down the bluffs, I was all soft earth, no trace of iron in me.

Nevertheless, by the time the river came into sight at the bottom, the park's familiar embrace had begun to work its comforting magic. My heart was beating at its normal pace again as I followed the road along the river, past a lone Parks Department worker, who was putting a new coat of paint on a very old metal slide.

I chose a parking spot near a grove of trees along the river, through which a small clearing could be seen, the trees an amphitheater and the river a stage. I'd come here countless times over the years to watch the show. Deer drinking. Fish leaping. Bald eagles swooping.

A wooden picnic table still stood in the center of the clearing. It was the very same table at which I'd sat on a Sunday morning more than twenty years earlier, struggling to pen my valedictory remarks for that afternoon's graduation ceremony. It too had recently received a new coat of paint, though no paint was thick enough to hide the indentations of countless carvings over the years. The initials of optimistic lovers bound together by plus signs and surrounded by hopeful hearts. Dates with no explanation, their significance carried away with the ones who etched them. Phallic symbols and breasts, the signature of the obsessed and rebellious teen.

I got down on my back and slid under the table, locating the date of my graduation, which I'd carved there after deciding what I'd say later that day. Only CH+MM had been similarly inspired to make their mark on the underside of the table. The three of us had been rewarded with a lack of paint and weather, and our carvings looked almost fresh. I ran my finger over the date, the hand that had carved it and the one that was tracing it separated only by the passage of time.

Until the last two days, I'd always thought of time as a river, bending in some places but mostly linear, carrying us along until we eventually disembark at our designated dock. It isn't true, though. Time is more like the place where the ocean meets the land. It isn't linear. The tide of it ebbs and flows. It waves and crashes. It has rip tides and undertows that can pull you outward into its expanse and downward into its depths. Your past isn't something you leave behind you, upriver. It's a pair of sunglasses knocked off your head by a crashing wave, seemingly gone for good, only to be washed up on shore a little way down the beach.

I was sitting at the picnic table, watching hawks circle the river in search of prey—and trying not to be pulled out to sea by the rip tide of my father's wink—when the tide of time came in again, washing a memory of Father Lou up onto my beach.

It's a Sunday morning, two decades earlier. My graduation ceremony is just hours away, and I'm sitting in this very same space when I hear him call out behind me.

"Elijah Campbell. What are you doing here on a Sunday morning? Shouldn't you be in church?"

I turn to see him walking across the clearing. Beyond him, I can see his car parked next to mine. The chatter in my head has drowned out the sounds of his approach.

I smile. There aren't many people I'd be happy to see on a morning like this. Father Lou is one of them. "Well, Father, I could ask you the same thing now, couldn't I?"

He laughs. There's delight in it. "Well-played, young man, well-played." He gestures toward the bench beside me. "Do you mind?"

"Not at all," I reply, sliding down the bench to make room for him.

He sits next to me, hands folded on the table in a prayerful posture, gazing out on the river. "Ah, beautiful," he says. "Now I see, you *are* at church."

My turn to laugh with delight. "It's comments like those that make my mom call you a heretic."

He nods. He knows what some in the town say about him. "It's remarkable, really, Elijah. Our faith tradition was founded by a man who was executed for heresy, and yet we go around executing those we deem to be heretics. It makes you wonder if our religion hasn't been turned a little upside down, doesn't it?"

Two things I appreciate in the moment: that he understands this amphitheater of mine feels like church to me, and that he isn't intimidated by my mom nor anyone else in town. It makes me think about getting up to speak at the graduation ceremony— intimidated by every pair of eyes on me—and I ask him for help with my speech.

"Father Lou, I'm giving the valedictory speech at graduation today, and I have no idea what to say."

"Mmmm," he murmurs, a sound that makes me feel like he understands and has maybe even been in my position before. He quietly watches the river long enough to make me wonder if I've misinterpreted his murmur, and then he speaks.

"I hope it doesn't sound like I'm disagreeing with you, but I think you do know what to say. You just haven't . . . how do I say it . . . located it within you yet."

I'm hoping for something more and I'm not ready to let him off the hook. "Well, Father, if you happen to have a map on you, feel free to let me know where *X* marks the spot."

The smile around his eyes tells me he appreciates my cleverness and persistence. His fingers begin to move slowly along the tabletop, first tracing the biggest initials on it, then tracing the heart around them. As his finger arrives back at the heart's point, he says, "That's your *X* right there, Elijah."

He looks me in the eye for the first time, seeing the confusion and questions there.

"It's the bottom of the heart," he explains. "You've probably heard that phrase, 'from the bottom of my heart.' It's a widely misused phrase. Came into popular usage sometime in the

Middle Ages. Nowadays, we usually take it to mean saying something positive with lots of sincerity. But do you know where the
phrase originated?"

I shake my head, but my hope is rising.

"Its first usage is traced back to an epic poem written by the
Roman poet Virgil, thirty years or so before the birth of Jesus. It's
about the rise of Rome from the ashes of Troy. In it he writes,
'Such words he utters, and sick with deep distress he feigns hope
on his face, and keeps his anguish hidden at the bottom of his
heart.' So, you see, to say something from the bottom of your
heart has nothing to do with saying positive things. In fact, it's
about giving up your positive persona, so to speak, and divulging
the secret anguish in your soul. Your pain. Your grief. And so on."

"You think I should talk about my pain today?" I ask incredu-
lously, thinking I've misunderstood him and inviting him to
correct my impression. He doesn't.

"Sure, why not? Most graduation speeches are rah-rah cheer-
leading routines, fun and forgettable. What if you got up there
and spoke from the bottom of your heart instead, sharing the
grief of the childhood you're leaving behind? You've all spent
years forming friendships, and now those friends will be scattered like pollen on the wind. Whatever safety your homes may
have afforded you will be taken from you as well. Everyone in the
auditorium will have the same grief at the bottom of their hearts.
Perhaps by sharing *yours* you will give them permission to feel
theirs." Father Lou continues, but the rest of what he says is soft
earth eroded by the flow of time.

And just like that, the tide of memory receded altogether.

Instead of being a kid with a graduation speech to write, I was
once again an aging man with a book to write.

On my graduation morning, after Father Lou left, I'd carved the date into the underside of the table, and then I'd drawn on our conversation to craft a graduation speech that made all those intimidating sets of eyes tender with grief. Twenty-one years later, I placed my finger on that same big heart on the table's surface. It was shallower with paint and time, but I traced it anyway, my finger finding the point at the bottom of it.

I got up, slid beneath the table, and used my car key to carve the date into its exposed underbelly, right next to the date of my graduation. Then, as I'd done on that Sunday morning years ago, I got in my car and headed home to the desk in my bedroom to write something from the bottom of my heart.

Finally, at long last, I'd write my book.

26

First Thing the next morning, I stopped by Books on Main for a cup of coffee and told Gus I was planning to stay in Bradford's Ferry until I finished my book. He told me there'd be a hot cup of coffee waiting for me every morning. I asked him if he'd be willing to read my work and give me feedback. He didn't hesitate.

"Just like the old days, Elijah!" He tugged out a drawer beneath the cash register, pushing around the detritus of a business until he found what he was looking for—a red pen. He held it up like you might hold the carving knife before Thanksgiving dinner, a look of gleeful anticipation on his face. "I'm coming out of retirement, my boy!"

And that's how it went, for the next eighteen days.

Every morning, I'd wake with the sun, walk to Books on Main and trade the previous day's pages for a cup of coffee to go, then walk directly back to my mother's house. Gus sensed there was little time for chitchat. Anyway, he was letting his pen do all the talking.

I'd write all morning, drive through one of several fast food places for lunch, write all afternoon, walk to Books on Main for its last cup of coffee of the day, retrieve the previous day's pages from Gus, walk across the street to pick up a sandwich at Sally's Subs, and then walk back to my mother's house, where I'd work well into the night incorporating Gus's suggestions. My old English teacher hadn't missed a beat—he was right every time.

Occasionally, the rhythm of it all would be interrupted by a call from Sarah. It was the only interruption that didn't feel like one. Her days were blending together into a mixture of sand, sun, and the sense of safety the Millers were so good at creating. My heart swelled with joy for her, but it broke on the distance between us and the silence of her mother. I used the brokenness of my heart to find my way to the bottom of it, and then I poured it into my manuscript.

My mother and I passed each other like ships in the night, even during the day. We'd find ways to barely miss each other in the house. I'd wait for the sound of her car pulling out of the driveway to use the bathroom, or she would hear my approaching footsteps and retreat into her bedroom. One time we ate dinner together and watched some HGTV afterward. Her presence ruined my dinner, and I imagine my presence ruined her show. We silently conspired to make sure it didn't happen again. I'm not sure which of us was the ghost in the home. Maybe we both were. Maybe that's the way it had always been.

Then, one morning, it was done.

I walked into Books on Main, and Gus greeted me with a bear hug. He drew back, holding me by the shoulders again, looking me directly in the eyes. "I'm *so* proud of you, Elijah. I wouldn't change a thing about your final chapter. It is finished." His words meant the world to me. The tears in his eyes meant even more.

"Celebratory cup of coffee, ceramic mug this time?" I asked.

A look of grave concern came over his face. "Have you looked at yourself in the mirror lately? You've barely slept in two weeks. You've been bleeding all over the page for most of that time. Instead of injecting more caffeine, why don't you put the finishing touches on this, send it off to Benjamin this morning, and get some *rest*." It was neither question nor command but simply the final suggestion he'd offer with regard to my book. Like all the rest, it was a good one.

I walked home. Checked formatting. Drafted a cover letter to my editor. Wrote a short email to Benjamin. Attached the cover letter and the manuscript. Hit send. I told myself I'd lie down for a few minutes to rest, then go grab some lunch. I never did. Instead, I fell asleep.

For the next twenty-four hours.

The vibration of my cellphone on the bedside table was my alarm clock. I reached for it, thinking I'd dozed off for thirty minutes, hoping Rebecca had finally decided to end her silence. The text wasn't from Rebecca, it was from Benjamin, and it was preceded by a half dozen missed calls from him. It read, *Talked to your mom. She says you've been sleeping for the last day. Well wake up, buddy. I've been looking for a reason to visit the Ferry again, and I've got a good one. I'll meet you at Books on Main in two hours. Text back to confirm.*

I texted back.

27

BENJAMIN ARRIVED AT BOOKS ON MAIN before I did. When the bell over the door alerted him to my entry, he turned on his heels and announced my arrival. "Elijah Campbell!" It had been a long time since he'd used my full name with a smile on his face.

He approached me with open arms and wrapped me in a warm hug, smacking my back several times, all affection, none of the aggression of just a few weeks ago. For the last ninety minutes, the reason for Benjamin's visit had seemed both obvious and impossible. I was on a pendulum again, daring to hope and then forbidding myself to do so. I played it safe and focused on the facts.

"Wow, you made great time, B."

His smiled reached all the way to his eyes. "Yeah, I broke every speed limit." With a dramatic flourish, he pulled a white envelope from a pocket inside his sport coat, holding it out to me. "I figured if I got a ticket, you could pay for it."

The pendulum swung all the way toward hope. It made my knees wobbly.

I took the envelope from him and looked up. Over his shoulder, Gus was looking at me expectantly, the way a parent might look at a child who is about to open the biggest present under the Christmas tree. The bell over the door tinkled again. This time, I was the one who swiveled on my heels. Father Lou walked through the door with a celebratory grin on his face.

My friends had orchestrated a surprise party.

"Well? Go ahead, open it," urged Benjamin. "I didn't risk my driver's license so you could stand here with that goofy look on your face!"

I opened the envelope. It held a check. The big kind that businesses use. The publisher's name in the top left corner. My name on the payee line. Today's date. The amount of it equal to the second half of my advance for *The Voice in the Void*.

"This is," I started, then trailed off. My jaw had dropped in cartoonish fashion.

"Unprecedented?" completed Benjamin. "Yeah, it is. I forwarded your manuscript to Jill yesterday, as soon as I received it. Apparently, she spent most of the night reading it, tried to hate it, but fell in love with it. In fact, she loved it so much I was able to convince her to cut you a check this morning. She says there will be a little cleaning up to do after she reads it through a second time, but it's your best work yet."

He turned to Gus. "And she says if *you* ever get tired of selling books and slinging coffee, they're always looking for good copyeditors."

Gus was shaking his head. "I only edit for geniuses, Benji!"

Father Lou spoke over my shoulder. "Elijah, I couldn't be prouder of you, son."

I turned around to face him. "I wrote it from the bottom of my heart, Father Lou."

A look of comprehension passed over his face. "I loved that graduation speech, son, and I know I'm going to love this book too."

I was about to thank him for his thread throughout my story when Gus smacked the counter several times, getting everyone's attention, and announced a round of caffeine on the house. In the corner, another table of retired men responded with hurrahs and calls for "Coffee! Black!" I invited Gus to whip me up something special and excused myself to the restroom.

I had no need of the toilet, but I was in desperate need of some space. Much had happened in the span of seconds. It was a lot to process.

I looked down at the check I was holding. There would be enough to pay off all the credit cards. To get caught up on our mortgage payments. To pay the hospital bill in full. There would be enough to buy Rebecca a proper tenth anniversary ring. There would even be enough left over to start that mythical savings account I'd been pretending about for years.

The thought of all my half-truths being turned into full truths made me realize I'd come to the restroom for a second reason. I wanted to text Rebecca with the good news in the hopes that her resolve had waned and she'd unblocked my phone number.

I wrote a short but sweet text this time, letting her know my book was finished and my advance was received. I hit send. The bubble was green instead of blue, suggesting my wife's resolve—which had never been known to wane—was following its typical course. *That's okay,* I thought, *I'll find a way to get the news to her.* It was going to take her a while to heal, and I owed her that time even more than I owed her a decent anniversary gift. I opened the door, ready to celebrate.

The mood in the bookshop, however, had been flipped upside down.

Benjamin, Gus, and Father Lou sat together at a table in what looked more like a graveside ceremony than a celebration. Each of them made eye contact with me before shifting their glances to a table on the other side of the café, where the county sheriff sat in full uniform, gold star gleaming over a breast pocket, Stetson hat sitting in front of him on the table.

My first wild thought was that Benjamin's speed had somehow caught up with him. A glance back at my friends told me Benjamin was not the one in trouble. Gus looked protective. Father Lou looked compassionate. Benjamin looked angry.

I looked back at the sheriff. Our eyes met. He stood up, picking up his hat and a white envelope hidden underneath it. He walked toward me, boots clicking on the floor, gun swaying in its holster at his waist, a look of regret rather than menace in his eyes. He came to a stop in front of me, holding the envelope out to me as Benjamin had done moments earlier.

"Gus here tells me you're Elijah Campbell?"

I nodded.

"Gus is a good man," he went on, "and he tells me you're a good man too, so it gives me no pleasure to be delivering these papers to you."

The envelope hung in midair between us, suspended there by his hand. I'd lost the use of my own hands. He filled the silence with details.

"We were informed that you're staying at your mother's house. I went there to give you these papers, and she told me I could probably find you here."

I didn't respond.

He filled the next silence with a disastrous attempt at becoming a therapist. "She seems like a nice lady, your mom. That's good. We need the support of loved ones during hard times."

Quietly, Father Lou had come alongside us and, at this, he intervened. "Thank you, sir," he said, taking the envelope from the sheriff with one hand, raising my hand with the other, and placing the envelope in it. "Eli has been served his divorce papers. You did this well, Sheriff. May God bless you and all those you protect today."

The sheriff seized on Father Lou's benediction and made a beeline for the door, tipping his hat at Gus on the way out.

Father Lou put his arm around me and walked me over to the table where they'd gathered. I sat down, placing the two envelopes on the table in front of me. In some ways they were identical. White. Business size. Privacy tint. The difference was that one held a future I'd been imagining with all my hope, and the other held a future I'd been denying with all my might.

My three friends looked at me, the same expression now on each face—lots of compassion mingled with lots of questions. This was Father Lou's territory, though. Gus and Benjamin deferred to him.

"Elijah, I think I'm speaking for all of us when I say how much I'm hurting for you right now. Hurt can be a bridge though, connecting people. You can tell us anything and we'll meet you in it."

Grace is a lot of things. It's three friends willing to witness your life crumble without looking away. Friends who will allow your ruined day to become their ruined day. Companions with urgent questions but the patience to wait while you search for your answers.

"Rebecca is leaving me." My face colored with shame as I admitted the obvious to my friends while admitting it to myself for the first time. "I didn't tell any of you because I didn't think it would happen in the end." Equal parts explanation, defensiveness, and apology. "We've been having financial problems and my focus has been on fixing them by getting this book written. I figured if I could make *this* happen," pointing to the envelope on the left, "I could prevent *this* from happening," pointing to the envelope on the right. "And I *did* make this happen." An edge crept into my voice as I jabbed with my index finger at the envelope from my publisher. Then, the edge was replaced by defeat. "I guess I just didn't make it happen fast enough."

The compassion and questions on Benjamin's face had been replaced by confusion.

"Wow, Eli, I'm sorry, man. This just doesn't sound like Rebecca. I remember the first time you brought her home to the Ferry. Remember that? She and I wound up dancing on the bar in the Den? She was so carefree. She's never seemed like the kind of person who would cling to material things. She loves that house of yours, but I can't picture her digging in her heels about it, you know? Did you ask her to leave her job to make more money elsewhere? Is that what did it?"

"No, that's the thing." The edge was back in my voice. "I've been protecting her from all of this. I didn't even tell her we were in financial trouble. I didn't want her to have to worry about it."

My eyes met Benjamin's and I could see the untruth in what I'd just said reflected back at me.

"Actually, you're right, she wouldn't have worried about it. What she would have done is offer to leave that job of hers to do something more lucrative. But she loves what she does so much, I couldn't bear to be the reason for her giving it up. This," I said, pointing again at the publisher's envelope, "means she doesn't have to leave that job."

"Elijah." It was Gus this time, his face now etched with the same look of confusion as Benjamin's. "I hope I'm not being obtuse here—I *have* lost a step or two over the years—but if Rebecca doesn't know about your financial problems, how can she be divorcing you because of them?"

For the first time in years, the heat of a spotlight induced prickles of sweat along my scalp. Like the keen editor he was, Gus had noticed an inconsistency in my story, and his question was like a red pen, circling something at the heart of my relationship with Rebecca and, indeed, at the heart of myself. He'd edited my book, and now he was asking me to edit my life, or at least the version of it I'd been telling myself.

This too was grace: my friends' insistence on loving me too much to be deceived by me, their gentle invitation to see the truth and maybe even tell it. Grace. It sounds great in theory, until it insists on looking at you so carefully and abidingly that it forces you to look at yourself. At first, grace is the feeling of light seeping into your shadowy places and your shadows pushing back. I was familiar with that feeling—I'd felt it in my last two sessions with Jeff. My shadows had rejected his persistent and patient light. Now, here I was, tempted to resist my friends' grace as well.

I looked at Father Lou, planning to reject Gus's editorial suggestion, but I saw in the crow's-feet at the corners of his eyes every version of him who had ever cared for me: the man with the bandage for my knee when I was a child, the advice that shaped my graduation speech, the comfort after my father's death, the wisdom about the ghosts within me that had unlocked the book within me as well. I owed him something more than my defensiveness.

Sometimes when our façades finally crumble, they crumble all at once.

"Gus is right, Father Lou. She's not leaving me because of our financial problems. As far as she knows, our finances are fine." I remembered the fire in her eyes on her departure. I remembered her words. "The last thing she said to me before she left with Sarah," I told them, "was that she can be alone all by herself."

Now, weeks later, with my guard down, as I said those words aloud, I truly heard them for the first time. I'd thought my heart was as broken as it could get. I was wrong. Father Lou broke it the rest of the way.

"It sounds like Rebecca never wanted your money, Elijah. She wanted your truth."

28

I DECLINED BENJAMIN'S OFFER of a ride home. I needed to walk.

He told me he'd be in town for a few days, tidying up his mother's house, preparing it for sale. She wasn't planning to return to Bradford's Ferry. Old bones and aging joints don't mix well with the kind of winter that once froze the Saukenuk and doubled John Marcus Bradford's business for a season. Mrs. Bruce had the money to stay warm, and she planned to use it.

I told him I'd started the yard work for him. He asked if he could thank me by buying a round at the Den in the next few days. I told him sure. That seemed to satisfy him. He congratulated me again on my achievement and then drove away in the direction of the bridge. I followed on foot.

As I approached the bridge, it occurred to me I hadn't dreamed my dream in weeks. Something worse was happening though. I was living it.

I stopped at the place where the sidewalk transitioned from solid ground to airborne bridge. It was the very spot where my recurring nightmare always began. I looked to the other side, almost expecting to see it shrouded in fog. It wasn't, of course.

The sun blazed. Cars reflected it. Traffic lights switched from red to green. The drive-through line at McDonald's wrapped around the restaurant. In my dream, I'd always been so concerned about surviving I'd never taken the time to wonder what was hidden in that haze on the other side. Probably not a McDonald's.

I looked down at my feet and saw concrete but imagined old, rotted boards with treacherous gaps in between. I jumped to the closest board and could almost hear it creak beneath my weight. A cyclist swerved around me, swearing something under his breath, glancing backward at the lunatic leaping over hallucinatory puddles. I couldn't blame him. For years, I'd forced myself to look like a solid, concrete bridge on the outside, while on the inside I felt rickety and rotting. I'd spent my whole life trying to avoid looks like the cyclist had just given me. But the papers in my pocket made it hard to care anymore.

As my mother's house came into sight, I prayed for her absence and, for once, my prayer was answered. I was able to bake a frozen pepperoni pizza without harassment, the oven dinging just as I heard her car pulling into the garage. I took the whole pie and a pizza cutter to my room and locked the door. The pepperoni was going to be painful.

I sat at my desk and ate the whole thing like it was a punishment.

Already regretting what I'd done, I placed the pizza tray on the floor and opened the laptop, which I'd used as a placemat. I needed to write something. Anything. Writing was how I coped, and I needed to cope now more than ever. As I stared at the screen, though, I realized there was nothing left to write. I was finished with my book. Rebecca was finished with me. There was no project left to complete. No pleading left to do.

I slapped the screen closed and tossed the computer onto my bed, where it triggered a series of ripples. Folding my arms on my desk, I lowered my forehead onto them. On the backs of my eyelids, I could see the scene from my dream in which the river begins to rise, though the river wasn't swollen with water; it was swollen with paper. A torrent of cash and divorce papers, flowing beneath me, rising, rising, threatening to sweep me away.

I shook my head, trying to erase the image, and in doing so, my elbow bumped something that came to rest against my skin. I raised my head to see what it was. And just like that I *was* falling, but not downward, not drowning. Rather, backward and remembering. A thin space on a golf course. My uncle's rage and remorse. A bunch of hot dogs. I had a choice: I could spend the rest of the afternoon in the painful present, or I could go in search of portals to the past.

I chose the past.

My mother was making herself lunch in the kitchen. I walked briskly through it, holding my stomach, declaring, "Ate a bunch of pepperoni, Mom, gotta go!" and strode out of the house. In spite of it all, I couldn't help but smile as I imagined her trying to sort out why I was leaving the house to use the bathroom.

⌣

The Hidden Links Golf Club was now more hidden than ever. Nestled into a patch of wooded land just outside Bradford's Ferry, it had been connected to the rest of civilization by a single gravel road. On summer mornings in its heyday, my grandfather and I would follow that narrow road through a grove of trees, canopies interwoven overhead, until the grove and the gravel gave way to a paved parking lot, with a large log cabin clubhouse standing sentinel on the far side of the asphalt. Compared to most golf clubs, it was relatively spartan. No driving range. No putting green. No frills. Just the feeling that you'd entered another world, one where human beings and the rest of nature still knew how to coexist.

The sign marking the entrance to the course had been removed several years ago, shortly after the club went bankrupt. Now, the place where the gravel road branched off the macadam country highway was nearly impossible to spot, grown over as it was with weeds and wildflowers. Nevertheless, two ruts connecting the highway to the forest still suggested its dying presence. I turned onto it.

As I entered the grove of trees, the tickling sound of undergrowth beneath the car gave way to the scratching and clacking of encroaching branches against its doors. Eventually, the old road opened onto the little parking lot, where thick, thorny things protruded from cracks in its pavement, reaching skyward, waist high. The pavement itself was being turned by neglect back into gravel. The clubhouse looked mostly as it once had, though one section of its roof sagged in an unpromising way. One more winter, and the clubhouse would have its first skylight.

I was looking for the sixth tee box.

Decades ago, I would have been able to walk directly to it, deriving my bearings from the closely mown fairways, tightly clipped greens, and the layout I'd memorized over the years. Now the fairways were almost indistinguishable from the rest of the land, and the greens were slightly less overgrown patches in the prairie.

I left my car in the parking lot and followed the fading asphalt cart path to the first tee box. The old wooden sign still stood there atop its post—a simple overhead diagram of the hole captioned by the words "Hole 1" and "372 Yards" and "Par 4." Though the paint was peeling, the diagram remained clear enough to remind me the fairway extended straight out from the tee box for the first two hundred yards before turning slightly left, concluding at an oval-shaped green protected on either side by two large oaks. The oaks looked like broccoli florets in the diagram.

Once reminded of the layout, I found it easier to discern the shape of the fairway and the location of the green, both clinging to whatever dignity they had left as the wild crowded in around them. I followed the first fairway to the first green, disturbing an entire ecosystem of insects, the sound of perturbed buzzing accompanying me along the way. Things slithered in the long grass. Several deer froze in the dopey hope I wouldn't see them. As I approached the two oaks landmarking the green, I veered off to the right of them, where the sign for the second tee box still stood. In this way, I slowly progressed toward the sixth tee box.

As I walked, the whole place got thinner.

When I was a boy, the Campbell family would gather in Bradford's Ferry every summer for an annual reunion, and this was where the men would spend their mornings. My grandfather, my dad, and my dad's brothers, Uncle Mark and Uncle Jerry. The regular foursome. When my cousin Jerry Junior—everyone called him JJ—and I were in about the third grade, they started inviting us along as caddies. JJ and I began every reunion a little shyly, having forgotten how much we enjoyed being together. By the end of the day or weekend, we'd be hiding his parents' car keys in the playful hope of stranding them in the Ferry forever. It was a boyish way of expressing our love for each other.

The Campbell men chose Hidden Links because of its informal atmosphere and relaxing pace of play. They were there to enjoy each other. However, my Uncle Mark had a hard time relaxing or enjoying much of anything. He was a nationally renowned pediatric neurosurgeon at the big children's hospital in Chicago. As a kid, I assumed that meant he loved kids. I found out later—at his funeral reception, actually—that he had little interest in children. It was, in fact, his disregard for them that made him such a good neurosurgeon; his emotions never got in the way. As a kid, he'd spent hours upon hours assembling ships in a bottle, and a high school guidance counselor had suggested he find a way to make money doing it. For Uncle Mark, every operation was just another ship in a bottle, and it had made him an exceedingly wealthy man.

I idolized my Uncle Mark. He lived in a penthouse on Lake Shore Drive with a majestic view of Lake Michigan. He drove flashy cars. His girlfriends were always glamorous. If expensive had a scent, it was the smell of his cologne filling every room he entered. He had season tickets to the Chicago Bulls—box seats— and a couple of times a year he'd give them to my dad and me. In the box, while I was feeding on desserts from the buffet, a bunch of strangers would tell me what a great guy my Uncle Mark was. I had no trouble believing them.

Every time he showed up in Bradford's Ferry, he'd come bearing gifts, usually some kind of NBA swag. The day he'd screamed at me on the sixth tee, he'd given me a Chicago Bulls wristband to atone for his transgression, and it had meant so much to me I'd refused to sully it with sweat. Instead, I'd propped it up on my desk next to my framed photo of William Perry, and there it had sat, undisturbed, for the last thirty years. Until today, when I had bumped it with my elbow.

Uncle Mark's pancreatic cancer was one ship he couldn't put back in its bottle. He died when I was in the seventh grade, an affluent and lonely man, overlooking Lake Michigan in the company of his hospice nurse. I wanted to talk to him again. As Father Lou might say, this time I wasn't interested in his money, I was interested in his truth.

As I approached the sixth tee box, a field of wildflowers beyond it advertised every color God ever created. This wasn't entirely new. Even when I was ten, the field had been a breath-taking vista, an unkempt boundary along the manicured course from which few wayward balls were ever retrieved, not so much because you didn't want to find them but because some kind of reverence in you hesitated to disturb the ground on which they'd come to rest. Indeed, after a few years with no disturbances, the field's color palette had become complete, and I couldn't take my eyes off it. We humans try to make things more beautiful by making them more ordered. Maybe God makes things more beautiful by letting them grow more wild.

As I gazed out on the field of flowers, the long brown prairie grass surrounding the sixth tee box disappeared, replaced in my memory by a vibrantly green and carefully manicured platform on which my grandfather and his three sons are standing, dis-cussing the details of their wager. JJ and I are sitting in one of the two carts parked next to the tee box, our jobs done for the moment, having handed the men their drivers.

The day is hot, and we've fished some ice from the cooler in the back of the cart. We hold it in our hands, placing one cube at a time in our mouths, sucking on it until it melts. We've had three hours to get reacquainted and we're old companions again. In boyhood, it doesn't take much to feel like you're the king of your kingdom for a moment or two. We're enjoying one of those moments.

My Uncle Mark is teeing off first, but I'm not paying much attention to what's happening on the tee box. I'm staring past it at that field of flowers. Just as Uncle Mark reaches the top of his backswing, JJ slips an ice cube down the back of my shirt, and I let out a shriek of surprise.

The result is predictable.

A low snap hook veering left, out over the wildflowers, clearly out of bounds. Two stroke penalty. My Uncle Mark looks at me and unleashes a series of R-rated expletives that age me a decade right on the spot. He's walking toward me, a bulging vein winding its way down the middle of his forehead, tendons standing out in his neck, still clenching his driver. It looks like he's going to use it on me. He's about three feet from the cart when my dad catches up with him and puts his hand on his shoulder. It breaks the spell. Uncle Mark stops in his tracks, his shoulders rising and falling rapidly with heavy breathing. The ice cube is already melting somewhere around my waistline. I think about throwing JJ under the bus and decide against it. I apologize profusely for what happened.

He turns away from me wordlessly. He'll give me the silent treatment for the next four holes. It's not until we're in the clubhouse, picking up snacks and sodas for the back nine, that he approaches me sheepishly. He buys JJ and me twice as much food as we can eat. Then he tells us he should have just taken a mulligan—a do-over—and holds out a wristband to each of us, not quite looking at us and not quite looking at the floor, saying, "I wish I had more to give you kids."

Those are the words I wanted to talk to my Uncle Mark about.

29

I'M STANDING THERE on the sun-bleached cart path, in the very space where I'd sat terrified in the golf cart so long ago as my Uncle Mark stalked toward me. I look up at the tee box, and there he is, larger than life, multimillion-dollar hands holding his driver. His skin is darkly tanned; it's not yet faded translucent gray by the chemotherapy still several years in his future. His hair is thick and black and slicked back. It, too, will fall prey to that chemotherapy. Is the tumor already growing in his pancreas? Probably. But also certainly not. A tumor can't grow within a memory. Cancer can't kill an apparition.

"Oh, Eli," he says in his deep baritone, tinged with a tenderness I never heard there while he was alive, "thank you for this chance to apologize to you for what happened here when you were a boy."

This is an unexpected start to our conversation. I feel vaguely uncomfortable about it. "Uncle Mark, I didn't come here hoping for an apology. In fact, it never occurred to me to ask for one. You showed us how badly you felt with hot dogs and wristbands almost right away. Apology can be spoken in many languages. You said yours with mustard and relish."

My uncle walks toward me. No stalking. No forehead vein. In fact, he looks peaceful. Halfway down the tee box's side slope, he sits down, cross-legged, placing his driver across his lap, his hands resting near either end of it. Jack Nicklaus meets the lotus position. After a brief pause, he says quietly, "You're very gracious, Eli."

My discomfort becomes less vague. If this conversation is happening in my imagination, then it stands to reason my uncle's compliments are actually compliments I'm giving myself. For a moment, I feel both silly and arrogant at the same time. Then I feel a cramp in my abdomen, and I'm reminded of the pizza with which I just punished myself. I'm not feeling any more forgiving toward myself than I was an hour ago—self-congratulation is not high on my to-do list this afternoon. So, something else must be happening here.

Uncle Mark's words must be coming from a part of me the divorce papers and the self-loathing and the pepperoni can't reach.

Uncle Mark nods his head, agreeing with what I haven't said. "Yes, that's right, Eli. You have blind spots. We all do. For instance, we think we know all the ways we were wounded, but really we've only cataloged a fraction of them." He has the apologetic look on his face of someone who knows they are the bearer of bad news. "And the wounds we *have* recognized? We think we understand them completely, but really we just know the who, what, where, and when of it. Usually, the *why* of it is completely hidden from us. Hidden within the untold story of the people who wounded us. And the *how* of it? *How* it continues to affect us in every moment of our lives? Well, we are oblivious to most of that. Blind spots, Eli. They're everywhere within us."

I can feel my ire rising. This is becoming a pattern in response to those who are trying to help me. Jeff. My grandmother. My grandfather. And now Uncle Mark. It occurs to me that my angry resistance to love is a blind spot of mine, but the thought just makes my ire rise faster.

"I can't have *that* many blind spots, Uncle Mark. I majored in psychology. I took advanced courses in it. I write books about the inner life. I spend all day every day reflecting on what goes on inside of me. All I do is think, think, think about life in general and my life specifically. How could I still be clueless about what is shaping me?"

He answers the question as if he's fielded it a thousand times. "We don't discover our blind spots by *thinking* about them. Rather, we *listen* for them. The problem is, when we hear them, we often plug our ears. For example, a moment ago, you heard me affirm your graciousness. You're not feeling particularly good about yourself today so the affirmation you heard within you, through me, must be coming from one of your blind spots. You see, Eli, that's the good news—the best news of all, really."

"What is?" I ask, my curiosity outweighing my resistance.

"Your biggest blind spot of all is your truest, worthiest, most lovable self. It's your soul. Your spirit. Your consciousness. Your essence. Whatever you want to call it. Every word falls equally short of capturing it. You can't see it because it's the part of you that sees. It's a sort of gathering place for everything that is good, true, and beautiful about you. It's the place where you store the love that created you, the love that has happened to you, and the love you are becoming. It's where I live within you, as a matter of fact. It's a space on the inside of you, and it's the thinnest of spaces."

His brow creases. "However, when you got wounded, you decided this space within you—this true you—wasn't worthy of love and belonging, so you moved the center of your identity out of that space, neglected it, let it collect cobwebs, forgot about it altogether. In the end, Eli, our biggest and most beautiful blind spot is our true self." His smile is like the field of wildflowers beyond us. "What a lovely surprise," he concludes.

I imagine my mother's reaction to this: woo-woo nonsense. I channel her, barely aware of plugging my ears, figuratively speaking.

"What do you know about it?" I challenge him. "You never seemed like you had any wounds. Your life was never a mess like mine. You had the reputation, the cars, the women, the penthouse. It sure looked like you lived your best life. What do you know about what I'm going through?"

He's undaunted by my anger. Indeed, he sets the driver aside and leans slightly forward, his voice becoming even more gentle. "Is that why you came here today, Eli, because you think I was perfect? Or is it because deep down you know I *perfected* the very façade you have been building for so long?"

My silence is my answer. The prairie grass sighs in the breeze. The wildflowers wave. The buzzing of cicadas in the treetops around us reaches a crescendo and then recedes, only to rise again. The air is pungent with summer.

"I was no less wounded than you, Eli, but I was exceptionally good at achieving my proxies for worth."

I'm immediately confused. In some golf tournaments, the closest ball to the pin on a particular par-three wins the "proxy contest." He's talking about something else though.

"Proxies for worth?" I ask.

"It's how we spend our lives, chasing our proxies for worth. You see, early in life, when we begin to doubt our true self is worthy of love and belonging, we start seeking substitutes for our worthiness. These substitutes—these proxies—vary a bit from person to person, but all proxies have a few characteristics in common."

I feel like he's about to do an autopsy on my life, and I cross my arms against it.

"First, our proxies are usually easy to quantify. We can tally them, measure our progress with them, compare that progress to the progress of others. A good proxy is like a good scoreboard; it tells you who is winning and who is losing in this competition to prove we are worthy. That's why so many people use money as a proxy for their worth. It's numerical. But any numerical thing will do. I used to track my personal records for quickest removal of a brain tumor, how fast one of my cars could go, how many women had spent the night. The better the numbers, the better I felt about myself. It's why your generation's social media has been such a smashing success. It's all numbers. Followers. Views. Subscribers. Likes. Shares. Numbers, numbers, numbers. All are proxies for worth."

It's hitting awfully close to home. I have my numbers too. Money is one, of course. Book sales another. And just this morning I had imagined buying Rebecca a tenth anniversary ring with a certain dollar amount attached to it.

He gives me the space to digest this and then continues. "The second quality of a good proxy is that it arises from our greatest giftedness. For instance, when my guidance counselor told me to make some money from my boat-in-a-bottle hobby, he was telling me to do something with my strongest skill: my dexterity. So I did. You have too, Eli. You have a way with words. And you have a gift for traveling inside yourself and putting words to what you find there on behalf of the rest of us. Those are your strengths and you have used them well. But you have also used people's reaction to those strengths as a proxy for your worth."

"Is that the third quality?" I ask. "The admiration of others?" My arms are at my side now, my resistance an afterthought.

He smiles. "That's right. When we're young and we get wounded, we watch for what gets loved around us. What do our people celebrate? What do they value? What do they treasure? Then we do what we need to do—and become who we need to become—in order to be celebrated, valued, and treasured. A good proxy is less a reflection of what *we* love and more a reflection of what was loved by those *around* us."

Again, it is quiet. In the thinness of the place, I can almost hear the *thwack* of golf balls being struck, the *clickety-clack* of old metal spikes on cart paths, the far-off cheers after a long winding putt finds its way into the bottom of a hole.

My uncle breaks the silence. "Proxies for worth weren't your reason for coming here today, either, were they?"

I shake my head. "You said something to us that day, Uncle Mark. In the clubhouse, after you bought us all those hot dogs and gave us those wristbands. You said, 'I wish I had more to give you kids.' For thirty years, I've assumed you meant more swag. After what happened to me this morning, though, I'm beginning to think you meant something else entirely."

His eyes become reservoirs. "You're right, Eli, I did mean something else, but what I really meant was coming from that big beautiful blind spot within me, so I didn't even know it."

"You know it now, though?"

"Yes, I do. And so do you. Listen to your blind spots, Eli. What did you want from me that day: a wristband or a hug?"

Now my eyes are reservoirs too. He continues.

"When I said I wished I could give you more, I meant more of *myself*. I wished I could show you the depth of my remorse. The fullness of my love for you. My sincere desire to be the kind of uncle who could make you feel like the most beloved nephew in the world. I wanted to embody my biggest and most beautiful blind spot so I wouldn't become another painful blind spot of yours."

I let myself feel it. His longing to give me a hug and my longing to be given one, and how neither one of us ever closed that gap while he was alive. The vapor of my love and my loneliness condenses, and my reservoirs become rivers. I'm not sure how much time passes as the rivers flow. When I look up again, the shadows have lengthened a little. My uncle still sits there, though, waiting for me.

"This is hard to hear, Uncle Mark. Good to hear. But hard."

His voice is so soft now it feels like the hug he never gave me. "I don't think it's the hardest thing to hear, Eli."

I look at him and I know what he's going to say next, and the sorrow of it feels like a veil about to be torn within me.

"I think you came here today because you and I have more in common than you'd like to admit: I didn't discover my blind spots until it was too late, and it seems the same is true of you."

The veil is torn. The foundations of my world shake with it. I know why I came. I may not be on my deathbed, but my marriage is, my family is, my future is, and the pain of what could have been is exquisite. The awareness that I no longer have the power to reverse my fortunes is like an anguished scream issuing from within me, the kind of scream that leaves your throat sore for days afterward. Uncle Mark gives me the space to silently scream. The shadows get longer. Gradually, my inner scream dies down, and it's replaced by a question. I look at my uncle, who can apparently see it coming.

"Go ahead," he says, giving me permission, "ask what you want to ask."

"Okay," I say, trying to gather my thoughts into something coherent. "You were really sick at the end. My dad told me that you were on your deathbed for at least a month before you passed. I just can't imagine what that month was like for you, with no more proxies to chase, with only time to think about the life you'd lived. I guess I'm wondering—were you able to make peace with it, or . . . or did you die wishing for a mulligan?"

As soon as the words are out of my mouth, I feel guilty about possibly stirring up that ugly reality for him, even though he's merely a memory. He doesn't seem to mind. He also doesn't seem interested in answering. Instead, he turns the question around on me.

"Search your heart, Eli. What do you hope I will say?"

What comes out next comes rushing out, like a dam has broken somewhere upstream and a whole reservoir is emptying itself all at once.

"I hope you will say that you did make peace with your life. That in your final hours you heard the whisper of your biggest blind spot, a voice coming from that graceful void within you. That you died knowing your proxies don't define you, but your mistakes don't either. That you died knowing you were defined by the love you longed to give, not the hugs you held back. That even though you couldn't go back and fix any of it, you somehow found a way to love all of it, exactly the way it was."

Uncle Mark looks at me, *into* me.

"That is *your* opportunity too, Eli. It is one of the gifts of what you're going through right now. You have an opportunity to love the life you've lived *before* it's over. This moment in your life—this opportunity—is a bridge. The toll is your willingness to accept everything that's brought you here. Not ignore it. Not tolerate it. Not even forgive it, though you must do that too. The toll is what it takes to *love* it. Then, on the other side of it, your reward will be the opportunity to start giving out hugs instead of wristbands, while you're still alive." He pauses and smiles one last time. "Not just when your nephew resurrects you with his imagination."

Then there was silence between us as his presence and the carefully manicured tee box were replaced by a mound of over-grown prairie. Some ambitious crickets joined the cicadas, and afternoon became evening. Some of the wildflowers began the long, slow process of closing for the darkness. I sat so still a family of rabbits dined several yards away from me without concern. I was frozen by despair as I found myself overwhelmed by yet another repetitive thought, this one far less pleasant than all others that had gone before it:

I don't have what it takes to cross this bridge of mine.

30

MY MOM, ON THE OTHER HAND, was in a festive mood.

She had managed to both intuit the reason for Benjamin's visit to town *and* ignore the reason for the sheriff's visit to her house. So she was ready to celebrate my accomplishment with a big dinner together and had no questions about why law enforcement had shown up at her door looking for me.

Furthermore, after finding the empty pepperoni pizza box and watching me run out of the house in a supposed digestive frenzy, she had put two and two together and concluded I really *did* have issues with meat, while simultaneously glossing over the question of why I'd run *away* from the bathroom in my moment of need. I thought of my Uncle Mark. Blind spots. My mother was riddled with them.

However, her blind spots had resulted in a trip to the grocery store for veggie burgers and, regardless of *why* she'd finally accepted the truth about my problems with meat, I was grateful for the gesture. At that moment, any kindness would do. She had a classic summer dinner planned: burgers on the grill, corn on the cob, potato salad, and hand-squeezed lemonade. My mother's grilling skills were second to none, and the aroma from the grill revived some of the appetite I'd lost along with my hope.

All in all, I figured, a good meal couldn't hurt, and it wasn't the worst consolation prize for losing at your life.

"We're eating in the dining room tonight!" she declared as she pulled her special occasion china down from the cupboard and her holiday silverware from a drawer. I was grateful for this too. My mom didn't mess around with "the good stuff," as she called it. Christmas. Easter. Birthdays. Graduations. Those were the only times I'd known her to use it. It was her way of acknowledging my big day, by placing it on par with those occasions. It was her way of loving me. For once, I let her.

"Go get cleaned up, dinner will be ready soon," she lilted from the dining room.

I walked into my bedroom. My laptop still lay on my bed. On my desk the old wristband rested on top of two white envelopes. Thanks to the wristband, those two envelopes no longer looked identical to me. In the publisher's envelope, I saw one of my proxies for worth. In the sheriff's envelope, I saw the once wonderful, now terrible, but always ordinary life I had lived, and which—according to my Uncle Mark—I must learn to love.

I opened the envelope with my ordinary life in it. Unfolded the papers. Scanned the pages. Our names: me, Rebecca, Sarah. Our address. Our county and our length of residence. The reason for the divorce: no one's fault, according to Rebecca. The division of assets: in true Rebecca fashion, she didn't want any help finding her way home from Italy. We would split the proceeds from selling the house and any other cash on hand, and otherwise she'd take care of herself. Custody was listed as to be determined.

My stomach cramped more viciously than it had on the golf course.

I couldn't love this. I couldn't even like it. I hated it. I hated that the most important people in my life were being taken away from me, and I was powerless to do anything about it. After Sarah's birth I'd often imagined what it must feel like in those moments after a child has gone missing, abducted, vanished, and there's nothing a parent can do to bring her back. Now I was experiencing only a hint of that, and still it was unbearable.

I went to the bathroom and slapped cold water on my face, a little too hard. It did the trick. A new mantra began repeating in my mind: *Get it together get it together get it together.* I could control almost nothing that mattered to me right now, but I could control how I showed up to this night. My mother was trying to love me, and just hours ago I'd become aware of one of my blind spots—my tendency to petulantly resist the love of others. So tonight, I'd stop resisting. I'd sit down at the table. I'd let her celebrate me in her own way and I'd be grateful for that. I'd start by learning how to love this ordinary night. I could do that much, or at least I could try.

My mother was already seated in the dining room off the kitchen. It was part of my father's first addition to the house, and it retained its original wallpaper, a sort of salmon color with a halfhearted gloss to it. Indeed, as I entered, I was struck by how the whole room was frozen in time. Same curtains on the bay window overlooking the backyard. Same oak table. Same chairs. Same tablecloth. I couldn't remember eating in here since my father had passed away. I took a deep breath as I took my usual seat across the table from my mother, preparing myself to make the best of the night.

Then, things got thin.

I looked up at her. Our eyes locked, and her eyes were like the room around us: unchanged. Sure, she'd added some crow's-feet over the years. A smudge of shadow beneath them. And they were recessed in more frailty than ever. But their walnut color remained her particular shade of brown, and they still evoked the sense that she wasn't looking at you *with* them but from somewhere *behind* them. Her eyes might as well have been a time machine.

I'm sixteen years old again, locking eyes with her during dinner on the day that orphaned me.

I'd walked home from my dad's office but couldn't remember doing so. Arriving home to an empty house, I locked myself in my bedroom and dropped onto my bed with my face buried in my pillow. I was trying to achieve pitch blackness, but the darkness behind my eyes was filled with images. Snapshots. A slide show—royal blue shorts, gray roots, wink, tilt—running over and over again. I screamed into the pillow, an agonized sort of howl, in the hopes of erasing the images with the sound of it. When it didn't work, I cried until I had no tears left to cry. The tears, too, failed to wash away the images. All that was left was to lie there, feeling empty of everything except the secret I'd been given to keep.

My mother had called me to dinner a half dozen times, but it wasn't until she pounded on my door and made threats about going to the DMV and revoking my learner's permit that I finally found the strength to lift myself from the bed. The walk from my room to the dining room was like a walk to an executioner's chair. I could hear my dad in there talking with her, intermingled with the clinking and clanking of food being dished out. I walked in and took my seat, careful to avoid looking at my father, who sat at the head of the table to my left. Instead, I looked up at my mom, and our eyes locked.

Walnut brown. There but not there.

I'm looking at her while at the same time seeing everything I saw at my father's office a few hours earlier. Though I know it's impossible, I'm convinced she can see it too. I'm both terrified of letting my dad down and desperate to do so.

My mother smiles, seeing nothing except my best attempt at nonchalance. She passes me a platter of asparagus and asks my dad about his day at the office. He launches into a litany of legalese related to some real estate closings he was involved with during the morning, before saying something that makes my heart slam against the inside of my ribcage like it's trying to get out. Again, I'm nonsensically terrified my mother will see its thumping through my T-shirt.

"Well," he says, "I probably shouldn't be telling you this, but you know Mandy Andrews, Eli's gym teacher?" My mother nods, a little wide-eyed. She always loved getting early access to town gossip through her husband's violation of attorney-client confidentiality. "Yeah, so she and her husband, Ed, are getting divorced. I spent most of the afternoon with her, helping her out with some things."

Helping her out. Some things. At these words, my heart hammers as hard as it did while I was standing back in his office, taking it all in. I can't believe his audacity. I'm astonished at how thinly he's disguised our secret. In spite of myself, I look toward him as he concludes his summary.

"Anyhow, I think she's more relaxed now," he says casually. He looks up, and it happens again.

He winks at me.

The whole day comes together in that wink. All of the pain. The shock at Samantha breaking up with me. The shame of it. The loss of it. The prom that would never happen. The confusion about the lowered blinds. The dread walking down the hallway. The much greater shock of what I found at the end of it. The sorrow and horror of his first wink. All that emotion consolidates in my gut, where it is lit on fire by rage about what my father has done and what he is doing. The rage takes over as I imagine myself reaching out and ripping his head from his shoulders, rolling it out of the dining room and against the far wall of the kitchen.

Instead, I eat because sorrow has no appetite, but rage is ravenous. I eat aggressively, spearing asparagus with loud cracks against my plate. Chomping on pot roast with my mouth open. Draining the glass of milk my mother pours at every dinner. I look at her and she looks a little startled, but in a good way. Her boy is clearly enjoying her cooking. What more could a mother ask for?

I'm done with my meal before my parents are halfway through theirs. I ask to be excused. My mother wonders if I'd like dessert. I turn to my father in exaggerated fashion and, looking him directly in the eye, I declare, "No, I think I've had enough for today." Then, dramatically, I wink at him. The look of uncertainty and fear I see come over his face is more satisfying than anything I've put in my stomach.

I get up from the table and walk through the kitchen toward my bedroom, stopping at the spot where I imagine my father's head has come to rest against the side door of the house. I stand over it, and I imagine kicking it, over and over, until it is unrecognizable with trauma, like me. I continue to my bedroom and slam the door loudly.

I slam a door within me too. I will never again feel grief about Samantha Stiller nor will I feel love for my father. I lock those feelings away in a blind spot within me. In the weeks that follow, whenever either one tries to emerge, I let my rage put them back in their place. Over time it gets easier. I forget they are there altogether. My dad, for his part, helps me forget—he'll die of a heart attack before we ever get around to talking about what passed between us that afternoon.

"Eli, you're creeping me out. Are you okay? What's happening?"

My mother's voice beckoned me back to the present. I'd been staring into her eyes for a while. Long enough to scare her. I looked to my left where my dad's seat sat empty. I looked back at her. The door on this particular blind spot was wide open. If there was ever a moment to unburden myself of the secret I'd been carrying for so many years, this was it. I opened my mouth to speak. My stomach cramped. My mouth closed, seemingly of its own accord. I'd come to this table to let my mother love me for a night, not to ruin her night, not to ruin her memory of her marriage, not to tell her the life she'd lived had been a sham.

"Sorry, Mom, it's been a long day. I think I'm just hungry. Let's eat."

And that's what we did. I attacked my potato salad as if it were that long-ago asparagus. I gnawed rows in my ear of corn like it might get away. I oohed and aahed over the veggie burger.

Just as I was finishing the last bite, my stomach cramped again. Followed by a second cramp. And a third. My mother could see I was in pain, and the next word she said was the most loving thing I'd heard from her in years.

"Pepperoni?" she guessed.

I nodded my head. It was more than pepperoni but not the kind of more I could tell her about. I stood up from the table. She clapped her hands and exhorted me to head for the bathroom, like a cheerleader at the Digestive Olympics. I did. It's where I spent most of the night. She checked on me every few hours. Every time I told her through the door I was fine and she could go to sleep. She never did. I learned something about my mom that night. She's good at loving those who are weak, such as a sick middle-aged man with nowhere else to go.

I also had plenty of time to think during the small hours of that night, though I suppose my Uncle Mark would say I was listening, not thinking. I heard a lot of things, but one in particular took me by surprise. I discounted the idea at first, but then I heard something else, which made the idea more plausible. I heard my Uncle Mark telling me it was the only way. Telling me I had to pay a toll, and the toll was love. I prayed sincerely for the first time in a long time. It went something like this: "Take this cup from my lips, but if there's really no other way to do it, so be it." Around five o'clock, exhausted and empty and wrung out, the rumbling in my stomach having finally subsided, no other options had presented themselves, so I surrendered to it.

With rumors of light in the eastern sky, I placed a phone call, got into bed, and fell asleep.

31

I AWOKE TO THE SOUND of Jeff's answering service calling me back.

Through gritty eyes I glanced at the time on my phone. Noon. A businesslike woman on the other end informed me that Jeff was out of the office. They were trying to reach him, but they couldn't guarantee he'd call me back today, and if I was in danger of hurting myself, I should go to the emergency room. I told her I wasn't and I'd understand if he didn't call me back *ever*, for a variety of reasons. She said, "Yes, sir," as if she understood, and hung up.

I was still lying in bed an hour later when he called.

"Elijah, this is Jeff. My answering service said you called." There was a mixture of kindness and caution in his voice.

"Jeff, hi, thank you for calling me back. I know you're out of the office today. I'm sorry for interfering with your personal time."

"It's all right, I wouldn't have called you back if I didn't want to, okay? It's actually great to hear your voice and to know you're alive and well. I've thought a lot about our last session, and I think I pushed you too hard."

"No, you didn't push me too hard, Jeff. You pushed me as firmly as I needed to be pushed, and in exactly the right direction.

I'm just sorry for storming out on you the way I did. I've discovered in the last few weeks I can be a bit of a brat toward people who are trying to love me by telling me hard things."

"Well then, what do you say we call it even?" he asked in a playful tone. "But just remember, the next time it comes to firing each other, it's my turn."

I told him he had a deal and asked if he had a few minutes to hear about what had happened since I walked out of his office. He did. I held nothing back. He sighed and groaned and lamented and cheered and made exasperated comments about my mom in all the right spots. It made me feel a little less alone in the world.

Finally, I told him my idea. "In my professional opinion," I said in an authoritative tone, pausing for him to laugh at my feigned grandstanding, "I need to have a different kind of conversation with my father, but I can't do so because the thin places around this town, where I feel most connected to him, are also traumatic places for me. The trauma overrides my imagination. It limits my freedom to experience something new. So I'd like to go somewhere I *don't* associate with my dad and try to have a conversation with him there."

"Makes sense to me," Jeff said, in a way that suggested he knew there was more coming. There was.

"And I'd like *you* to be the voice of my father in that conversation." As I said it, I expelled a bunch of air and tension I hadn't known I was holding. There. It was out there and it was a big ask and I'd be devastated if he declined but I'd also understand, even though I'd be back at square one with no idea where to go next. Jeff didn't hesitate though.

"I'm honored and humbly accept your invitation, Elijah. When and where?"

"Well, I think the when should be up to you. The where is up to me, I know, but to be honest I don't have a clue."

I could almost hear him thinking through the phone. Then, "Elijah, when was the last time you visited your father's grave?"

I felt momentarily disoriented by the unexpected obviousness of it. The truth was, I hadn't visited my father's grave since the burial service, and yet doing so had never occurred to me. Big blind spot. Chalk one up for Uncle Mark.

Then Jeff laid out the ground rules. First, when he called at four o'clock, I'd be waiting for him at the gravesite and I'd simply pick up the phone, say "Hi, Dad," and he'd take it from there. Second, he asked me to acknowledge out loud that whatever I felt during the conversation, I was feeling toward my father, not toward him. And finally, I consented to neither one of us breaking our roles—he would be my father, and I would be my father's son, until we hung up the phone. We could debrief the call at our next appointment. Having reached our agreements, I thanked Jeff for going along with this ridiculous notion of mine. He thanked me for trusting him enough to invite him into it.

~~

I arrived at the cemetery a little early because I had only a vague sense of where my father's grave was located, and I wasn't about to ask my mother. I began my search beneath a sprawling oak tree that dwarfed every other tree in the cemetery, because I remembered looking up at its swaying branches during my father's burial service. The mourners in attendance had probably seen a grief-stricken son searching the heavens for answers.

However, I hadn't been looking *up at it*, I had been looking *away from him*, as I'd done in every moment together since his last wink at the dinner table.

I walked in concentric circles outward from the oak tree until I came to my father's plot. It was marked by a large rectangular slab of gray granite, about a foot high, inscribed with his name— Steven Campbell—and the dates that had bookended his life. The epitaph read, "He lived and died in the spirit of this town: in service to those around him."

The cauldron within me was roiling again. I read the epitaph aloud. A laugh with no laughter in it escaped me. "Yeah, he served Mrs. Andrews all right."

I was overcome by an urge to call Jeff and cancel the whole thing. My Uncle Mark's challenge—to cross this bridge in my journey by loving the life I'd lived before it was over, and to pay the toll by embracing everything that had brought me to this moment—seemed an absurdity. Staring at my father's gravestone, I didn't think I was capable of paying the toll, nor did I even *want* to pay it.

I took out my phone, my thumb hovering over Jeff's name in my contacts, before putting it back in my pocket. I decided to put my hope in Jeff's ability to work some kind of miracle here. After all, I told myself, it couldn't hurt to try, could it? The answer, of course, was yes, it could hurt very much. I waited for the phone to ring.

At four o'clock and zero seconds, it did.

32

"HI, DAD."

"Hi, Eli."

I placed the phone on top of the gravestone and stepped back, standing at the foot of the plot, only my father's body lying between his voice and mine.

After so many years, there was so much to say, and yet I had no idea where to begin. Only social pleasantries came to mind, such as, "So, how are you, Dad?" I imagined Jeff responding with, "Well, I'm sort of dead," and it stirred a strange, unhinged kind of laughter within me. It subsided, and I was reminded of why I'd brought Jeff into this experiment. Clearly, I was not capable of having this conversation on my own. So I gave up and waited for my dad to speak. I was beginning to wonder if the cellular service had failed, when he did.

"I can't believe how long you kept our secret, Son."

I was surprised by the automaticity of my rage. "First of all, don't call me 'Son.' Call me 'buddy.' Call me 'friend.' Call me your partner in crime. But don't ever call me 'Son.' And second of all: seriously? After all these years, that's what you're going to start with?"

My father seemed unfazed by my reaction. "Well, I figured you didn't come here to chitchat."

Of course he was right, and it pissed me off even more. I stewed.

He continued. "When you winked at me at the table that night, I thought for sure you would tell your mom before the weekend was out. But you never did. So I assumed my body wouldn't be cold before you'd spill the beans upon my death. But you never did. You've never told *anyone*. Not your best friend Benjamin. Not even your wife—and she's a looker, Eli, I don't know how you keep anything from her. I want to thank you, Son. A man couldn't ask for a more loyal friend."

This wasn't going the way I'd thought it would. I'd pictured something warmer. More tender. Touchy-feely. Redemptive. Something more like the conversation with my Uncle Mark. Something that would drain away my anger, not add to it. Instead, he was ignoring my demand to stop calling me Son, and he was ogling my wife with his rotting eyes. Enough was enough.

"You're right, Dad, I didn't come here to chitchat, but I didn't come here for a pat on the back, either, for God's sake." I was spitting the words out like bug spray that had wandered onto my tongue. "I came here for an *apology*. I want you to apologize for what you did to Mom. I want you to apologize for what you did to me. I want you to apologize for what I saw. All of it. Mrs. Andrews. The wink. The other wink. The assumption I'd keep your secret for you. I want you to get down on your dead knees and beg me for *forgiveness!*" The words echoed in the cemetery air.

His response was ruthless. "*Our* secret," he said.

Those words rattled me, like a left hook to the temple I hadn't seen coming. "*What?*"

"*Our* secret, Eli, not *my* secret. Yes, I'll take some responsibility for what I did with Mandy Andrews, but as soon as you saw it, it became *our* secret. You could have told anyone whenever you wanted. In truth, a part of me hoped you would. Living that kind of lie is a burden you'll probably never be able to understand."

I couldn't believe my ears. "Self-pity makes for a pretty pitiful apology, Dad." The word *Dad* was spoken in air quotes.

"That's because I apologize for nothing, Eli."

I was speechless, my jaw hanging lower than when Benjamin presented me with the royalty check.

"Son, you have no idea what was happening behind the scenes of my marriage to your mother, if you can even call it a marriage. We never divorced, but we'd been emotionally separated for a long time before you stumbled on your gym teacher and me. I deserved to find comfort somewhere. A little consolation for a lifetime spent serving others. I don't apologize for Mandy Andrews. And for all you know, she was one of many. I stand by my actions. Of course, I wish you hadn't witnessed what you did, but frankly, you should have knocked."

I took a step toward the gravestone, planning not to hang up the phone but to fling it into the trunk of that great oak. Then I froze, remembering the agreement I'd made with Jeff. I was impotent with rage, and I looked up into the branches of the tree and screamed for real this time—an agonized, guttural, full-bodied, and ultimately failed attempt to expel what I felt toward my father. At that very moment, an invisible wind rushed in from somewhere providential, bending every branch of the oak tree in a swirling, whooshing vortex. I took it as permission to scream again. Somehow, the second one was louder.

As my scream and the inexplicable wind faded, my father's voice became a little more kind for the first time. "Eli, you think you need me to apologize in order for you to forgive me, but you don't. In fact, if I apologized, you'd reject it out of hand. No, Son, you need something else to happen in order to forgive me."

Hoarsely and hopelessly I asked, "What?" expecting the answer to be as unsatisfying as the rest of our conversation had been. It was.

"You need to betray me."

The words hung in the still air between us. A million insects buzzed in the summer heat, adding up to a low hum all around us.

"You need to tell our secret, Eli. Until you do, it will be impossible to forgive me, because every day you keep our secret you continue to participate in the very thing for which you want me to apologize. What good would it do for me to apologize for the secret you kept today, if tomorrow you're going to keep it all over again?" I could hear an attorney's reasoning in this argument. He sounded pretty satisfied with himself, as well he should have been, as it let him completely off the hook.

"Are you giving me permission to tell the secret?" I asked, daring him.

"Never," he responded immediately and emphatically. "I wouldn't have given you permission in life, and I won't give it to you in death. If I'd wanted this secret told, I would have told it myself while I still could. No, Son, you'll never get my permission. Like I said, if you want to unburden yourself of our secret, you will have to *betray* me."

At those words, my rage melted into a loneliness so deep I felt like I might fall into it and never stop falling. The racking sobs that came with it were rendered silent by the pain. Just a collapsing of the shoulders. A rhythmic jerking of the torso. A cessation of breath. A surrender to gravity, as I found myself kneeling in the grass. I felt like I might cry forever, but within a minute the sobbing subsided. I gasped at air, eventually catching my breath, and tried to put into words what the sobs had been saying.

"Dad, you were never a dad to me. All I ever had was your friendship. If I betray *that*, there will be *nothing* left of you. I will be all alone."

The voice may have been that of a middle-aged man, but the words were those of a sixteen-year-old boy who was beginning to understand why he'd *really* carried a secret around with him for almost a quarter of a century. And they were the words that finally gave me—the older man who was already all alone and thus had nothing to lose—permission to do what I'd wanted to do since I was a sophomore in high school.

I was going to tell my secret.

33

THE TOLL WAS ACCEPTANCE and the cost was high indeed.

I hung up the phone without saying goodbye and without my traditional, "Love you, Dad." The conversation had not changed my love for my father—I would always love him the way a son always loves his father: truly and helplessly. I'd expressed that love to him countless times before, in words given and words hidden. However, for the first time, I could see that the love my father had given me in return had been something less than true—he'd taught me love was loyalty to a person rather than faithfulness to the truth. I'd spent a lifetime rehearsing that lesson, protecting everyone from my inconvenient truths, and calling that love.

I was done with that definition of love.

I pulled into my mother's driveway. Out of habit, I was steering the car toward my spot next to the garage when my father's words, brought to life through Jeff, echoed within me: "You need to betray me." I pumped the brakes. Turned the steering wheel. Pulled into the empty space in the garage next to my mother's car. For decades I'd deferred to my father, even in his absence. I'd preserved the empty spaces he'd left in our lives. Twenty-three years was long enough. It was the smallest of betrayals—a parking spot—but the cost was high. As I turned off the ignition, grief welled up within me, like a tumor on the move. It filled everything between my throat and stomach, and I had difficulty breathing beneath its mass.

Echoes:

"If I'd wanted this secret told, I would have told it myself."

"No, Son, you'll never get my permission."

"You'll have to betray me."

I entered the kitchen, where I found my mother in the same position I'd found her weeks ago upon my arrival in Bradford's Ferry—her back to me, preparing dinner. Not everything was the same though.

"Well, hello there," she chimed, glancing at me briefly over her shoulder. "I was hoping you'd make it home in time for dinner. I saw the way you scarfed down the veggie burger and the corn last night, and I had to admit to myself, 'Annie, maybe you've been a little stubborn over the years.' So I made a grocery run and tonight we're having a salad. Grilled tofu and chickpeas on romaine. I've made an amazing vinaigrette. You're going to love it!"

Upon leaving the cemetery, I'd thought my resolve was as solid as the granite beneath which my father was buried. Now I wasn't sure if it could withstand a few garbanzo beans. I needed to say something quickly before it crumbled for good.

"Mom, we need to talk." I tried to put some unmistakable gravity in my voice, something that would suggest to my mother the weight of what I was planning to say. She, however, seemed immune to gravity, floating somewhere up in her own space.

"Sure, let's talk!" she said brightly, her back still turned to me, drizzling the salad with vinaigrette, picking up two wooden tongs, beginning to toss it. "No global warming talk, though, let's keep it light tonight!"

Oh boy.

"No, Mom, I mean we really need to *talk*." I paused. Then, with the tremor of a little boy in my voice, I elaborated. "We need to talk about Dad." She jerked to a stop in midtoss, several wet pieces of lettuce escaping the salad bowl and finding their way to the counter and the floor. "I went to his grave today."

"Oh, did you now?" Her back was still to me. Her voice was striving for singsong and falling just a little short. She ignored the fugitive lettuce and resumed her tossing, even more vigorously than before.

I tried to go on. Struggled. "Geez," I muttered, more to myself than to her, "I've rehearsed this a thousand times over the years, and I still don't know how to start it."

"Well then, perhaps you should rehearse it a thousand more times and try again a few years down the road!" She laughed, but it was a fragile laugh. Toss-toss went the salad.

"No, I have to say this now, Mom. I've spent so much of my life opening my mouth to say one thing and never getting it out, and it's made a mess of things."

"Oh nonsense," she retorted quickly. "Your life is wonderful. Look at you. You're an accomplished author. You've just finished another book. You've got a pocket full of cash. You've got a beautiful family. Not such a mess, if you ask me." The leaves of lettuce were bruising and wilting beneath the trauma of her tossing.

"Mom. The sheriff yesterday. He was looking for me. He gave me divorce papers. Rebecca is *leaving* me." There, finally. A little bit of truth. It was a good start. She'd have to listen now.

Or not.

"Oh well, that. Yes, I figured. But you two will work it out." The best she could muster was a patina of nonchalance.

"I don't think we will, Mom." There was a forcefulness in my voice that usually accompanied my journeys away from truth, not toward it. For the first time, however, my anger seemed to be repurposed. It wasn't a veil. It was fuel. The energy I needed to push me over the hump of my hiding. "I've been lying to Rebecca for years. About important things." I paused on the fulcrum of my relationship with my mother, hesitating one last time, then finally tipping into my fullest truth. "And unlike you, Mom, she doesn't ignore the lies she's being told."

She whirled on me, wielding her salad tongs in front of her like weapons, vinaigrette spattering the refrigerator door. "Shut *up*, Elijah!"

My mother had never revealed her rage to me. In that instant though, I understood I'd always *sensed* it. Right there, just below the surface of her. In the wordless abyss of childhood, I'd made an unspoken pact with her: I'd intuit the limits of what she would tolerate, and she'd reward me by keeping her rage in a cage. I'd just violated our contract for the very first time.

She glanced down at the oversized utensils, apparently surprised by her own aggression. She dropped them to her side. She didn't need them—her eyes were dangerous enough. "How *dare* you suppose you know what I ignore or don't ignore. And for your information, I don't ignore *anything*."

"You're right, Mom, I'm sorry. I shouldn't have started off by talking about you." Backpedaling, but sincerely, not fearfully. "I want to tell you about *me*. I'm just not very good at it. Not much practice, you know?" I chuckled, trying to lighten the mood. For a moment it seemed to work.

"Well, I'd be happy to hear about *you*, Eli. I thought you wanted to talk about your dad, and I don't see the point in that, the man is dead and gone, but yes, you, I'd be happy to talk about you." She turned quickly back to the assault on her salad, suggesting her eagerness to hear about me was somewhat less enthusiastic than her words had indicated.

"That's the thing, though, Mom. What I need to tell you about me will mean telling you something about Dad." She stopped tossing the salad again, this time releasing the tongs and placing her hands on the counter on either side of the bowl. "I saw something, Mom. Something I've kept to myself since I was sixteen."

"Don't, Eli." Plaintive. "Just don't. There's no need for this. The past is the past. Leave well enough alone." She leaned forward onto her hands, using the counter for support.

"That's the thing, though. The past *isn't* the past. It's *not* behind us. It's right here, right now. In *me*. I've been carrying it around all these years, and I can't carry it around anymore. I have to tell someone, and I think that someone should be you, Mom, because it's the truth about your life, too."

"Shut up, Eli." Quieter this time but somehow scarier as she lowered her head and leaned even more heavily on the counter.

"The Friday before sophomore prom, the day Samantha Stiller broke up with me, I walked to Dad's office after school."

"Shut up, Eli." I could barely hear her over the whirring of the refrigerator.

"I got to his office and the blinds were down and I was confused but I went in anyway."

"I'm warning you, Eli, stop this now. This isn't necessary. We have tofu and chickpeas."

I heard it and didn't hear it at the same time—my mother's warning that soybean curd and garbanzo beans were the best she could do for me. I continued, "When I got inside, I heard noises and—"

It was as far as I got. My mother reared up and spun around. *"Shut up, Elijah!"*

No tongs this time. Again, she didn't need them. They were blunt instruments compared to the weapon she would wield now: her words.

"You want the *truth*, Elijah? Really? You want the *truth* to be told here today?"

"I'm your only child, I think I *deserve* the truth!" I bellowed with every ounce of defiance I could muster.

Before the words were out of my mouth, though, I realized I'd miscalculated. At my father's grave, when I'd imagined there was nothing left to lose, I'd been wrong. The look in her eyes said there was plenty left to lose, and she was going to take it from me.

Then, she told me.

34

Dear Rebecca,

I'm not sure if this letter will be passed on to you. I hope it will. I have a lot to tell you.

Before I say anything else, though, I want you to know this is not my way of trying to change your mind. It's my way of saying goodbye. For years, I've tried to give you the best of me, never understanding what you really wanted was the rest of me. That's what this letter is—the rest of me. All those parts of my story and our story I've hidden from you. You've always deserved the truth. Here, at the end, I'm finally able to give it to you.

That word: hidden. It will be easier for me to write this letter if I call what I did "hiding" rather than "lying." To lie, one must know they are lying. But I didn't realize I was lying to you; I thought I was loving you by protecting you from unnecessary truths. I'll certainly understand if you prefer to call it lying, however. Not that you need my understanding now. At any rate, I want to tell you the whole truth, in parts, beginning with us.

I hid small things from you, and big things. Let's start small.

My hiding from you began in our very first moment, when you put that lovely leg of yours in my lap. We laughed a lot over the years about your audacity and about how I got all mumbly and bumbly in the midst of it. I let you assume my discombobulation was due only to your forwardness, but it was also due to my hiddenness. Just a few hours earlier, my roommate had set me up on a blind date for that evening. She and I had traded numbers and, just before I microwaved that mystery meat of mine, I'd sent her a text confirming a date for that evening. As soon as your leg came to rest in my lap, it became something you didn't need to know. Growing up, I learned love keeps everything as simple as possible.

Now, I understand, love is about more than simplicity. It's about honesty.

Here's some more honesty. You thought we kept getting lucky in those early months of our relationship, always winding up directly across from each other in our classes, exchanging knowing looks and glances throughout our lectures. The truth is, I figured out where you liked to sit in each of our classes, and I got to the classroom early every time in order to snag the seat with the best view of you. I hid this because it seemed creepy.

The night you were hit by the drunk driver, I'd been a drunk driver myself. I'd gone out with some of the other guys who had nowhere else to go for the holiday, and we'd celebrated our alienation with a few too many drinks. The ride home had been a blurry one. I hadn't hurt anyone, but when I got the call from your mother the next day, I was sick with guilt anyway, and I vowed never to drink and drive again. You've always admired that policy of mine, and I've always been too ashamed to admit the reason for the thing you loved.

Later that day, when your parents gave me the key to their house, the first thing I did upon entering was chip the decorative vase you bought your mother in Italy. In those days, she displayed it on the sideboard in their entryway. Well, when I turned to close the door, my duffel bag brushed up against it. It wobbled and toppled, and I dove. I got my hand under it in time to cushion its impact on the tile floor, but a piece of the lip splintered off. I found some super glue in a kitchen drawer and repaired it as well as I could. Your mom displays it on the fireplace mantel now. If you look at it closely, you'll find the crack. Every time your dad started a fire over the years, I imagined the heat melting the glue and the whole thing coming apart in front of our eyes. It's another metaphor for our relationship, I guess.

Not everything I hid from you was that dramatic, though. Most of it was pretty ordinary. I hid it anyway. Habit. For instance, I sometimes picked my nose and wiped it on the bottom of the driver's seat. You'll find the evidence there. Sorry. I sometimes pretended to be sicker than I was because you were so good at caring for sick people. I thought Mariah Carey's last album was great. I never really liked your veggie tacos, but I liked you, so I swallowed the truth along with the soy crumbles.

Rebecca, I could go on and on about the small things, but my time is short, and there are more important stories to tell . . .

35

YOUR PAST IS A CITY YOU CONSTRUCT within yourself, block by block, neighborhood by neighborhood, over many years. It has buildings made of memory. They are monuments to your life—skyscrapers made of stories, tenements made of tales—that no wolf could blow down. They are timeless landmarks, orienting you to where you've been and to where you're going.

Like a hurricane meeting the coastline, though, my mother's fury leveled all the existing structures within me. Everything I'd believed about my family was reduced to a landscape of jagged debris. No memory was left untouched, each one so thoroughly decimated it might never have existed at all.

I tried to board up the windows of my selfhood against the onslaught, but it was futile. The force of her gale was just too powerful. Her truth too devastating to withstand. Everything was torn down.

Then, as quickly as it began, her winds receded. Like a tropical storm churning inland, she moved on to some distant land within herself, an apocalypse spent of its energy, now only capable of drizzling in some other place. She snatched her purse and walked out of the house.

I sat staggered within the aftermath, staring at that soggy bowl of tofu, chickpeas, and romaine. It was bruised and beaten. Inedible and useless. Suitable only for the compost pile. My mother had left us in similar conditions.

The house was still. Ten minutes passed. Thirty. An hour. Gradually, a chasm opened within me.

I remembered the first time I flew on a plane. A distant relative was getting married, and my parents had seized the opportunity to travel the skies. The midday flight would mean a very late lunch or an early dinner on arrival. We boarded the plane on schedule. Already, I was hungry. Then our departure time came and went. The pilot announced the cabin wasn't pressurizing properly. We disembarked. The repairs failed. While we waited for another plane to arrive, I got hungrier. My parents window-shopped several restaurants in the terminal. Too expensive. The hunger within me grew. Eventually, we got on another plane. Lifted off. Magic. I forgot the ravenous void opening within me. Then the flight attendants started handing out snacks. The picture on the package made it look like manna from heaven. In actuality, and to my horror, it tasted like black licorice, and it made my gorge rise. A three-hour flight. Baggage claim. The hunger expanded, devouring every nook and cranny within me. We waited for a rental car. We traveled highways with interstates and exits with numbers attached to them but nary a McDonald's in sight. The emptiness within became everything; nothingness became the most voracious of somethings. We arrived at the hotel. My parents checked in while I stood fixated by some candy bars in the vending machine by the elevators. Within me—a cavernous need. Within the machine—the satisfaction of that need. Separating us—a thin pane of glass about which I could do nothing.

As I sat there in the kitchen, the minutes ticking by, my loneliness was like that hunger. It was nothing and everything all at once. Within me—an infinite void, a gaping maw. On the other side of the glass—the people who might have loved me, if only I could have reached them, if only they had been inclined to reach me.

The strangest thing—it didn't feel like a feeling. It was more like a sound. A scream issuing from the very center of me. Not a cry for satisfaction, though. A cry for release. I recognized its voice. I'd heard it for the first time just a few weeks earlier, in my bathtub. It was Jah. He didn't want to *fill* the void; he wanted to extinguish my ability to *feel* it. The very thought of it brought such relief that anything else was inconceivable.

I was no longer safe in my own presence.

When whole communities are leveled by storms, you hear stories of people calling out from beneath the wreckage, pets scraping their way out of the debris, creation stubbornly resisting its demise. It makes little sense, this dragging of oneself back to a life that has been destroyed. And yet these creatures claw toward the light. Some of them even find it, only to expire a little while later from their mortal wounds. That's the only way to explain what I did next.

I texted Benjamin.

館

Though I left my mother's house shortly after texting him, Benjamin was waiting for me when I arrived at the Draughty Den, sitting at that copper-topped bar with his back to me. Behind the bar, a young, copiously pierced guy leaned against the far end of the copper, engrossed in his phone, ignoring everyone. The only other patrons were the same group of guys I'd seen there several weeks earlier. Once again, they acknowledged me with head nods as I entered the bar.

Benjamin noticed the nods and turned around. He gave me the kind of look you'd give a widow at her husband's wake. I appreciated it and hated it.

"How are you, buddy?" he asked gingerly as I took a seat next to him at the bar.

"About how you'd expect," I replied, sounding as chipper as I could. "What does a guy need to do to get a beer around here?"

Benjamin smiled dubiously and waved at the bartender. The kid was oblivious, grinning at something on his phone.

"Excuse me?" Benjamin called, waving again.

Nothing. The kid laughed out loud this time.

"Hey, we'd like to get a couple of beers," Benjamin added, a little more loudly.

The kid switched his grip from one-handed to two-handed so he could use both thumbs to tap out a message of some kind. Benjamin opened his mouth to try again.

I slammed my open palm on the top of the bar, rattling everything on it, and the kid returned to the analog world with such a fright he lost his grip on the phone and bobbled it several times before finally securing it. The guys at the end of the bar chortled at the scene.

"We're ready to order," I said. Even I was a little surprised by the murder in my tone—I hadn't known Jah could speak out loud—and it had the intended effect. The kid hustled toward us.

"Yeah, uh, sorry, I uh, was catching up on my feed, you know?" He looked like a fourth grader called into the principal's office. I ignored his apology.

"I'll have two fingers of your best Scotch, neat."

"Uh, okay." Long pause as he searched a dusty mental Rolodex. "I think we've, uh, only got one kind of Scotch."

"Well then, that's your best, isn't it?"

It was Benjamin's turn to be slack-jawed, and his eyebrows were raised in a question. I answered it.

"I changed my mind, not in a beer mood tonight."

He required no further explanation. "I get that," he said. Then, looking at the bartender, "Make that two." In that moment, I loved my friend with my whole heart.

The bartender put the two drinks in front of us. Benjamin raised his glass. "First, we toast to what is good. Congratulations on your manuscript, Eli."

We clinked glasses. He took a sip of his. I tilted my head back and emptied mine. The bartender's eyes went wide. My chest burned and my eyes watered. It was the first glass of Scotch I'd ever drunk. It wasn't going to be my last.

"Another," I commanded without looking at the bartender. "Next round's on me, B," I declared, holding my glass up to him, wagging it with my thumb and forefinger, before passing it back to the bartender. The kid complied and once it became clear I wasn't going to guzzle the second one, he backed up cautiously toward the end of the bar, giving us some privacy.

"Eli, are you okay? I mean, I know you're not okay-okay. Who could be okay after what happened yesterday. What I mean is, are you *okay*?"

I understood the question, but I didn't know the answer, so I responded with a question of my own. "Do you remember the night we asked Johnny Mathers to go out on the river with us?"

The booze was already reaching my bloodstream, and I wanted more of its gauzy comfort. I took another big swallow.

Benjamin eyed the glass with concern as I returned it to the copper surface, but there was hope in his voice as he responded to my question. "Of course, how could I forget it? Epic night. Geez, he gave us a scare, didn't he?"

～～

It was Labor Day weekend, a couple of weeks into our freshman year of high school. A Sunday night, with a day off on Monday, and I was spending the night at the Bruces'. We'd pitched a tent in his backyard along the Saukenuk River, gathered stones to ring a campfire, and cooked our hot dogs over it as the sun set. By our freshman year, it was already uncool to admit any sort of romanticism about a moment. Fortunately, Benjamin and I had agreed long ago no such rules applied to our friendship.

"Do you ever wonder if this is what it felt like to be John Marcus Bradford, his very first night on the banks of the Saukenuk?" I asked, turning over my hot dog while imagining it to be venison or rabbit.

"Ever?" he replied instantly. "I was wondering it just now." Our friendship was built on synchronicities like that.

The sun set on a moonless night, and the sky darkened toward an inky black. Around the fire, we traded our early impressions of high school and our hopes and dreams for the year. As we talked, the surface of the Saukenuk smoothed out to the same flawless glass that Bradford had enjoyed centuries before. Around eleven o'clock, sounds began to drift down to us from somewhere upriver. Quiet at first, and then gradually more raucous. We walked to the river's bank and strained our eyes to see what could be seen. In the distance, the faintest glow of another campfire. Shadows moving around it. Benjamin recognized the location.

"That's the Lambert family campsite. I bet Tommy and his buddies are getting smashed."

Tommy Lambert was a senior and one of the more unpredictable guys in school. If you were on his good side, he'd see you in the hallway and slap your back so companionably your skin would sting all the way through the next class period. Tommy's friendship hurt, but his bullying hurt a lot worse. If you somehow managed to get on his bad side—and few people ever understood how they got there—the high school hallways could become a dangerous place. Legend had it he'd cut a kid in middle school and was itching to do it again. Already we'd seen him bloody one freshman's nose. We were only a couple of weeks into high school, and so far he hadn't noticed us. We both wanted to keep it that way, and yet the spirit of John Marcus Bradford was coming over us.

"Are you thinking what I'm thinking?" I asked.

By way of answer, Benjamin looked a hundred yards down the river's edge to where the next home stood. He pointed at a light in an upstairs window. "Johnny's still awake."

Johnny Mathers lived close to Benjamin, but he might as well have lived in a different dimension. Mrs. Mathers was so anxious about tragedy befalling her kids that her strictness was legendary in the Ferry. Benjamin and I had always liked Johnny, but she'd never allowed him to hang out with us. The look in Benjamin's eyes suggested it was finally time to defy her. And I understood the reason: Johnny Mathers had a canoe.

We crept through the long grass growing along the riverbank toward Johnny's house. In that moment, I couldn't have told you whether we were Bradford or the Native Americans he befriended. It didn't matter. The place was thin and we were an echo of something timeless. The plan was obvious to both of us without stating it—find small pebbles, toss them at the window, and talk him into taking his canoe out on the river.

Clink. Clink. Clink. Benjamin and I looked at each other in surprise, both of us impressed with the other's accuracy. Some magic in the night had imbued us with ancient skills we hadn't really earned. A week later—when the Mathers were out of town—we'd go back and try again, never hitting the window once, quitting after fifteen minutes. Strange magic.

The window opened with a howl of wood on wood. It must have been years since it was last opened. Clearly, Johnny was not in the habit of climbing down the side of his house.

We whispered up to him, explaining what we wanted to do—canoe upriver, eavesdrop on Tommy Lambert and his cronies, and hopefully get some dirt on them that could later be used to negotiate for our safety if push literally came to shove. We'd assumed he'd require some convincing, but Johnny climbed through that window like a zoo monkey whose cage had been left open. It was fourteen years of imprisonment expressed in a single jailbreak. Benjamin and I looked at each other, surprised again. Strange magic indeed.

Not all of Johnny's mother was left behind, though. He insisted we put on the life vests stowed in a bin next to the house. Benjamin and I suggested they first be rubbed in river mud to disguise their orange glow. Also, it felt like the kind of thing the

Native Americans might have done had they come a-spying on Bradford or that army fort upriver.

Though the Lambert campsite was hundreds of yards upstream, we approached it quickly because the late summer current had slowed to a near standstill. As we drew closer, the images around the campfire became clearer and the voices almost intelligible. It was indeed Tommy Lambert with a half dozen of his friends. We could see firelight glinting off brown beer bottles strewn around the campsite.

It quickly became clear, however, that we had a problem—to get close enough to hear what they were saying, we'd have to expose ourselves on the open water. In whispers, we agreed on a solution. There was a slight bend in the river just before the Lambert campsite. We'd navigate close enough to shore that the bend would hide us from view, then two of us would remain in the canoe paddling to keep it in place, while the third would swim around the bend to do the eavesdropping.

I prepared myself for a lively debate about who would get stuck with the risky role of swimmer, but once again the night worked its magic. Johnny immediately volunteered, shedding his life vest, T-shirt, shoes, and socks. In the dark, I couldn't see Benjamin, but I could imagine another surprised look on his face. What kind of reckless creature had Mrs. Mathers wrought?

Johnny slipped over the side of the boat like he'd done it a thousand times and, with just a few breaststrokes, disappeared into the darkness that enveloped us. Benjamin and I paddled and waited, hearts racing. A minute passed. Two minutes. Three. Then it happened—shouts of alarm from the campsite. From our vantage point, we could see a beer bottle thrown into the river, end over end, splashing violently on impact. A moment later, the beams of several high-powered flashlights lit up the water's surface, moving back and forth, like a search party. It seemed Johnny had been spotted.

Wordless minutes passed in the canoe. It was too dark for Benjamin and me to exchange glances, and we were too afraid of discovery to exchange words. After five minutes of scanning the water and coming up with nothing, Tommy Lambert and his buddies gave up the search and went back to their hooting and hollering around the campfire. Then came the really scary part.

Johnny didn't return.

Five minutes passed like an hour, thirty minutes like a day, forty-five like a year. Benjamin and I paddled, not knowing what else to do, our shoulders growing sore, shivering in the coolness of the September night. Almost an hour had passed when two hands broke the surface of the water and gripped the lip of the canoe, scaring us half to death with shock and relief.

Johnny pulled himself in, explaining in hushed whispers that once he'd been spotted, he'd managed to stay submerged in the water with just his mouth and nose above the surface, taking in air and the occasional mouthful of the Saukenuk, waiting until it felt safe to return. Of course, as soon as he *did* return, it became inconceivable to us that he might not have, so we had never talked about that hour in which it seemed like we'd led Johnny Mathers to his death.

~~

"Do you remember what he said to us, right before he climbed back through his bedroom window?" I asked Benjamin.

He laughed. "How could I forget it. 'The Saukenuk tastes like John Marcus Bradford's armpit, fellas.' That kid. I bet we'd still be friends with him today if his mother had let him hang out with us."

I took another big swallow of Scotch. Its uncomfortable burn had already morphed into a soothing warmth. "You didn't hear? He drowned in his own backyard a few years ago. Family pool. Autopsy showed a heart attack resulting in death by aspiration of water. Sort of ironic, don't you think? For an hour, we thought he'd drowned, and that's ultimately what got him." More Scotch. "Anyway, we never talked about that hour in the canoe. We never talked about what it felt like to have killed a kid."

Benjamin was quiet. I knew he was considering his response. It's the kind of rhythm you learn to trust in a friendship over time. Eventually, he spoke.

"Dude. That sucks about Johnny. And to be honest, I'm not sure this is the best conversation for you to be having tonight. But if there's one thing I know about you, Eli, it's that you're going to have the conversation you want to have, no more, no less. And I suppose tonight of all nights you've earned the right to that."

I leaned on the bar, settling in to listen.

He took a sip from his Scotch. "What did I feel that night while we waited? I guess I felt the grief of his death, though I wouldn't have known to call it grief at the time. There are five stages, right?"

I nodded.

"Right," he went on. "I'd say for the first fifteen minutes or so I was in denial, just assuming he'd be back any minute. Then, when he didn't come back, I was pissed at Tommy Lambert and his buddies, as if their flashlight beams had stabbed him to death. Then," he laughed, almost to himself, "I suddenly became a praying man. I remember promising God I'd go to church every Sunday if only he'd return Johnny to us. I was just getting around to feeling sick to my stomach when Johnny grabbed the edge of the boat. Then, pure relief, Eli."

He paused, considering whether he should do the obvious thing. Then he did it. "How about you, what was it like for you?"

I drained the Scotch and held my glass aloft. I had to give the kid credit—he wasn't going to make the same mistake twice. He approached us briskly, refilled the glass, and retreated to the end of the bar once again. I took another swig and looked at my friend.

"I skipped right to the sick stomach, Benji. For an hour, I assumed Johnny Mathers was dead. It's an hour that's haunted me for years, but I hadn't realized it until this evening."

Swig. I looked at Benjamin. Any hint of hope was quickly fading from his countenance, replaced only by concern.

"You see, I spent that hour imagining what his death meant for us. I imagined having to go back and tell your parents, who'd have to go tell Mrs. Mathers, who'd call the police and organize a search party. I imagined how it would alter the future of our lives forever. We'd always be the kids who killed Johnny Mathers."

I paused, searching for words. It was the first time I'd expressed aloud something I'd known for decades but never known I knew, until my mother's hurricane.

"It wasn't just our future, though, Benji. It was our *past*, too. Some things don't just change what is to come; they work their way *backward* into what has already happened. It's like a new lens, a new angle from which you can see your story, and it alters everything about it. I knew Johnny's death would be a ghost, haunting every memory I had of the Saukenuk, every fondness

I felt toward the Ferry, every moment of friendship shared between the two of us."

I took another large swallow, draining off most of my refill.

"But that isn't what's *really* haunted me about that hour. What's always haunted me most is that I wasn't more concerned for Johnny Mathers. My thoughts didn't gravitate toward grief like yours did. They gravitated toward myself, toward the things that would die for *me* if Johnny was indeed dead. They gravitated toward self-preservation."

Benjamin started to open his mouth, and I cut him off.

"Yeah, yeah, I know, we were kids. A little selfishness and self-preservation is normal. Grace upon grace. I get it. But the truth is, my entire life has been organized around self-preservation. I've known it ever since that night, and I've managed to *not* know it, all at the same time. We keep secrets from ourselves, B. Blind spots, as my Uncle Mark would say."

I finished off the third glass. The room was beginning to rock ever so slightly, like we rocked during that interminable hour on the Saukenuk. Benjamin was silent, surrendered to my sodden soliloquy.

"A couple of hours ago I sat in a canoe again, man, powerless to stop the rearranging of my past, to stop the altering of my future. And this time, Johnny didn't come back to the boat. He picked up his purse and walked out of the house."

I laughed, a harsh sound that triggered a look of confusion from the bartender.

"But it was a *good* thing, B. A good thing. Because for the first time in my entire life, I feel no instinct for self-preservation. You can't preserve a self that no longer exists. There's nothing to protect. Nothing to shave." I was starting to slur but sober enough to be aware of it. "Nothing to *save*," I corrected myself. "It's quite a relief, actually, this freedom to not care about what happens to you."

I stared at my empty glass, through it, beyond it.

After some silence, Benjamin was tentative. "Eli, I'm worried about you. First the divorce papers, then whatever happened this evening. You have a therapist, right? Do you think you should call them?"

I smiled wryly. "Oh, I called him today. It was quite a conversation. But I don't think you're hearing me, B. No more cages. No more fences. No more walls. They all protect you, but they also imprison you. I'm free. This is *good* news."

I stood up as I announced the gospel according to Eli, and almost fell backward.

"I think it's time for me to go home," I said as I slapped several twenties on the bar and pointed at the bartender. "Tell Mr. I'm-Checking-My-Feed to keep the change." My first step toward the door looked more like a lurch.

Benjamin spun around, grabbing my arm and steadying me. "I don't think you're in any condition to drive, Eli. Or walk for that matter. Let me take you."

I also wasn't in any condition to argue.

If Benjamin were a therapist, he'd have taken me to the hospital. Instead, he was a friend. So he took me home.

36

Rebecca, our story has a subplot I've kept you completely unaware of.

No, there weren't other women. In fact, there were fewer women than I led you to believe. I'm not sure if you remember, but on the walk home from our first lunch date at McDonald's, you confessed you'd been with several men, and you asked me directly about my history: "All right, out with it, Elijah Campbell, how many notches are on your proverbial bedpost?" I mumbled and bumbled again before telling you there was one notch on my bedpost. It wasn't true. I'd never been with another woman. You were my first and only. I feared you'd interpret that as some sort of defect, though. After all, your life had been exciting and exotic—jumps from airplanes and solo trips home from Italy—and mine lacked even the excitement of my first time. So I hid the truth and told you what I thought would keep you interested in me. Again, I'm sorry for the hiding.

That lunch at McDonald's. It was the beginning of the subplot I've hidden from you. I insisted on paying for both of us that day. The truth is, even though it was McDonald's and we'd ordered value meals, it was money I didn't have. However, I figured "without a penny to his name" wasn't one of the boxes you were hoping to check in your search for a boyfriend. So I put it on a credit card and forgot about it. The interest was worth it to me because I thought I was exchanging it for your continued interest in me, and I told myself it would never happen again.

It was merely the first shovelful of dirt tossed on a truth I've been burying for years now.

Don't worry, there were no dark addictions or ugly habits. Just my addiction to ignoring reality and my habit of hiding the truth. For instance, that first Christmas when we bought our first car together, you knew I couldn't really afford it. I explained it away by saying my dad had a life insurance policy I could draw from. He didn't. The truth is, the next day when you went back to class, I told you I wasn't feeling well and was going to stay home. I didn't. I went to the bank and took out an additional loan.

I paid off that loan when my first book advance arrived in the mail. We splurged at Haute Cuisine that night to celebrate. I was going to tell you the truth about how I planned to spend the advance, but at dinner you toasted to "finally having a little cushion in our savings account." I kept my mouth shut as we finished a dinner we couldn't afford. Every time something made you happy, I assumed it was also making you love me. To risk your happiness was to risk our togetherness. It was a spurious correlation, but it felt so true at the time.

It went that way for years. Every time you thought we were building up reserves, we were really paying off bills and paying down credit cards. I was constantly moving our debt around, taking advantage of cards with zero percent interest and no transfer fees, consolidating some loans while paying the minimum balance on others, never quite getting ahead. Every time I tinkered with it, I thought about telling you, but unhiding gets harder over time.

Do you remember when I got all my suits dry-cleaned? You asked if somebody had died or was getting married because I hadn't worn a suit in years and had no need for one. Well, I made some crack about getting married to you every day if I could—it was true, but it was also a distraction, and it worked. You laughed, I walked the suits out the front door, and you never asked about it again. The truth is, I needed a clean suit for job interviews.

The Whisper in the Wind was selling steadily, but it was clearly going to be years before I earned out my advance, and we needed cash right away. And I actually got a job—a nine-to-five kind of thing, entering data for a big company. We would have needed to find afterschool care for Sarah, and I would have been forced to reveal years' worth of truth and hiding. I was planning to start on a Monday morning.

By that Sunday, I still hadn't said a thing to you. You might remember it. I made a big deal about dropping Sarah off at church for Sunday school and the two of us sneaking out for coffee. You weren't thrilled by the idea, but you went along with it because I told you there was something important to discuss. We got our drinks and sat down. You stared at me. I stared back. You said, "Well, Campbell, what's the big deal?" I opened my mouth to tell you about my new job, and what came out was an idea for my next book. You stared at me again for a moment—as if to say, "Really, this is why we're abusing the church's Sunday school program?"—but then you did what you always did. You listened to me and loved me.

I called the company on Monday morning and fired myself.

Creditors have been calling, Rebecca, but my most recent advance will wipe out all our debt. However, the savings accounts you imagine are just that—imaginary. I suppose the lawyers will discover all of this in the weeks to come, but I wanted you to hear it from me first.

Keeping it hidden from you has become a part-time job, and I could spend pages telling you about it. Instead, I'd like to tell you about another important secret I've kept from you. It's about my dad. From time to time, you questioned my estrangement from him. I gave you answers that never really satisfied you, and rightly so. They weren't the real answers.

I have better answers for you now. . . .

37

BENJAMIN CAME TO A STOP at the bottom of the driveway, his headlights illuminating an open garage door and two empty spaces. My mother was still gone. I reached for the door handle.

"Wait, Eli." There was a desperate tone in his voice. "Are you *sure* you're going to be okay here tonight? I mean, you're welcome to crash at my mom's house. Heck, we can pitch a tent down on the river and throw rocks at old lady Mathers's windows if you want. I'm up for anything."

It's hard to resist the pull of a friend, especially when that friendship has gathered gravitational force over the years. The booze, however, had left me mostly untethered from all loving forces.

"Yeah yeah thanks buddy but I'll be fine you don't have to worry about me."

I was working hard to enunciate, but it still came out sounding like a single word. I knew I needed to slow myself down so as to not worry him more.

"I appreciate the offer, B, but I think what I need is a good, long sleep, you know? Actually, I think I'm going to take a hot bath first, then get some sleep. Besides, like I said, I feel great. Nothing to protect, remember? The end of self-preservation!"

I feigned jubilance and reached for the door handle. Benjamin tugged my elbow in a wordless request to stay a little longer. I figured that was the least I could do for my friend. Besides, the house seemed a long way away.

"That's the thing that's bothering me, Eli. The self-preservation thing. I know it can be hard to walk around feeling protective all the time, but self-preservation is the reason we've survived, isn't it? It's knit into the species. It's evolutionary. It's a God-given instinct, and I just don't know if it's a great idea to look that kind of gift horse in the mouth." He paused. "I guess what I'm trying to say is, I *want* you wanting to survive, because I want my friend around for a very long time."

His throat tightened on that last word, and it came out sounding like a man choking back tears. I looked at him for the first time since we'd left the Den. His eyes were glistening with something extra I'd never seen there before in all my years of friendship with him. I fought with my own emotions, which were threatening to gather in my eyes as well. I won the fight.

"Well, shucks, buddy, you're giving me all the feels," I said brightly. "I love you too, man. And I will think about what you said."

Before he could tug my elbow again, I got out of the car and walked into the house.

38

When I was sixteen, I witnessed my father having an affair with my gym teacher. At his office. On his desk.

My mother wanted nothing to do with this part of my truth, so besides Jeff, you're the only person I've ever told. Telling you is even harder than telling him, in part because I only hid it from him for six months, but I hid it from you for twelve years. Putting it down on paper is even more painful too. It's like I've got a sixteen-year-old boy in me who is still terrified of betraying his father, and by writing it down I'm making the betrayal official. What a conundrum you find yourself in as a kid—you only get one dad, no matter how unfatherly he happens to behave.

Rebecca, my dad wasn't a father. He was a friend. I think it's the only thing he knew how to be, and it might have worked out okay for all of us, if only he'd known how to be a true friend. The real problem, I think, was my father saw friendship as a finite resource. It was a competition among companions for a limited amount of love. In other words, being friends with my dad meant neither one of us could be friends with my mom. He had all sorts of ways of subtly encouraging this—secrets we kept from her, jokes we made about her, rebellions we directed toward her. For sixteen years, I reaped the rewards of that arrangement. Clandestine ice cream and R-rated movies. Waterbeds and stereo systems. Closeness and comfort.

When I walked in on him with my gym teacher, I discovered the real cost of those rewards.

I'm telling you this now because—and this is so hard to admit, even to myself—I've replicated some of my father's fathering. I've sought to be Sarah's friend, at your expense, and I've done so in countless ways. We went out for ice cream every Wednesday after school. We always used the dumpster behind her school to dispose of our evidence. We laughed at how clever we were. On Wednesday nights, when you were mystified by her lack of appetite at the dinner table, we'd sneak a knowing look at each other. Not a wink. Never a wink. I told myself that somehow made it okay. I feel sick to my stomach just writing it down.

Sometimes she'd confide to me something hard that had happened to her at school. We'd talk it out and I'd comfort her and she'd be fine. For reasons I didn't understand at the time, I'd remind her how tired you could be after a day at work, and I'd suggest we spare you the stress by keeping it between the two of us.

She's saving money in a shoebox in the back of her closet. I never stopped to wonder why nor to ask her about it. It was sufficient that I knew about it and you didn't.

We pretended to watch *Frozen* with you for the first time on video. We'd already seen it in the theater.

As I write these things down, I feel all the anger toward myself that I felt toward my dad in his final years. I never figured out how to forgive him. I hope you'll eventually find a way to forgive me. I'll understand if you don't.

It's important you know these things because, once I'm not around, the work of being her mother may be more complicated than you realize because of the way I've fathered her. I know it's not anything you can't overcome, of course. You're Rebecca Miller, and she's her mother's daughter. You two will find your way home from Italy together.

Rebecca, I wish this secret about my father was the last of my parents' secrets. It isn't, though. Nor is it their biggest secret. My mother, in a fit of transparency she no doubt regrets, confessed something to me that happened long ago, before I was born. Something with the power to reach forward through time and into my life . . .

39

You don't realize what a thin place a house is until you contemplate entering it for the last time. Then memories bombard you, like you're the only light in a dark space filled with moths. They flutter around you, brush up against you, and, if you are very still, they land on you, covering you in the dust of their delicate wings.

In such a moment, a house becomes more than a thin place; it becomes *many* thin places—every room an entryway into its own set of stories. Kitchens and basements, bedrooms and living rooms, dining rooms and dens, each a time machine unto itself, transporting you along your mortal coil to a different destination.

Your last time in a house is a finite time—a time that is, by definition, soon coming to an end. The memories that fill the air may be countless, but your minutes are numbered. You must be selective about which moths you draw to you. Or perhaps, when time is precious, it is the memories themselves that choose you. Probably it is some mysterious mixture of the two. I suppose that might be the ultimate measure of a soul: which memories does your light attract in the end as the darkness is closing in?

As I walked into the house, the air was thick with them.

I went to the basement game room first because Benjamin's choked uttering of the word *time* was still fresh in my mind, and it was the space where Benjamin and I had spent most of our time in the house. Hours of video games on an old Nintendo. Hours of table tennis on my parents' makeshift Ping-Pong table. Hours of homework and gossip, television and movies, bingeing on Pringles and Pepsi. I went there, too, because I assumed it to be the place in the house where the moths would be most benevolent. I was right.

Sitting on an old solid oak entertainment center was an ancient tube television, weighing so much even the thick oak slabs sagged a little beneath the weight of television and time. The TV had been made in an era before remote controls, so Benjamin and I would sit in beanbags in front of it, perfecting the art of changing the channel on the keypad with our toes. The beanbags were gone, but the coffee table we'd leaned them against was still there. I recalled reaching backward for cans of soda and handfuls of popcorn, our eyes glued to a horror movie we were forbidden to watch.

The old Ping-Pong tabletop had been removed from its sawhorse legs and leaned up against a far wall. It was too heavy to lift alone, but my memory was strong enough to return it to its rightful position on the sawhorses, which had miraculously held their position through the years. One lovely moth landed on me.

Benjamin is at the far end of the table, closest to the television, facing me. It's a week after Johnny Mathers informed us about the unique flavor of the Saukenuk River. It's a Friday night—the night the stars aligned and Samantha Stiller sat down next to me on the bleachers at our first high school football game. I'm bursting with happiness and, perhaps even more importantly, Benjamin is bursting for me. Literally. He lauds me for my composure throughout the game as he pauses our volley to take a drink of Pepsi. Mid-gulp, I tell him how I really felt. "Dude, I don't care what Johnny says about the flavor of the Saukenuk, it tastes like Pepsi compared to what I dropped in my pants when she sat down." His laughter sprays Pepsi all over the table. It's the most delightful mess either one of us has ever cleaned up.

∿

I walked over to the table, running my fingers along the edge of it, and I could have sworn I felt stickiness here and there. Spots we missed in our hastiness to resume playing decades ago. The past is always behind us, but it is also, always, within us, as sticky as Pepsi and laughter.

Retreating from the room, I turned off the lights in the basement and climbed the stairs to the living areas. I steeled myself for the memories that would find me up there. Like a moth, a memory can't bite you, but it can scare you half to death by flying out of an unexpected place.

The stairs led to the living room, where an unanticipated memory landed on me, though it was the welcome kind of surprise. In the darkened living room, I saw the lights of our Christmas tree. A Christmas tree is an especially thin place in a home. The consistency of its location and decor over the years makes it a superhighway into the past, with many exits to choose from. I took the earliest exit I could remember.

∿

I'm seven years old. It must be late on Christmas morning, because I can already smell the turkey roasting in the oven for that afternoon's feast. I'm virtually swimming in wrapping paper. My parents are sitting on the couch, a little closer than usual, and a lot happier. My father is holding a fancy goblet full of something red. I'm assembling a massive Lego creation—an Ewok village? the Millennium Falcon? G.I. Joe's headquarters?— and he's making well-timed suggestions while making my mother feel loved. It's warm in the house. It's even warmer inside of me.

That warmth brings with it another memory.

It's Sarah's first Christmas, and Rebecca and I are gathered around the very same tree with her and my mother. Now I'm the one sitting on the sofa with my wife, a glass of red wine in my hand, making suggestions to my mother about how to assemble a new rattle with lights and batteries. She is showing Sarah a tenderness I've never experienced from her myself. It's a gift to see it expressed now toward the little girl I love so much. Rebecca senses my gratitude, squeezes my hand, kisses my cheek, snuggles in. From my mother's old turntable, Judy Garland is singing "Have Yourself a Merry Little Christmas," and I feel a peacefulness that has eluded me for most of my life.

∿

I took the next exit back to the present, where the tears I'd successfully fought back in the car with Benjamin finally triumphed. I walked into the kitchen, where the bowl of beaten salad still sat forlornly, the large chef's knife my mother had used to cut the romaine still sitting next to it on the cutting board, flakes of dried lettuce crusted on it. I braced myself again, expecting to relive the evening. Instead, I looked at the kitchen sink and was ambushed by another moth with laughter in it.

It's a few weeks after our honeymoon, the night of the wedding reception my mother hosted for us in Bradford's Ferry. A humble but happy affair. I'm aware it's my mother's least favorite thing— this socializing with anyone but her closest friends. Nevertheless, for an evening the house has been filled with my favorite people: Benjamin, his parents, Gus, Father Lou, and a host of friends from high school. Even Junior made an appearance.

The guests have all departed and it's just my mother, Rebecca, and me in the kitchen.

We're retelling stories from the night, piecing together from each of our experiences a complete picture of the evening. My mother, in spite of herself, has gotten caught up in the celebration. Suddenly, she looks at the remaining half of the sheet cake on the kitchen table and declares she will never be able to resist so many senseless calories. She lifts it over her head theatrically, walks it across the kitchen, slams it into the sink, and begins shoving it down the garbage disposal, but not before taking a fistful and shoving it in her mouth, mostly with accurate aim, but with some icing smeared from mouth to ear on either side.

In this impetuousness, she's speaking Rebecca's love language, so Rebecca gets up and strides across the kitchen, snagging her own fistful of cake. I'm helpless to resist the shared playfulness of the woman who defined so much of my past and the one who will determine so much of my future. I end up with cake in my ears, but not enough to block out the sounds of our collective laughter.

It was a really good memory. Too good. The return to the present moment felt like a crash landing. I had not been prepared for my mother to show up so fondly in my memories. I had not been prepared for Rebecca to show up so consistently, especially in this house. These two women. One was planning to leave me, and the other, I'd found out only a few hours earlier, had never really been with me.

I didn't think about what happened next, which is to say there was no choice in it. I floated somewhere above it, in a space where it felt like a fact that had already happened. Jah was in charge. My feet walked across the kitchen to the cutting board. My hands lifted the chef's knife. My body walked to the sink, squirted Palmolive onto the blade, scrubbed it clean with a sponge, dried it off with a dish towel, and took it to my bedroom.

Standing in the doorway, I looked at my desk where I'd spent so many hours of study in my high school years. My eyes rested on what all those hours—and the many hours of desk work after them—had resulted in: two white envelopes. I sat down at the desk, placing the knife next to me. I had a few things to write down before I took a bath.

40

Rebecca, I'm aware this final bit of unhiding is as much for me as for you, but it is the only way to be completely rid of my secrets. You have given me countless gifts over the years. If you have indeed read this far, thank you for this final one.

Do you remember learning at UPenn about flashbulb memories? Memories of events that are so emotional and consequential that every detail remains seared in your mind like a snapshot, such as where you were when the planes hit the towers. Well, my conversation with my mother is a flashbulb memory for me.

It began with trying to tell her the secret about my father. She refused to hear it. I realize now she was refusing not because my father successfully kept it from her, but because it was a secret she'd successfully kept from herself. My mistake was thinking I could force her to acknowledge it. To her credit, she gave me fair warning, which I ignored. Then she did something I couldn't ignore. She asked me if I really wanted the truth to be told, and I said I was her only child and I deserved the truth.

That was when she told me I wasn't her only child.

"The truth is you had an older brother!" she shouted. "And he died, and it was my fault, and I never really loved anyone or anything else ever again, and you were born less than a year later, and I'm sure you're smart enough to figure out what that means about my feelings for you, Elijah!"

Then her rage morphed instantaneously into shock. I think the last part—about never having loved again—was news even to her. She turned back to the salad she'd been mixing for us and leaned on the counter again with her back to me.

It was too much for me to process, so I did what I often do when I don't know what to feel: I asked for more information.

The voice that came over her shoulder was the voice of a skeleton. There was no flesh and blood in it, only hollowness, only a void. It was the voice of a larynx fully disconnected from its soul. It gave me chills, Rebecca.

"Do you really want the details of it, Elijah?" she asked. "Isn't it enough for you to know that I loved my dead baby but not my living one? You've been vindicated. All those times you suggested I was giving you something less than love, you were right. All your instincts were correct. I had a dead son and you had a dead mother. All your loneliness was real. Every time you told yourself you could make me love you more by being a better boy or a more successful man—it was all a waste of time. You were never going to make me love you. You only ever reminded me of what I'd lost, and I was never going to love that loss. So there, you win. Every veggie burger I refused to buy, every hamburger I insisted on grilling for you, I was never really serving you. Every time, I was serving the boy I imagined Benjamin might have become."

Have you ever been so disoriented the room seemed to actually tilt? I always thought that saying—he almost fell out of his chair—was a cartoonish phrase. It's not. You can hear things that are so terrible and so disconcerting that your whole world is turned on its side metaphorically, and your body honors the metaphor. All I could do was hold on and repeat the name "Benjamin" as a question.

"I hate your books, Elijah," she replied, turning around. There was poison in her voice again. "All this nonsense about a benevolent universe, a loving God, a tenderness at the center of everything. You came home after your first day of kindergarten and told me about your new best friend. His name was Benjamin. The name of my dead son. It felt like the hounds of hell were chasing me. Then you made good on your declaration, and Benjamin Bruce became your lifelong friend, and every time I heard that name—thousands of times over the years—I heard the barking of those hounds. Every time I saw your best friend, I saw the God of the universe. But he wasn't tender, Elijah. He was a torturer. I hate your books, not because they're bad but because they're wrong. At worst, at the center of the universe is a psychopath. At best, it's just empty, and every horrible thing is just happenstance."

Her hate activated my anger and I realized I did want the details, in part because they were a part of my own story, and in part because I wanted her to feel the pain of sharing them. I defiantly answered her rhetorical question and told her yes, give me the details.

Her voice was skeletal again, though this time she continued to face me. "Your father was in law school at the University of Chicago. I was waitressing to pay the bills. We were living in a flat in the city, and we were as happy as a young couple can be. One night, we got a little careless with our happiness. Nine months later, Benjamin was born. Your father still had two years of law school ahead of him. We agreed I'd stay home with Benny, we'd rack up a little debt, and when he graduated, we'd move back to Bradford's Ferry, he'd start his practice, and we'd live happily ever after."

She paused. I thought she might cry. Instead, her voice got colder.

"Benny was three months old when our anniversary rolled around. We decided to celebrate by getting a babysitter and going out on our first date in months. We agreed we wouldn't talk about Benny all night. That lasted about thirty minutes. We spent the whole evening imagining our future with him." Her words had become a whisper. I had to lean in to hear her.

"We drank too much. Went home and paid the sitter. I was still nursing Benny, and he was sleeping with us most nights. I told myself one booze-filled meal wouldn't hurt him. While he was nursing I passed out. When I woke up hours later, he . . . he wasn't breathing. We called 911. An ambulance came. There was nothing they could do. The coroner determined the cause of death to be sudden infant death syndrome, but SIDS is a description, not a diagnosis. I believed that I rolled over in the night and suffocated my baby boy. Your father disagreed. I didn't care. And that is how our marriage went. I was never touchy-feely, but Benny had brought out what feely-ness I had, and he took it with him when he went."

She looked me in the eye then, and the animosity was back in her voice.

"I'm not quite sure what you were so eager to tell me here tonight, Elijah, but I bet I've got the gist of it. Your father lost a son and a wife that night. I tried to do wifely things for him afterward. You were the result of one of those wifely things, just two months after Benny died. When I found out you were in me, I dreaded you. When you were born, I realized the best thing I could do for you was tolerate you. I mustered the same kind of tolerance for your father. Eventually, he gave up on getting any affection from me. I'm guessing he found other ways to get it. I don't blame him. The truth is, I was just relieved he was no longer looking to me for it. So, there. You have your details. Your mother ruined four lives. Now, don't you wish you'd just eaten the damn salad, Elijah?" She laughed harshly when she said that.

I told her no, I didn't wish I'd eaten the salad; I wished she'd give herself some grace. I told her none of it was her fault. I told her the days of excusing men's philandering were behind us, and my dad was responsible for his own actions. I told her the death of Benjamin hadn't hurt our family as much as her unwillingness to forgive herself for it had. I told her it's never too late to begin healing. I told her even if she'd never really loved me, she was my mother and I still loved her. I told her she had another chance to receive that love, if only she could accept that bad things happen but she's not a bad person. As I said all of that, her face got flushed and her eyes filled with tears. There was a moment, Rebecca, when I believed restoration might be possible. Then, she finished what she'd started.

Her voice was quiet again, but the ice in it had become sharp and jagged. "Don't you think I know that, Elijah?" she hissed. "Do you think I haven't told myself that a thousand times, a million times? Do you really think *you* saying it is going to be the difference maker? Don't fool yourself, Elijah, your words aren't *that* powerful. Quite a God complex you've got. If I was Rebecca, I'd have left you, too."

Then she got up, slung her purse over her shoulder, and walked out of the house.

41

I PUT DOWN MY PEN, got up from the desk, and crossed the hall into the bathroom. Standing in front of the bathtub, I looked down and was surprised to see the kitchen knife in my hand. It was a vaguely pleasant surprise, like shaking a milk carton you thought was empty and discovering there's still a little left in the bottom. My surprise took the form of something that was both word and sound—"Huh!"—as I lifted the knife to eye level. I could see three knives. I laughed.

"One fer each glash of whishkey," I announced to the empty bathroom. I laughed again at the sound of my slurring. Jah wasn't laughing, however. His voice within me was calm and focused. "You cut yourself with the middle one."

For a moment, it seemed unfathomable that I would follow Jah's instructions. I thought of Rebecca receiving the news. I thought of her having to deliver it to Sarah. I thought of my mother getting home eventually, finding me in the tub, the horror of the scene. Then Jah spoke up again, repeating her words: *If I was Rebecca, I'd have left you, too.* My mother thought she'd had the last word.

Jah was planning to prove her wrong.

He continued, repeating her words to me. *I hate your books, Elijah.* Jah believed his way was the only way. *When I found out you were in me, I dreaded you.* He was building his case. *Don't fool yourself, Elijah, your words aren't that powerful.* As I stood there, swaying slightly in front of the tub, his case seemed air-tight. *Now, don't you wish you'd just eaten the damn salad, Elijah?* A lifetime of confusion and loneliness and pain coalesced—a cyclone of anger and sorrow—and at the eye of the storm was the image of my mother finding me in the tub. Jah smiled as he captioned the scene with *his* last word:

Now, don't you wish you'd just kept your damn mouth shut, Mother?

I placed the knife on the toilet seat, turned on the tap, and clumsily disrobed. It took a while. Eventually, I lifted one leg over the side of the tub. The water was too hot. I didn't care. I dropped myself into the tub a little too quickly and water sloshed onto the floor. My discarded clothing soaked it up.

With my eyes closed, I reached for the edge of the tub, my hand searching for the knife. Nothing. I opened them. I spotted it across the bathroom on the toilet. I'd have to retrieve it. It seemed like a Herculean task.

Déjà vu.

Last time it had been Rebecca's razor blades in a drawer at the foot of the tub. This time a knife on the toilet. Both times, an overwhelming fatigue brought on by booze and warm water. Last time, I'd closed my eyes and dreamed that terrible dream, which had sent me on this search for peace and healing, this wild goose chase that had only deepened my pain and thrown salt on my wounds. I closed my eyes. This time, I told myself, I'll gather my will for a moment—gather my Jah—get the knife from the toilet, and finish the job.

Instead, once again, I dreamed.

42

I'M AT THE RIVER'S EDGE once again.

At first glance, everything looks the same: the rickety bridge and the rushing water, sunlight where I'm standing, and fog on the far-off bank. However, on closer inspection, not everything is the same.

First, as I look down at my feet, I see they are no longer a boy's feet, and they are no longer clad in those tattered tennis shoes. The sneakers have been replaced by a pair of flip-flops that reveal a man's feet—bigger, with tufts of hair in various places, veins raised and blue through the skin. They are the sandals I wore to my father's gravesite and during my mother's hurricane. Beneath them, I can see the same pavement as always, but in the warped what and when of the dreamworld, I know the ground beneath me is also the grass in front of my father's grave, and it is the tile in my mother's kitchen. I know it is every ground I've ever stood on. I know this bridge is every path I've ever walked.

Second, I no longer feel alone in the dream. There is a presence behind me, presumably somewhere on Main Street. Except that's not quite right. There are presences behind me, plural. I don't know who or what they are, but like so many new things, they inspire uncertainty in me, and the uncertainty triggers anxiety, *and the anxiety makes me want to avoid their source. I decide not to turn around.*

Third, I'm thrilled to discover my anxiety about the presences is my only anxiety. Looking out on the rotted boards and the frothy water beneath them, I feel no fear of the river. It's not that I believe the bridge will hold me, or I'll reach the other side, or the water is somehow less dangerous. No, I still believe the bridge will break, and I'll be swept away to my untimely death. The difference is . . . I don't care. As in the real world, my instinct for self-preservation is gone from the dreamworld.

And so I begin.

Not slowly this time, however. I quickly step to the first yellowish board with the two rusted nails in each of its ends. I'm absent of thought. I'm all movement. The board sags. No problem. I know how this goes. I step to the next relatively healthy-looking board. And then the next. And the next. I've done this a dozen times. A hundred times. A thousand times. Muscle memory propels me onto the dark board lying at the impossible angle, and I know the cracking of it is coming before I even hear it, so I immediately leap to the board just ahead of me.

I'm not walking, I'm dancing.

I see the two-foot gap between me and the really rotted board, the gap between it and the tantalizingly pristine board onto which I must leap, as well as the gap beyond that one. I don't think twice. I make the leap. I stick the landing. As always, the water begins rising, but this time I'm not bothered by it. It's a contest now. Will I get to the other side before the water reaches me? The outcome seems irrelevant. I'm enjoying the freedom of the game.

I leap to a board I've never reached before. I hesitate for a moment in this new space, and I become aware once again of the presences behind me. They're following me. No, they're chasing me, closing the distance between us. Suddenly, I'm both a little free and a little afraid. I leap to the next board, and the next, and the next. For the first time ever, the opposite shore is drawing closer, though it is no less shrouded. The presences are upon me. I feel breath on the back of my neck.

I leap again and, in midair, I look down at the board I'm about to land on—it's got the mushy consistency of oatmeal, and I know it cannot hold me. Sure enough, as my foot makes contact, it passes right through the board, like a spoon through porridge. I feel nothing but relief. As I begin to fall, I think, It's over. Finally, it's over.

Except it's not.

I keep falling, face upward toward the sky, arms and legs flailing. The water is only inches from the bridge, so the impact should have been immediate, and yet I continue to fall and fall and fall. I freefall through eons of dream space, and suddenly all my old fear is back and a terrified scream erupts from me, the same word as always. I scream for my mother, and her name is still on my lips when I feel the impact.

It's a splash of sorts, but not into water. Into bedsheets.

In contrast to the thrashing of my fall, I'm lying preternaturally still, in the dark. The top sheet is hanging off the side of the bed, exposing me completely to the movement of the murky midsummer air around me. A box fan in the window at the foot of the bed is set to low, barely pushing the air around, humming quietly. It blows the sound of crickets into the room, too. Otherwise, the night is completely silent.

My eyes adjust and I can see the darkness is accentuated by deep brown faux wood paneling on the walls. The door to the bedroom is ajar. A dim light from another bedroom filters down the hallway and through the door, penetrating only a few feet into this room before gradually waning to almost nothing.

I look down at the sheets. I see figures and faces there and, though it's too dark to see them clearly, I know who they are— Luke Skywalker and Princess Leia, Han Solo and Chewbacca. I've fallen into my bedroom in the house my parents rented during the fifth year of my life. I can't tell if I'm imagining or dreaming. I can't tell if I'm asleep or awake. My arms and legs feel impossibly heavy. I look down at them. I couldn't move them even if I wanted to. I glance again toward the door and, suddenly, I very much want to move.

Standing in the doorway is my mother's disembodied bathrobe.

Not my mother—just her bathrobe. Blue terrycloth, old and pilled, belt cinched around the waist of a body that cannot be seen. It appears to hover there, though presumably resting on the woman I cannot see, have never been able to see, and never will be able to truly see. My five-year-old bladder constricts, and it is no small effort to keep the bed dry. I want to sit up and back up into the corner of the bed that sits against the corner of the room farthest from the door. But I can't. I'm paralyzed with fear.

Then the bathrobe begins to move toward me. Its hovering is nothing like walking; it is undisturbed by the swinging of arms and legs, and no human ever walked this slowly. Its progress is nearly imperceptible. My fear goes to eleven. Still, it approaches. My terror goes to twelve. Thirteen. Fourteen. The space between my back and my mattress is a sweaty swamp as the bathrobe finally reaches my bedside, leaning forward ever so slightly and completely silently. Then, nothing. She, it, whatever, seems to stare at me with an eyeless gaze.

I open my mouth to scream my mother's name again, this time not a plea to rescue me but a command to get away from me. However, just before I unleash the scream, the apparition speaks. It is a voice without body—without time or place or space—and though I know it comes from the thing in the bathrobe, I hear its utterance first and foremost somewhere else. Somewhere in the center of me. It speaks for a minute, an hour, a day, a year; it speaks slowly and forever, drawing out each word, guaranteeing I won't miss a single one of them.

All in all, there are four.

43

I AWOKE IN THE BATHTUB as utterly still as I'd been in the dream, though instead of feeling fearful, I was peculiarly peaceful.

I looked around, taking an inventory of the situation. The darkness outside the high bathroom window. The quiet of the house. I felt surprisingly sober, which suggested many hours had passed. However, the water was still warm—the temperature of bedcovers, not river water—which suggested I'd been asleep relatively briefly.

I reached over the side of tub. Retrieved my still soggy blue jeans. Extricated my phone from a pocket. It was just a few minutes past midnight. I'd been asleep less than an hour. Apparently, the adrenaline of my nightmare had nullified the effects of the whiskey. I set my phone on the edge of the tub. Settled back into the bedcover-warm water. Shifted my inventory inward.

I'd had *two* recurring nightmares in childhood. Blind spot.

The second nightmare—the one about a bedroom and a bathrobe and a boogeymom—I'd dreamed no more than a handful of times, and never once after kindergarten. Nevertheless, during the year I was dreaming it, every night when the lights went out, I'd pull the bedcovers over the top of my head and lie as still as I could in the hopes that, if the wraith actually appeared, she'd fail to notice me. I would eventually drift off to sleep like that, completely scared and completely hidden. In a way, I'd never really come out from beneath those bedcovers.

On Main Street, a teenager stomped on an accelerator, and the growl of a muscle car traveled across the Ferry, penetrating the walls of my mother's house.

I continued my inner inventory. Upon waking from the bridge dream a month earlier, I'd resisted its wisdom with all my might. I'd fought back against its pull on me, trying to turn it into quick-fix inspiration rather than allowing it to be what it was—a deep inner knowing, a revelation that it was time to return to the Ferry, time to face my pain. In contrast, after the recurrence of this bathrobe nightmare, there was no fight in me whatsoever. I was surrendered to it.

Surrender. Typically, we think of surrender as a bad thing—a loss or a defeat. The truth is, though, surrender is only a bad thing if the thing we've been resisting is also bad. However, if the thing we've been resisting is a good thing, then surrender is a very good thing indeed. For instance, when you are surrendering your secrets—those you've kept from others and those you've kept from yourself—you are surrendering your resistance to reality, to truth, to honesty and authenticity and vulnerability. That is not a bad surrender. It is a sacred surrender.

More sounds from Main Street. This time someone goosing the kind of motorcycle Benjamin and I used to call a crotch rocket. The Doppler effect made the whine of it come and go. The revelation I was surrendering to, on the other hand, came and stayed, and it sounded like this:

Not all my ghosts are dead.

For three weeks, Bradford's Ferry had become like Swiss cheese to me, with holes here and there through which I could slip into and out of the past. Each time, I'd encountered a loved one of mine who'd passed from this life into the next one. My mother, though, had passed long ago from this life without ever entering into another one. She was a soul suspended between worlds. At the age of five, I'd already sensed she was there but not there. It had haunted me, and that haunting had been reflected in a dream. My mother had been my very first ghost and, unbeknown to me, I'd been conversing with the ghost of her my whole life.

From Main Street, the sounds of police sirens filled the night briefly before dying abruptly midhowl. A dog in the distance joined the chorus of machines and men.

Its howling drew my thoughts to the barely human voice emanating from the ghostly bathrobe in my dream. The apparition's utterance still echoed within me. Four words: *I am your freedom.* Considering the source, they were strangely comforting words. In the echoing of them, I heard hope and perhaps even a way forward. They had awakened within me a longing, not to *have* the last word but to *hear* the last word. I simply wanted my mom to apologize so I could forgive her and be free of her haunting at last.

However, after what had happened just hours ago in the kitchen, I knew I'd never have that kind of conversation with her in flesh and blood. She simply wouldn't allow it. The image of her as a ghost, though, had given me another idea. I could have a different kind of conversation with her in my *imagination*. A month earlier, I would have considered the idea foolish. After my conversation with my "dad" in the cemetery, however, I believed in the power of memory and imagination to change the course of a person's life.

The water was no longer warm. I stood up. Aside from a dull ache behind my forehead, I felt as clearheaded as I'd felt in weeks. I dried off and dressed in what had been passing for pajamas while I'd been in Bradford's Ferry. I picked up the kitchen knife from the toilet, shivered once, and walked it back out to the kitchen where I dropped it into the sink.

Back in my bedroom, I picked up from my desk what I'd written an hour earlier, reviewing it. I congratulated myself on a job well done.

Then I sent Benjamin a text. *Thwop.* The sound of it being delivered was still repeating in my echoic memory when three dots appeared below it, followed by three words: "See you there!"

I set the alarm on my phone, making sure to charge it in preparation for the following day. I closed my eyes, a man without a destination but at least with a direction.

Sleep came quickly, but not before I heard two things. The first was the sound of my mother pulling into the driveway and entering the house. The second was a voice, beginning somewhere at the edges of my awareness, then whining to a crescendo like that crotch rocket before quickly fading off into the distance. It said the plan to talk with my mother the way I'd talked with my father was a good one, but I would do well to remember that the conversation with my father hadn't been as pleasurable as I'd hoped.

44

FOR THE THIRD TIME IN AS MANY DAYS, Benjamin beat me to our destination.

I'd awoken to my alarm at eight in the morning, showered, dressed, and emerged from my room prepared for another encounter with my mother. There were signs of her presence. The salad rotting in the trash. The dishes done. The kitchen counters immaculate, as if the entire evening before had been a dream as well. That's what I was prepared for—my mother pretending our conversation had never happened. Fortunately, I was overprepared because she'd already left again. No note. No acknowledgment of my existence whatsoever.

Books on Main was busier than usual, and Gus had his hands full behind the counter. He cast me a smile, clearly relieved I hadn't cracked up completely after what had happened in this space just two days earlier. Benjamin had already staked out a table in the corner farthest from the door, and I could see my mug sitting in front of an empty chair, steam rising from its surface. Friends show up when they're called on, but best friends show up early and with a hot cup of coffee.

He was dressed for work in gray slacks and a sky-blue sport coat, his thick head of hair slicked back in what he called his "deal-making do." His smile as I approached the table leaned heavily in the direction of relief. He pushed a chair out with his foot, and as I took my seat, the relief came through in his voice.

"You scared the hell out of me last night, buddy. After I dropped you off, I couldn't sleep. I wasn't sure if I should leave you alone, call the cops to request a wellness check, or call 911 to order up an ambulance. I was just about to get back in the car to check on you myself when I got your text."

"I noticed you replied right away," I said with a grimace. "I'm sorry to have put you through that, B. You were right to be worried about me last night, and it wasn't fair of me to keep you completely in the dark about why I was such a wreck. After everything we've been through, you deserve an explanation. Do you have a few minutes?"

A few minutes turned into thirty as I finally opened up to him about my writer's block, the nightmare that had driven me back to Bradford's Ferry, Father Lou's recommendation for reviving my spiritual life, and the ensuing conversations with my grandmother and grandfather that had inspired my manuscript. I told him about my disastrous attempt to have an actual conversation with my mother the night before, omitting most of the details—especially about a baby named Benjamin—deciding it was kindness, not hiddenness, to spare him the knowledge that my mother had been tortured by his presence. Last, I told him about my most recent nightmare. I spared none of its details. He involuntarily shivered at the description of my mother's ghost.

I finished. Took a deep breath. Scanned him for signs he might still be thinking about requesting a wellness check. Instead, I saw on his face the delight of someone who'd just found a puzzle piece underneath the sofa months after it went missing. He finally had the whole picture and was just glad he could understand me again.

It occurred to me just then that the longing to understand someone may be the purest expression of love. In that sense, I guess, the opposite of love isn't hating someone, it's hiding yourself from them so you can never be known. And the completion of love isn't satisfaction, it's seeking to know someone in return. In that sense, I owed Benjamin some attention—it had been a while since I'd focused on my people more than my problems. Benjamin, however, didn't seem to be keeping a tally, and I suppose that is love's highest expression of all.

"Eli, thank you. I needed to hear this, buddy. I missed you over the last year. It's good to have you back. I *do* have you back, don't I?"

He did, almost. Showing up completely, though, would include more than just sharing the past. It included what I was thinking about doing next. I opened my mouth to do so, when a hand gently squeezed my shoulder and Gus swung around the table, taking a seat next to Benjamin. His usual jocularity was subdued by concern.

"Elijah, you have had me up at night. When I put myself in your shoes, I don't know how I'd handle what happened to you in here. Benjamin's good news, the sheriff's bad news. My goodness. How are you hanging in there, my boy?" He leaned forward on his elbows.

I admitted that, for a while, I'd hung on by a very thin thread indeed, but I told him I'd finally let go of the thread and the falling was feeling better. He sat back, clearly more relieved but also a little unconvinced. He wanted to understand me better, and in order to close the circuit on the love he was offering me, I needed to unhide myself even more.

"Gus, you remember the conversations I wrote about in my manuscript? With the 'ghosts' of my loved ones?"

He nodded.

"Well, those conversations didn't end with the manuscript. After I walked out of here two days ago, I had a conversation with my Uncle Mark, and then I did something really bizarre."

I paused, glancing at Benjamin, hoping what I'd say next wouldn't finally trigger that wellness check.

"B, do you remember right before we left the Den last night, you asked me if I should call my therapist and I told you I already had and it was quite the conversation?"

Benjamin nodded.

"Well, the conversation I was referring to was at my dad's gravesite. I asked my therapist to be my father's ghost, to talk with me about our relationship and some of the ways I'd been hurt by it. It was hard, really hard, but it started healing something within me."

I checked both of their faces again. They were listening, not judging. More grace. I felt safe enough to tell them what I was hoping to do next.

"So, I'd like to try the same kind of conversation with my mother. If I can't have a meaningful conversation with the living version of her, maybe I can at least have one with the imaginary version of her. I'm just not sure where to have it, and I'm not sure who I could possibly ask to stand in for her."

I sat back, waiting for their reaction. I didn't have to wait long. Instead of questioning my plan, they started helping me with it. Gus was the first to make a suggestion.

"Why not ask your therapist again?"

"I thought about that. First of all, I feel like I've abused that poor man's patience enough over the last month. But even more importantly, he did too good a job. I'll always associate his voice with the voice of Steven Campbell."

Benjamin chimed in. "Makes sense. But the location is a little more obvious, isn't it?"

Gus and I both looked at him, awaiting his revelation.

"You've got to return to the scene of the crime, or last night's dream at least. Figure out who lives in that old house your parents were renting when you were five, and ask them if you can borrow one of their bedrooms for an hour."

He sat back, crossing his arms over his chest, pleased with himself.

I sighed. "That's actually a great idea, B, but one stranger already let me use her home for one of my conversations. Her name was Mabel, and I scared that poor lady half to death. I'm not sure I can ask yet another person to play host to my absurdity."

Gus leaned in again. I thought he was going to ask me about the dream Benjamin had mentioned, but he had another question on his mind. "I think I remember where you and your parents lived in those days. They'd just moved back to town and your dad had started his practice but hadn't found office space yet. He helped me out with the purchase of my first home at the time and had me swing by your house to sign some papers. Little one-and-a-half story bungalow on the corner of Miller and Prospect Streets, right? Painted white and green back then, and still to this day?"

"Yep, that's the one," I said, marveling at another blessing of small-town life but still not sure where his inquiry was leading.

The clouds on Gus's face cleared and the sun came out. He held up his finger in a just-wait-one-minute gesture and bounded off, circling around the coffee bar where he pulled a thin phone book from beneath the counter, flipping through it rapidly. He fingered a number, tapped it into his cellphone, and smiled at us across the café as it rang.

Benjamin and I exchanged curious glances and strained to hear what Gus was saying into the phone, but the store was too loud to make it out. He lowered the device, triumphantly punched the end-of-call icon, and gave us an exuberant thumbs-up. He started to walk back around the bar, halting mid-step, lifting his phone again, tapping something into it, and then returning to the table where he took his seat, a goofy grin on his face. We waited for him to explain himself. He just kept grinning. Finally, I gave in.

"Well, Man of Mystery, are you going to explain what just happened?"

He laughed. "Do you remember your old high school math teacher, Nan Gathers?"

"How could you forget Mrs. Gathers?" Benjamin and I asked in unison, our amusement multiplied by our hallmark synchronicity.

Mrs. Gathers had been a mythic figure around the high school. With her wild and whitened hair, she looked like Albert Einstein minus the mustache. Always covered in chalk and a zeal for quadratic equations, she'd loved any kid with a knack for numbers and had little use for the rest. I was among the rest. She'd spotted my ineptitude from a mile away, and it had been confirmed by my first exam in sophomore algebra, at the top of which she'd written in her signature purple pen, "C-" and "distributive law!"

I had no idea what she meant, and she'd had little interest in me for the rest of the year.

Gus, on the other hand, had been a colleague of hers for decades and, he explained, even though Nan Gathers had no love for the subject he'd taught, she'd been pretty sweet on *him*. So he'd just called his old friend and placed a strange request. Fortunately, she was still no stranger to strangeness, and she'd agreed. She was expecting me later that evening, around sundown. The whole endeavor was starting to feel real, and I was starting to feel sick to my stomach. Which is probably why I pointed out another problem rather than expressing my gratitude.

"There's still the issue of who will be the voice of my mother in the conversation."

Gus's smile stretched wider. "I solved that one for you, too, my boy!"

I thought of the text he'd stopped to send on the way back to the table.

"Who did you text?" I asked with both wonder and dread.

The dread, it turned out, was unnecessary. The bell over the door tinkled. Gus looked up and then looked back at me, beaming. I turned.

Father Lou walked in.

45

FATHER LOU HEARD my confession.

Shortly after his arrival, Benjamin said his goodbyes and departed the Ferry for some meetings in Chicago. His mother's house would go on the market that day. Gus, too, returned to his work, wishing me well in that evening's conversation, giving me the hug of a father sending his son off to college, or marriage, or the delivery room.

Then I told Father Lou all of it from the beginning, and sequentially.

I began with the death of my brother, Benjamin, and the trauma it had inflicted on my mother and her marriage and me. Then I betrayed my father again, telling Father Lou every detail I could recall about the afternoon at my dad's law office, about the wink at the dinner table, about my conversation in the cemetery with Jeff. I admitted to a decade's worth of hiding about my finances. I took responsibility for the demise of my marriage—love is the longing to understand, I told Father Lou, and by hiding myself I'd resisted Rebecca's love. I told him about both of my nightmares, the one-word scream in the first one and the four words spoken to me in the second one.

He asked me a lot of questions in preparation for our conversation later that evening. I answered them as honestly as I could. He sipped his coffee quietly for a while. Then he told me he would do his best to represent everyone involved. I almost asked him what he meant by everyone but decided he'd earned my trust and stayed silent. On the sidewalk outside the bookstore, we confirmed cellphone numbers and the time of our call, and he, too, gave me a fatherly hug before parting ways.

When I arrived at my mother's house, her spot in the garage remained empty. That was good. The next time I talked with her, I wanted her to be speaking to me in Father Lou's deep baritone. We'd laughingly agreed that, in his attempt to personify Annie Campbell, he could forgo his falsetto.

I entered my boyhood bedroom, walked to the side of the bed, and turned the temperature dial to off. I gathered my things—a few stray items of clothing, my laptop, the two envelopes on the desk—and packed them into my bags. After my conversation at Nan Gathers's house, it would finally be time to go home. To face the toothbrush holder with a single toothbrush in it.

I stopped in the doorway, scanning the room one last time. On my desk, the Bulls wristband sat propped up against the photo of William Perry. I walked across the room, picked it up, and pulled it onto my wrist. It looked ridiculous. I didn't care. I walked out of the house, got in the car, and proceeded to spend the rest of the day with my other best friend, Bradford's Ferry itself.

I traveled from thin space to thin space, not encountering any of my ghosts this time, just appreciating the town itself, this constant companion of mine. Like any true companion, she held my memories within her, the painful ones and the beautiful ones, and I revisited them all, including an old kindergarten play-ground, once gleaming steel now painted in primary colors. And the tree in my grandparents' yard, where an apple bushel had once been nailed. And the law office that, one afternoon, had been transformed from the source of my greatest pride to my greatest pain. And the clearing in the park, where a picnic table stood with two dates carved into its underbelly. Beneath it, several rabbits were nibbling on weeds as the sun tipped toward evening.

Finally, I grabbed one last sandwich from Sally's Subs and turned in the direction of the home where I'd once dreamed about a boogeymom.

46

I PULLED UP TO NAN GATHERS'S HOUSE as the sun was setting beyond the rolling western hills of Bradford's Ferry. The horizon was stamped with a blackened tree line on a crimson background. The undersides of high clouds were etched with burning oranges and royal purples. Toward the east, the dome gradually transitioned to deepening hues of blue. There, a single star could already be seen in the coming darkness.

I knew she was expecting me, but still I felt nervous, as if I were back in sophomore algebra. The past is behind us, but it is also, always, within us. I rang the bell.

Nan Gathers had not changed a bit. It was as if sometime in early adulthood she'd aged fifty years all at once, and time was still catching up to her. White hair still flew in every direction. Her eyes were still wild with passion. She even had a smudge of what looked to be ice cream at the corner of her mouth. It might as well have been chalk.

"Hi Mrs. Gathers, I'm not sure if you remember me. I'm Elijah Campbell." I found myself looking down at her feet, like I was fifteen again. If I'd had a hat, it would have been in my hands. "Thanks for agreeing to this. I sure am grateful."

"Elijah Campbell," she said as if she was still trying to place me, which must surely have been an act given she'd had hours to jog her memory. "Ah, yes, I seem to recall you struggling with the distributive law. Can't remember much about you beyond that." I was certain *that* was true.

"Yes, ma'am," I said, looking up at her. "I hope you'll forgive me. I still have no idea what the distributive law is."

She erupted in cackles of delight. "Give me a few more years, and I won't have any idea, either!"

She cackled some more while her shoulders bounced and her hair rearranged itself. This was a version of herself she'd saved for the teacher's lounge. I could see why she and Gus had gotten along so well.

"Well, come on in with yourself now, and quit being so sheepish. Houses! We think we own them, but mostly it's the bank that owns them, and if a fire comes along, you learn real quick that no one really owns any pile of lumber except the good Lord himself. You lived here once. This is as much your house as mine. Now I don't know what you're planning, and I don't want to know," she said, wagging a finger at me, "but would you like a bowl of ice cream first?"

My eyes had not deceived me—ice cream was the new chalk.

"I'm okay, Mrs. Gathers, but thanks."

"Nan. You start calling me Nan or so help me God, I *will* kick you out of here."

She cackled to show me she was only kidding. The adult version of me believed her. The algebra student in me wasn't quite so sure.

"Yes, ma'am. I mean, sure thing, Nan. I'll start calling you Nan."

"Now there we go," she said, pleased. "We're friends now. You see, when you teach for nearly fifty years in a town, most everybody sees you as their oddball teacher, and you've got to retrain them to see you as a *person*. Most of them aren't as easy as you," she declared, poking me in a rib and cackling again when I jumped. "Now, about that ice cream?"

A bowl of Rocky Road later, she led me up the narrow stairs to the second floor.

The landing in the upstairs hallway was barely big enough to turn around in. Opposite the stairs, a door led into the bigger bedroom. To my left was my old bedroom. It was dark, in part because the sunlight had completely bled out of the night and in part because the room had never been renovated. The same muddy-brown faux wood paneling lined every wall. Another bit of Bradford's Ferry had resisted the tides of time.

"Well, I'll leave you to your business," Nan called over her shoulder as she retreated down the stairs. "Take as long as you like. I'll be down here. There's a John Nash documentary I've been wanting to get around to. That should tide me over for a couple of hours!"

Before I could tell her I was planning to be quick, she was gone.

I turned back toward the landing, surveyed it, and decided to make a couple of adjustments, turning on the light in the bigger bedroom and turning off the light in the hallway. Now it looked just right.

I stepped into my old bedroom, slid my hand along the wall, and found the light switch by muscle memory. A single low-wattage bulb in an overhead fixture came on, giving off a sickly, yellowish light. The basin of the fixture was dotted with the silhouettes of dead insects resting inside it.

The faux wood paneling had never been particularly glamorous, and several decades had done it no favors. In places it was coming loose from the wall beneath it, warping and bending.

Bright silver dots in several spots suggested Mrs. Gathers— Nan—or someone before her had tried to extend its life by nailing it back in place.

A twin bed still inhabited the corner of the room farthest from the door. No Star Wars bedspread, though. This one was plain beige with white floral stitches along its edges. I looked to my left. The window was open, as it had been in my dream, but there was no box fan. Tonight the air was free to come and go of its own volition. Mostly it just stayed in place, unmoving and heavy. Between the thinness of the room and the thickness of the air, I was having a hard time drawing a breath.

I pulled my phone from a pocket and texted Father Lou. *Are you there?*

Immediately: *I am.*

Are you ready? I asked.

I am, came the reply.

I switched off the bedroom light and lay down on the bed. As an adult you grow taller, so you see the world from a different angle. Lying down, however, returns us to the perspective of our youth. I turned my head to look at the door, and the gray light seeping in from the hallway caused time to collapse completely. I closed my eyes briefly, and the disembodied bathrobe was already floating on the backs of my eyelids. I opened them and looked toward the door and there it was. There *she* was.

I had no bedsheets to lift over my head this time. Instead, I lifted my phone and called Father Lou. As it rang, I tapped the speaker button and heard the sounds of a phone call being answered. Father Lou said nothing, the only indication of his presence the subtle static of cellular silence. He was waiting for me to begin the conversation.

But I couldn't.

It seemed my imagination had gone rogue. The disembodied bathrobe was already beginning its slow, ethereal advance toward me, and every adult thing I wanted to say was trapped behind a five-year-old's silent scream. The specter arrived at the bedside, and I could see the bathrobe was just as I remembered it—a purplish-blue terrycloth, worn and pilled. It leaned over, stopping at an angle above me. In the midst of a dream, you don't doubt its reality—in the moment, I didn't doubt the reality of my imagination either.

"Mom . . ." I croaked, my voice sounding as worn and tattered as the bathrobe itself. I swallowed hard, generating just enough saliva to try again. "Mom," I said a little more clearly.

I'd planned to open with something positive and true. I'd planned to say I love you. Instead, three very different words came out of my mouth.

"You scare me."

I heard those words, and they surprised me, but they also calmed me. I was telling the truth. No hiding. That was good.

Father Lou remained silent. I waited for him to say something. Nothing. I decided to continue with the next thing that came to mind. The time for secrets was behind us. I looked up into the not-face of the thing staring down at me.

"When I was a boy, shortly after we moved out of this house, you and Dad left me with a babysitter one night, and she put on a movie for me. *Invasion of the Body Snatchers*. It terrified me and, for years, I assumed my terror was about having my body hijacked by an alien. Last night, though, I realized the real reason for my fear—the movie explained my experience of you. It seemed like an alien had snatched your body from you. Like my mother was gone and some other creature was looking out at me from behind her eyes. It explained everything about the absence I sensed in you. That was scary. But it wasn't the scariest part. The worst part was knowing I loved you anyway. No matter how alien and foreign to me you might be—no matter how little you loved me—I knew I would cling to you anyway, like a baby clings to the shirt of his mother while being carried. Only, you weren't carrying me. I was holding on to you, but you weren't interested in holding me. Do you have any idea, Mom, how hauntingly lonely it was to be your son?"

My heart was hammering with the effort of honesty, but I figured Father Lou's response would give me time to calm down. I waited. In the waiting, I could feel all my hope gathering. I hoped he would be able to find in himself the words my mother had been unable to find in herself. I hoped he'd build those four dream-words—*I am your freedom*—into something that would help me to forgive her and to let go of her. However, as a minute passed and then another—with the specter hovering over me—my fear and sadness and hope morphed into agitation.

"Father Lou, are you there?"

The phone vibrated on the bed beside me. I lifted it. "I am."

Like Jeff in the cemetery, Father Lou and I had agreed not to break character, but I was beginning to wonder if he was missing the point of this bizarre exercise. I considered saying so but thought better of it, deciding once again to trust him. I gave it another try.

"Mom, all of the anger and judgment and resentment you must surely have sensed in me over the years, it was just my backward way of showing you that I loved you and that I wanted you to love me. All I ever really wanted was to feel like your beloved son, and I didn't know how to express that except to make you feel like my disappointing mother."

There. I'd kicked off the expression of regret and remorse. It galled me a little that I'd had to go first, but I trusted it would be worth it. I waited for Father Lou to respond. Once again, nothing. I checked the phone. The call was still connected. Just to be sure, I asked again into the darkness, "Are you still there?"

A moment, then another buzz. "I am."

With each of my other ghosts, I'd become frustrated when I hadn't heard what I was expecting to hear. This time, though, my frustration was doubled because I'd expected it to be different with Father Lou. His words and his presence had always comforted me, and I felt decidedly uncomfortable about what was happening. It was time to tell him so, even if it meant breaking character.

"Okay, Father Lou, this is frustrating. You're going to have to say more than 'I am' if we're going to get anywhere."

A moment of silence. Then he spoke. "I imagine you are getting frustrated, Elijah. I imagine that's how Moses and the Israelites must have felt, too, when they asked God for his name and he refused to give it. Instead, he simply replied, 'I AM WHO I AM.' Can you imagine how frustrating that must have been at first?"

My ire was up. "Father, I always loved your sermons but I don't need one now. I need a *conversation*. I need my mother to apologize so I can forgive her and move on. I'm sorry if I wasn't clear about that."

I didn't sound sorry.

He was silent for a while before responding in his kindest tone. "Elijah, I spent most of the afternoon praying about this conversation. What I discerned is that it's not my place to speak words on your mother's behalf that she is not willing to speak for herself. I think that does a disservice to her. But even more importantly, I think it does a disservice to *you*."

My response was instant and petulant. "How could helping me to forgive my mother be a disservice to *me*?"

He was prepared with an answer.

"Because if you need an apology to forgive someone, you aren't really forgiving, you're winning."

He let that pronouncement stand on its own for a while before continuing.

"You aren't revising a wrong, you're simply revising the scoreboard. Sure, an apology is a necessary part of reconciliation because it's a sign that hurtful ways may yet turn into healthy ways. However, you aren't interested in reconciling with your mother, Elijah. You want to forgive her so you can be free of her. You don't need an apology for that."

It was a strange thing to feel like I'd been punched in the gut by Father Lou. It was an even stranger thing to punch back.

"I know that, Father. That's basic Psych 101. When you forgive someone, you're not necessarily doing it for them, you're doing it for yourself. Yada yada. I get that. That's why I'm here."

He stayed patient, which was its own kind of irritant.

"Well, I guess that's the problem, Elijah. Psych 101 gets it wrong. You see, every time you forgive someone, it *is* for yourself, but it is *also* for them. When two things are tethered to each other, you can't free one without freeing the other. When you cut the rope of resentment that ties you to your mother, you will be freeing yourself, but you will also be freeing her. The only difference is you will be able to feel your freedom, but you will not be able to feel hers. *She* will, though, somewhere in her soul. She won't understand what has happened to her, of course. She'll simply wake up one morning and the birdsong will sound a little clearer, the sunlight will seem a little brighter, the entire weight of life just a little lighter. Your freedom is tied to hers."

I was silent, and nauseous.

"And here's the thing, Elijah, you *know* all of this already. Not in your head, but in your heart. At some level, every single one of us knows this. The blueprint for existence is written on every soul. Perhaps not on its outer rings, where we're all banged up and bruised and ashamed and abandoned and messed up in a million little ways, but in the quiet and sacred center of it where no pain can reach. *That's* why we all struggle so much to forgive freely, without an apology to justify it. We know the other has not earned the freedom we are about to grant them, so we refuse to give it. And in doing so, we are refusing ourselves the very healing for which we so deeply yearn. Elijah, you can't just free yourself, you must free your mother, too, without her having done anything to deserve it."

A summer breeze stirred the curtains on the window, and a long silence fell between us as the bathrobe hovered mutely over me. Gradually, an inner breeze stirred something within me, something like anguish and despair.

"I don't know if I can do that for her, Father. I don't know if I have it in me."

My condescension was gone for good. I hoped he could hear the apology in my voice. Even if he couldn't, though, I knew he'd already forgiven me. He'd already freed me. I could feel it.

"I understand, son, I really do." He paused, the long pause of a poker player who is deciding whether to go all in. Eventually, he pushed all his chips to the center of the table.

"Are you up for talking to this old man a little while longer?"

I pushed all mine in too. "Yes. Of course."

"Thank you," he said, as if *I* was the one doing *him* a favor. "Elijah, I think you're having trouble forgiving your mother because you've always believed the best measure of your love is the strength of your grip. You've loved your people by doing whatever it takes to hold on to them. Hiding was just your most reliable way of holding on. Your secrets were simply a symptom of what you've believed about love—that love clings to the object of its desire, even if it costs everyone dearly. Even if it costs the truth."

The blind spot he'd just articulated was so big it felt apocalyptic. If I allowed myself to truly receive his observation, there'd be no going back from it. What came out of my mouth next felt like something I was hearing rather than saying.

"I'm trying to release my mother by repairing what is broken between the two of us, which is not really letting go. It's just another way of holding on."

"That's right," he said gently. "And I believe the voice in your dream was inviting you into a love that lets go. 'I am your freedom,'" he said with awe in his voice. "What a grace."

"I am your freedom," I repeated. "You've lost me again, Father Lou."

"Elijah, for thousands upon thousands of years, human beings have been debating the nature of God. Then, in our Scriptures, one human being named John appeared to end the conversation altogether when he wrote, 'God is love.' Mic drop, right? Except appearances can be deceiving. I don't believe John's description of God was intended to *end* the conversation. It was intended to *reframe* it around a new question."

"What is love?" I ventured, struggling to catch up with him and just barely doing so.

"That's right, Elijah. And it's the most graceful of questions because answering it is not an intellectual exercise. It's an experiential one. As we come closer to truly answering that question with our lives, we actually draw closer to God. You drew closer to God when you rejected the false notion that love is loyalty. Now you are coming even closer to him as you reject the false notion that love is a leash tethering everyone to you."

"I AM," I breathed, more sigh than speech, recalling his refrain at the beginning of our conversation. It hadn't been an accident. "I AM WHO I AM," I breathed again, remembering the parallel he'd drawn between my frustration and the Israelites'. "I am your freedom," I repeated one more time, recollecting what he'd said earlier that morning about representing everyone involved. "You believe *God* was speaking to me in my dream?"

He chuckled. "Here I am, saying I can't speak on behalf of your mother, but I can speak on behalf of the Almighty. You'll have to forgive me. It's a job hazard. But to answer your question, yes, I believe God was speaking to you in your dream. And I believe it was the same message God has been trying to deliver to humanity for millennia."

"Which is?"

"God holds us completely, without holding *on* to us at all, because that's what love does."

I was quiet, but Father Lou interpreted my silence accurately. I wanted him to say more.

"Elijah, I believe we are, all of us, always, resting in the great cupped and loving hands of God. We are born right into the center of this divine presence, into a gracious space filled with joy and sorrow, pleasure and pain, hope and despair, love and loss. We live there and we die there as well. We hurt and we heal there. We rejoice and we lament there."

The wonder in his voice tapered off as he downshifted into a more somber-sounding gear.

"And, inevitably, we make *demands* there. Mostly, we demand God become something smaller than the hands that hold us, something we can hold *on* to. So we populate the space we've been given with our own smaller versions of God. Then, as those little gods die off—as they always do when confronted with our reason and experience and science and so on—we call that empty space a void. We say God is dead or perhaps never existed at all. In the meantime, God just keeps holding us in those cupped and ever-present hands, waiting for us to notice that we are held by love in every moment."

It was my turn to chuckle. "I'm following you again, Father Lou, but you're reminding me of that old Sunday school song, 'He's Got the Whole World in His Hands.'"

Instead of laughing, his tone grew even gentler.

"Thankfully, there are many metaphors for this bigger God, Elijah."

He paused for a moment, searching for one. He didn't have to look far.

"I remember so clearly the morning of your high school graduation, sitting there at the picnic table, looking out on the Saukenuk with you. I remember thinking you *were* at church, because rivers are such a splendid metaphor for our life in God. You see, most of us are focused on how much of heaven seems to be flowing through us. We rejoice at feeling flooded, and we lament at feeling all dried up. But the truth is, God isn't the water. *We* are the water.

Life is the water. Being *human* is the water. God is the *banks* of the river, holding all of it and all of us. And when we dry up from time to time—when the flow ceases for a while—the banks still remain, abiding with us during every season of drought, as well."

I remembered Father Lou speaking at my high school baccalaureate ceremony. In the middle of it, he'd departed from his prepared notes, swept along by his intoxication with the magnitude of the God he'd experienced. I could tell Father Lou had abandoned his notes once again.

"The great call of the spiritual life is to see the banks beyond the river. To see the hands doing the holding. To see God beyond the void. Around it. Containing it. Speaking to us from the edges of it." He laughed to himself. "Of course, we human beings tend to be a little hard of hearing, so there was this one time when God came particularly close in the hope we'd hear the message particularly clearly."

"Jesus," I volunteered.

"Jesus," he confirmed. "He tried to tell us about the mystery of it all. 'I am in my Father, and you are in me, and I am in you,' he said. Of course, instead of living into the mystery of those words, it seems many of us put him on a leash and made him yet another object to which we cling. I imagine if he could be here with us now, he'd be saying something like, 'Don't cling to me, *rest* with me in the cupped and tender hands of God, and learn to love each other as freely as you've been loved by God.'"

Twelve years earlier, Rebecca's words—"I don't know, Campbell, what are *you* doing this evening?"—had caused the twin threads of hope and fear to wrap themselves around my heart and cinch it so tightly I could barely breathe. This time, it was Father Lou's words that triggered those twin threads. The freedom he was describing sounded both exceptionally easy and, at first, exceptionally painful. For a moment, my fear won out.

"How can I be the cupped and loving hands of God to anyone, Father? I've been nothing but a clenched fist for so long. It's hard to imagine becoming anything else."

"I understand, Elijah. Can you believe there was a time I felt exactly the same way about myself? Nowadays, though, I have one meditation, which I return to in as many moments as possible, and I'd like to think it's making a difference in my life."

On my first date with Rebecca, in McDonald's, I'd found the thread of hope disentangled from fear, and I'd tugged on it. I did so once again. "What image?" I asked.

"It's an image I borrowed from one of my favorite authors. He said that many human relationships are like the interlocking fingers of two hands. In our loneliness, we cling to each other, and this mutual clinging creates more suffering than it could ever prevent because it doesn't take away our loneliness. These interlocking relationships, so to speak, often fall apart because they become suffocating and oppressive. He said human relationships are meant to be like two hands folded together, which can move away from each other while still touching at the fingertips. By doing so, they can create space between themselves. A little tent, he said. A home. A safe place to be."

He let that sink in before pronouncing a benediction on my life.

"Elijah, I believe your dream is calling you into the freedom of loving beyond clinging. Loving like a tent, like a home, like a safe place to be."

I found myself finally and fully surrendering to Father Lou's words, but it didn't feel like relief. It felt like grief—the feeling of truly letting something go. It was an agonizing ache somewhere deep in my bones, the most exquisite of growing pains. Yet for the first time, I could imagine what my life might become after all the growing.

"I've done that to all my people, haven't I, Father? My dad. My mom. Rebecca, especially. Rather than touching my fingertips to hers and making our marriage a space of freedom, I tried to interlock our fingers and hold on to her with all my might. I clung to her with my secrets and called that clinging love, didn't I?"

"Yes, you did, Elijah. And *of course* you did. Holding on to each other is how we begin. You said it yourself—a baby clings to its mother at first. It's only after the child has been held really well for a really long time that it begins to trust it's safe to let go. A few of us develop that trust as children in the arms of a loving parent. Most of us have to learn it much later in life, among our chosen companions. Learning how to *hold* each other without holding *on* to one another. It's why we're here. It's why we've been given each other."

Silence fell again.

I lay completely still, just as I'd done near the end of every bathrobe nightmare. However, my mother's ghost had vanished, and I didn't feel like I was waking from a nightmare; I felt like I was awakening to my *life.* Most such awakenings look pretty ordinary, I guess. For instance, they look like a middle-aged man lying on a bed, for the first time appreciating the space in the room around him, space comprised only of air no person can hold on to for longer than one good breath.

Lying there, recalling Father Lou's recitation of Jesus—*I am in my Father, and you are in me, and I am in you*—I simply allowed myself to be *in* it all, and I gave that sense of being a word I'd never given it before: love. It was just a start, and a small one at that, but that was okay. For almost forty years, I'd rehearsed one way of loving; it might take another forty to learn a new one.

After all, the day doesn't dawn all at once; it dawns by degrees.

47

Rebecca, after my mother grabbed her purse and walked out, I was in a dark place, and I met Benjamin at the Den. I drank a bunch of cheap Scotch and for a couple of hours I contemplated not being here anymore. In that dark place, I romanticized it as my way of letting you go. In truth, it would have been avoiding the pain of *actually* letting you go.

At any rate, near the end of those hours, I sat down at my desk, signed the divorce decree, and listed on the back of it every bank account, username, and password I could recall. Fortunately, I then passed out and had a nightmare. Strange as it may sound, I awoke from it with a glimmer of hope, which grew into a glow over the next twenty-four hours.

I left Bradford's Ferry last night—after an extraordinary conversation with Father Lou—planning to drive home to our house for a good night's sleep. Instead, I drove past the exit and just kept on going. I wrote each part of this letter at a different rest stop along the way. One in Indiana. One in Ohio. *Two* in Pennsylvania—that state is *wide*, especially at five in the morning. And now here I am in Seaside, eating lunch at Dani's Deli, finishing this letter.

Do you remember the first time we ate here, that first Christmas after your accident? Your jaw was still super sore and you were having difficulty eating solid food, but you wanted me to taste your favorite sandwich at your favorite restaurant in town. I was loving it but it was hard to watch you there, unable to share it. So I asked the kid at the counter to blend it up for us, and she thought I was crazy, but I *knew* I was crazy—about you—so it didn't matter. Anyway, this restaurant is a thin place for me, a crack in time through which the joy of the past is oozing, even as I anticipate what must come next.

Your parents' house is less than a mile from here. I'm going to finish this letter, and then I'm going to deliver it and the divorce decree to the house. It's midday on a Saturday, so you'll all be gone at the beach. Your mom will check for mail when you get home. She'll find the divorce decree and the letter. I'll just have to hope she passes the letter on to you.

Rebecca, I haven't shared any of this to elicit sympathy from you, nor in the hopes of changing your mind. I didn't come here to win you back. In fact, the purpose of this pilgrimage has been exactly the opposite. I'll never stop wanting you, but I have to stop holding on to you. I hope that frees you from the bondage of what I've called love. I hope it frees Sarah to truly love her father rather than to simply be loyal to him. And I hope it frees me to find my way home from Italy on my own, like you did once upon a time.

I don't think it's an exaggeration to say that two nights ago I experienced the darkest night of my soul. Last night, though, I saw it for what it really was. In a dark night of the soul, you feel like you've lost God. You haven't. Rather, you've lost all the little gods to which you were attached and to which you'd assigned lordship. Then what you're left with is a void, but it's not a void that exists without God; it's the space that exists *within* God. In a dark night of the soul, you realize it's just you and the great I AM. Then, the day starts dawning.

I love you, Rebecca. I always will. *And* I will release you.

Eli

48

SEASIDE, MARYLAND, AMOUNTED to a single intersection and its ripple effects. A coastal highway running north and south, parallel to the Atlantic, intersected at the town center with a two-lane road that crossed the highway and dead-ended at a boardwalk, a well-preserved relic from another age. The inland road had been laid down specifically to generate tourist traffic from parts west, especially Washington, DC. It had worked. By midday on a Saturday, the pilot of the biplane flying up and down the coast trailing a banner advertising happy hour at The Beached Wail—a weekend hotspot featuring loud local bands—would be hard-pressed to glimpse a single patch of sand, and still the traffic streaming in from Virginia would be backed up for miles with families who had gotten a late start for one reason or another.

Dani's Deli was located just north of that intersection. For that reason, I knew Rebecca and her parents wouldn't fight its crowds on the last weekend of summer, and for the same reason I found myself mired in the sludge of traffic on my departure from the restaurant. Green light, red light, green light, red light. With each change in the signal, I inched closer to the inter-section, closer to the road that would take me to my family at the beach if I turned left, or closer to the delivery of my envelope if I continued straight.

Green light. Finally, it was my turn, and the choice presented itself—get into the left-turn lane or stay straight.

Several years ago, the car we'd bought after Rebecca's accident had started to show its age—for some reason, it only wanted to turn left, and you had to fight it with all your strength to keep it straight. That's how it felt now, like some ghost in the machine was tugging the wheel toward the left-turn lane. I knew where my family would be on the beach—right next to the beach um-brella stand where Sarah and I had built sandcastles on dozens of hot summer days. To be with them again, all I needed to do was allow the pull of the ghost in the machine. However, the last month had taught me a lot about listening to ghosts. So I lis-tened to this one too. It was telling me I still had a lot of letting go to do.

I chose the lane with the straight arrow and passed through the intersection.

To find the Miller homestead from there, you simply turned several times in the direction of fewer people. It took me five minutes and almost fifteen years to get there, because as I drew closer to their home, the world got thinner and time got slippery again. It was, of course, the day I would finally surrender to my divorce. It was also the day I drove there to ask Mr. Miller for Rebecca's hand in marriage—the day he said I needed to quit calling him sir, to call him Dad, or at least Brad. It was our wedding day and Benjamin was next to me and I was still pinching myself and he was reassuring me Rebecca was for real. It was a week or so after Sarah's birth, and she was dozing in her car seat, just minutes away from meeting her grandparents for the first time. It was the last time we'd all been there to-gether, in the spring for Easter, the whole town of Seaside en-joying the final days of its off-season lull. It was every summer vacation we'd ever taken there—all those sandcastles. It was every Christmas holiday we'd ever celebrated there. It was my life coming unpaused all those years ago as Rebecca Miller hit the play button on my heart. It was the entire album of our life together. It was the sound of the needle reaching the end of the album.

When you let go of something big, you are also letting go of all the little things hiding out in its nooks and crannies, and it feels more like a tearing than a releasing. Nevertheless, *that* is why I'd come. You could put a stamp on an envelope and drop it in the mailbox and fool yourself into thinking it's just another afternoon. But there was no mistaking this for an ordinary afternoon.

It was the day, finally, I'd let the rushing river get me.

One final stop sign. One more turn left. One big bend in the road. Then the whole world seemed to open up into ocean and sky. Like a gateway to the wild windblown dunes beyond it, the Miller house stood forth at the end of the lane, its two stories some unique mixture of Cape Cod and farmhouse, with a wide front porch stretching the length of the home. To the left of the house, a driveway bent around it, leading to a rarely used garage hidden from sight. I expected the driveway to be half-empty.

It wasn't.

Next to Rebecca's red SUV was her dad's old, beat-up Land Rover. It was the quintessential beachmobile. Plenty of room for boogie boards and beach chairs. Tourists could ding it. Seagulls could dump on it. Sand could litter the inside of it. Every time

I'd gone to the beach with the Millers, one of us had driven it. I couldn't imagine a scenario in which they'd gone to the beach but the Land Rover hadn't.

A hundred thoughts collided into mental paralysis, and my body took over. My foot pumped the brake, bringing the car to a jolting stop. I tried to breathe and barely succeeded. I looked down at the gear stick and shifted into reverse. My foot eased off the brake. I looked up, glancing again at the Land Rover. It was sitting in the very spot where it had been parked all those years ago on my first arrival here, alone. The world grew thin once more as I recalled letting myself in, knocking over the vase, diving for it, mostly saving it, and hiding the crack.

I pressed the brake again. Put the car in park.

The day I broke the vase I'd had no choice—hiding had been my one and only instinct. However my freedom of choice had been restored by the month in Bradford's Ferry. I could choose to once again hide from the crack I'd created in the middle of my life, or I could take responsibility for it. I could hide from this moment, or I could show up to it.

I felt my body settle into the simplicity of that choice. I realized how much I'd still been hiding out in the plan to stuff the divorce papers through a mail slot in my in-laws' front door while everyone was out getting a tan. It would be another thing entirely to look someone in the eye while I handed them over. I imagined it would be more painful for them and more painful for me, but it was the pain of letting go, and that, I was learning, was a sacred kind of pain—while it seemed like it was reducing your life, it was actually expanding it.

I shifted into drive.

For the first time in a month, instead of time folding backward, it folded forward, and I could see what was about to happen. Rebecca's father had only two real priorities in his life—protecting the planet and protecting his family. On a Saturday afternoon, if he wasn't at the beach with them, he was home with them, and he always had one eye on the lane leading to his house. He would see me pull up, and he'd protect his daughter from her pain by meeting me on the front porch. I parked in the driveway behind the Land Rover and waited.

The door opened, and Brad Miller stepped out.

I reached for the envelope in the passenger seat. It was thick with the divorce decree and the pages of my letter, heavy with the weight of surrender. I got out of the car and walked toward the porch, my eyes on the ground, watching my feet carry me down the front walk, up the porch steps, and to within a yard of his own sandaled feet. Along the way, my search for something to say had come up empty.

I lifted my eyes to his, taking in his beach shorts and an old, frayed T-shirt proclaiming that sticking your head in the sand had gotten a bad rap. With his bronzed skin, square jaw, and salt-and-pepper hair swept backward in perfectly coiffed dishevelment, he looked almost exactly as I remembered. However, his eyes appeared to have aged a decade since Easter. Underscored by dark shadows and framed by red rims, his eyes looked like those of a man haunted by a loss.

He tried to say something and choked on it. He tried again and could manage only a strangled sound. Giving up, he opened his arms wide, stepped toward me, wrapped me in an embrace, and cried like a little boy. The loss that was haunting him was me.

To have someone grieve you is to be loved with a depth most people never get to know in this life. It's the funeral you never get to see and the eulogy you never get to hear. In his grief, I could feel my own grief surfacing within me, like a beach ball I'd been pushing beneath the surface of the water for far too long. Time folded forward again. I saw myself fully feeling the loss of Rebecca before finalizing the loss. I saw myself folding into the arms of a father for the first time since I was sixteen and losing my resolve altogether. I saw what I needed to do, and I did it. I pushed the beach ball back down one last time.

The rush of his grief slowed to a trickle, and we slowly stepped back from each other.

He pushed the tears from his eyes with the backs of his hands before trying to talk again. "Eli," he said, thick with nasal congestion, "I can't let you see Rebecca." There was a heartbroken apology beneath the words.

"I know, Brad," I replied, my voice cracking with the effort of keeping the beach ball beneath the surface. "Actually, I'm here now because I assumed you'd all be at the beach and I could drop off this," I raised the envelope, "without making a scene."

I could see gratitude soften his features further. He'd been wondering if he'd have to fight me off, and it was the last thing he wanted to do.

"Well, you were right to assume that. We planned to go." He looked down at his clothing as if to present evidence to the court. "We told Sarah to slow down on the pancakes this morning, but she's got a lot of your wife in her and she couldn't be deterred. Sure enough, she developed a stomachache. Rebecca is upstairs napping with her right now. Also, if you don't start calling me Dad on a day like today, you never will. Do it for me, Eli."

For years I'd been trying to call him Dad, but I'd never been able to do so for reasons that were inexplicable to me at the time. Now I knew it had been my misplaced loyalty to my biological father. Calling anyone else Dad had felt like a betrayal. It no longer felt that way.

"Okay, I'll call you dad, Dad."

Tears irrigated my eyes. His eyes started to shimmer again too. He held out his hand.

I pushed down on the beach ball with all my strength, and I passed him the envelope.

"The divorce papers are in there, signed. On the back, I wrote all our financial information, so Rebecca can give it to her lawyer and get things rolling. There's also a letter in there. I wrote it to Rebecca on the drive here last night. I know she's been clear about not receiving any communications from me, but I hope you'll pass it on to her. It's my way of saying goodbye in a way I think she'll actually be grateful for. Of course, I'll understand if you respect her wishes."

He slid the envelope into the cargo pocket of his shorts. "We love you, Eli. We always have and we always will. You're our son. In here." He pointed at his chest. "This divorce will change a lot of things, but it can't change that."

"Thank you," I said, before adding, "Dad."

He opened his mouth, made another choking sound, wrapped me in a final embrace instead, and then turned around, disappearing into the home and closing the door behind him. I turned around too, staring at the steps leading down to the front walk. They would be my first steps alone in thirteen years. I took the first one. And then I took another. And another. And with each one, I took my hands off the beach ball of grief within me.

I released it to do what it was designed to do, which is to surface. And surface it did.

I got into the car, placed my head on the steering wheel, and I wept. I wept for my wife. I wept for my life with my daughter, which was about to be severed in half, at best. I wept for my mother and my father and for a baby named Benny and for all the years of hiding and clinging. I wept for the pain of my past and the death of the future I'd envisioned.

The grief flowed freely for a minute, five minutes, perhaps ten minutes, and then it began to ebb again, and my chest heaved and my head throbbed and my eyes burned and I was completely wrung out. Within me, there was only emptiness. A strange emptiness though, not like any I'd ever felt before. A relatively peaceful void, which felt a little scary but also a little spacious. There was room in me to receive whatever happened next, no matter how painful or wonderful it might be. Reaching for the ignition, I sensed motion on the porch. I looked up.

The front door opened.

THE DOOR SWINGS INWARD, and she's standing there, cloaked in the shadows of the home. Enough light filters in for me to see she's holding an empty envelope in one hand and a clutch of papers in the other. A divorce decree and a letter. Her head is bowed over the papers. My chest is supposed to be tightening, but it's not. The opposite, actually. Something is expanding within me. Opening. Preparing to embrace this, whatever it is.

She drops the envelope and with her free hand lifts the top page, shuffling it to the bottom of the stack. Her head remains bowed. As she reads, she steps forward across the threshold, onto the porch, into the light. Her dark chocolate hair has been bleached to milk chocolate by a month of sun. A beach sarong hides a bathing suit but exposes a pair of legs every bit as bronze as the day she first placed them on my lap.

She slips another page to the bottom of the stack and with her free hand pulls on the door behind her, leaving it only slightly ajar. Several seagulls mark the skyline. The ocean glitters in the distance. Dune grass dances in a cooling breeze off the water. I don't know what to do, so I do nothing.

Another page moves to the bottom of the stack, and she takes another step forward, head still down. She lifts the back of her free hand to her eyes, the way her father had moments ago. The gesture sends my own vision swimming. I don't know if our tears are sorrowful or joyful, but of course they are both. They are always both.

This time, she pulls the top page free with one hand and holds it separate from the rest as she reads the page beneath it. The pages in both hands are fluttering. I look at the dune grass. It is still. The breeze has gone back out to sea.

Both of her hands drop to her sides and her chin drops to her chest and her shoulders bob rhythmically. The hurt my hiding has caused her comes in like the tide. For the first time, I know the true absence of self-preservation—I'd give my life if it would take away her pain. It wouldn't. I feel my powerlessness. I try to make space for it too.

Her shoulders grow still and slowly, ever so slowly, she lifts her chin, and for the first time I see her face. It is like the ocean— salt water glistening on its surface. I search it for some sign of sunken treasure and there is none to be found, except the slightest of movement at the corners of her mouth and the subtlest of crinkling at the corners of her eyes. As she continues to cry, I recognize the pairing of that crinkling and crying. I recognize it from that moment when I stood at the altar and the doors opened and she appeared all in white and took her first steps down the aisle. I recognize it from the delivery room where I was still holding the scissors—the rubbery relent of Sarah's umbilical cord still felt in my fingertips—and her daughter was being placed in her arms for the first time. I recognize it from that afternoon, not so long ago, when the Hallmark card arrived in the mail from a former client, letting her know that, because of her, he was in college instead of a morgue. I recognize it as the look of a woman who is right where she wants to be and over-flowing with the satisfaction of it.

Suddenly, time speeds up and the door behind her is being pulled inward and a young lady who looks so much like her is rushing outward and Sarah is bounding down the steps and I'm getting out of the car to meet her and I'm on my knees and she's wrapped around my neck and all a-chatter—*I missed you, Daddy!*—and Rebecca is taking one small, slow step forward—*Grandma made so many pancakes!*—and Rebecca is descending the porch steps—*I put on too much syrup*—and she takes the last two steps in one stride—*my stomach hurt so bad*—and she's rushing toward us—*but now I feel so much better, Daddy!*—and then Rebecca is with us and she's down on her knees too and I take in the scent of her and there is so much space in me for it and yet all of me is filled up.

And for the first time,

I hold my ladies,

without holding on to them at all.

EPILOGUE

WHAT DO WE MEAN, EXACTLY, when we say something is a dream come true?

Usually, it means we've imagined our lives getting better in some particular way, and then one day the thing we've been imagining actually happens. Dream jobs. Dream houses. Dream vacations. These are the things that come to mind. When what we *acquire* matches what we *desire*, we say a dream has come true. It's a thrilling thing when our inner world and outer world sync up like that. Of course it is.

For a little while.

The problem is, if you trace almost any dream back to its source, you will find at its origins a wound. The blind spot in the job-and-house-and-vacation kind of dream is the hurt it is trying to heal, or at least hide. More often than not, a dream coming true is a way of trying to put the past behind you. But you can't put something behind you if it is also within you.

I chased my dreams, and I even caught a few. When I married Rebecca, it was a dream come true. When I published my first book. When Sarah was born. When we bought that house in the suburbs with the soaker tub. All of them were dreams come true. What a thrill. And yet, it seems, each time one came true, my pain became more restless.

I remember a long car ride once with Rebecca and Sarah when Sarah suddenly screamed out from the back seat. Startled, we asked her why she'd screamed, and she said simply, "It's been a long time since anyone listened to me." I guess my pain finally screamed out from the back seat of my soul, because I hadn't listened to it for a while. After all, who has time to listen to their pain while they're chasing their dreams?

So my past and my pain screamed out through the leaving of my wife and the crumbling of my life, through a long-ago nightmare and some long-lost ghosts. More and more, I think that kind of scream is what we call a midlife crisis. *Midlife* is probably a misnomer, though, because you don't always hear that scream around the midpoint of your life expectancy. *Crisis* is probably a misnomer, too, because if you listen to the scream instead of doubling down on all your dream chasing, it doesn't become a crisis; it becomes an awakening.

At any rate, when my past and my pain screamed out from the back seat of my soul, I tried to ignore it at first. Most of us do. That bridge in the middle of our life looks too rickety to be trusted, and the river of pain running beneath it too scary to be felt. Eventually, though, the people I've loved—and the God I've come to love all over again—did something very unexpected. Instead of rescuing me from my pain, they pushed me into it. I resented each and every one of them for it at first, until I finally surrendered to the truth:

The only way to peace is through the pain of the past.

So I went there. I walked out onto the broken bridge in the middle of my life, and I discovered something entirely un-expected while I was on it—you can either spend your life making your dreams come true, *or you can allow your dreams to become truer.* The former, more often than not, is a waste of time, while the latter can redeem *all* your time—the past that lurks within you, the present that is all around you, and the future that is eventually shaped by you.

What does it mean to allow our dreams to become truer?

Sarah is starting to learn cursive in school. It was a struggle at first, but her teacher was patient—day after day he expressed confidence in the students' ability to make their handwriting better. And with practice came some modest improvement. Then, her teacher changed his approach. Instead of telling the class to make their handwriting better, he encouraged them to make it *beautiful-er.* Well, that was all they needed to hear. She came home that night with pages full of swirls and swoops and loops and, in the beauty of it, I could actually make out the meaning of the words more clearly.

Our dreams become truer when they become beautiful-er. If we listen to the scream, and if we walk out onto that bridge, and if we face the pain rising beneath it, then gradually we begin to dream different dreams. Our inner world gets rewritten in cursive, and we begin to make out the meaning of our life in words like feeling and grieving and surrendering and forgiving and falling and dying and resurrecting. When that happens, you don't need your dreams to come true around you anymore because they've already come true within you.

That's what happened to me, and every day my swirls and my swoops and my loops are becoming a little more beautiful. Every day I'm able to make out a little more of the meaning in this one hard and holy life I've been given to live. I've begun to dream that nightmare again too, the one with the bridge in it. Though it doesn't feel like a nightmare anymore.

It feels more like a dream becoming truer.

I'm at the river's edge once again.

A few nights in a row now, I've found myself here. Then a dozen nights. A hundred nights. A thousand nights. Every night it is the same, and every night it is grace.

I look down at my feet, and they are the feet of a man in a well-worn pair of flip-flops. Somehow, I can also see in them the tender feet of the boy he once was, and the gnarled toes and joints of the old man he will become. They are the feet of yesterday and today and someday.

I can sense a presence behind me. Presences, plural. I'm never alone in the dream anymore. This no longer scares me. In fact, it comforts me because I know who they are and why they are here.

I look out on the bridge and the river, and everything is exactly the same, yet nothing is the same. The bridge is rickety and the rotting boards lie dangerously distant from one another. The water is as muddy and as threatening as ever. Nevertheless I feel no fear, not because I want to die but because I want to be resurrected.

And so I begin.

I go slowly. I'm not trying to save myself; I'm trying to savor the moment. I step onto the yellowish board with the two rusty nails at the end. I listen to the subtle screeching of the nails as the board bounces slightly beneath my weight. They make a music I enjoy for a little while, until finally the board settles in place. I move on, picking out the healthiest-looking boards, leaping from one to the next.

The presences behind me advance along with me, though they are weightless and cause no screeching of nails nor creaking of boards.

I prance onto the dark board and off it before it can crack and fall into the water. Then I'm faced with the two-foot gaps before and after the really rotted board. As always, I leap across both gaps and stick the landing on the other side. As always, the water begins to rise. I look down at its unfathomable depths and I smile, not because I'm in a race I can win but because I know I will lose and the losing is a better kind of victory.

The water continues to rise. I make several more leaps before I'm faced with the rotted board I once fell through on the darkest night of my soul, sending me falling into another dream entirely. I've never made that mistake again. Just beyond it is a startlingly yellow board, and I leap to it, landing safely. There is breath on the back of my neck once again.

From here I can see a pattern of healthy boards I know for certain will allow me to complete my journey across the bridge and into the mysterious shroud of fog on the other side. However, I also know what is going to happen next.

I begin to feel the presences behind me move alongside me, around me, past me. They are not floating, but they're not walking, either. Their backs are to me at first. Then, one by one, they begin to turn, facing me. I watch them as they reach out to each other, taking each other's hands. They are all here. Rebecca and Sarah. Benjamin and Gus. Jeff and Father Lou. My mother and my father and a little boy I never met. My uncle. My grandfather. My grandmother.

They are not here to help me cross the bridge. They are here to prevent me from doing so.

Suddenly, their presence is inverted, and I can see through the space they are taking up, as if they are a window into the fog itself that lies just beyond them. In the fog I can see every tantalizing thing. It contains all my dreams—indeed it contains every human dream—and in the fog they have all come true. Then, just as suddenly, the window closes and I can see my companions again, and in their gazes I can see why they are barring the way. They are refusing to let me settle for what is in the fog. They are here to usher me into something more. They are here so I might experience the grace of death and resurrection.

The water is at my ankles and rising quickly. I look down at it, and its brown hue takes my breath away. Every night it takes my breath away. Because it's the color of caramel.

I look up at my grandmother, who stands at the edge of this barricade of companions. One of her hands is holding on to my mother's. The other hand is free, thumb and forefinger rubbing rhythmically together. We lock eyes as she smiles and nods.

"Underneath the caramel," I murmur.

"Underneath the caramel," she agrees.

It's all the encouragement I need to surrender to the rising water. My companions rise with the surface of it, but I don't, and it's at my knees and my waist and my chest and my chin, and the last thing I see as the water covers me is them looking down on me, and the look is love.

I sink beneath the surface of the water and discover right away this is a very strange river indeed. I feel no fear because my fear was my resistance to the river of pain, and my resistance is gone. I feel other things, though. Indeed, I feel all other things. I feel all the lonesomeness and abandonment and shame and anger and hurt and pain and grief and sorrow of a human life. My whole being is filled with it, and it is excruciating, but I also have enough space for it, and I know how momentary it is compared to what will come.

The river's strangeness also means I don't get swept away in it. I just keep sinking, deeper and deeper into the pain, until no light from above can penetrate its murky depths and everything is darkness. And still I sink. I sink through ages and eons until I sink beyond time itself. I sink through molecules and matter into an ether beyond substance itself. On and on I sink, until finally I feel my feet exiting the water, then my knees and my waist and so on, like the river is a great cloud and I'm a raindrop departing it.

And then I'm falling again through this other ether, but much faster, plummeting toward terminal velocity, and my ears are full of the wind of it and my eyes are squeezed tight in preparation for the impact of it, and then as quickly as the fall began, it halts, somehow both suddenly and gently, and I'm overcome by a sensation of hovering and I tentatively open my eyes and I'm on my back looking up at an azure sky clearer than any atmosphere I've ever witnessed. My arms are open wide.

Slowly, I turn my head to the side, and I can see what I'm hovering over. It's a field of wildflowers so vivid and various in color I have to squint at first against the power of it. Gradually, my eyes become accustomed to the brilliance surrounding me, so I open them all the way, and I can see it's not just any field of wildflowers. It's that field of flowers beyond the boundaries of an old, dying golf course. Now, it's also a field of flowers beyond the boundaries of my old, dying life. And the whole field is humming with something, every flower vibrating with sound, and the sound is singing, and the song is grace, and it resonates with the tuning fork that is my soul, sending ripples of joy throughout me and to the edges of me and beyond me.

This goes on for a long while, and it never gets old.

Then I'm waking and I'm leaving this place, and a part of me resists the departure, but the rest of me receives it because I know I will come here in my sleep again and, even more so, I know I can never really leave it, even in my waking. This is the grace at the bottom of all things. It is God underneath everything.

And it is beautiful-er than anything I can imagine.

ACKNOWLEDGMENTS

MY LAST BOOK, *True Companions*, concluded with an epilogue that pushed the boundary of nonfiction and fiction. In it, I imagined an inner reunion of all of my companions—past, present, and future. The scene played with the malleability of time and space in the realm of memory and soulfulness, and it experimented ever so briefly with an imaginary conversation between my grandfather and me. In other words, it had the seeds of this novel in it. However, I'm certain those seeds would never have sprouted and flourished if my agent, Kathryn Helmers, hadn't kept watering them with a repeated question: "What if?" Kathy, this book exists because you believed in it and in me, and your talent, insight, and wisdom are threaded throughout it. You're the field of wildflowers beneath my writing career.

There was a handful of friends who prepared the soil for Kathy's influence. They reached out to me after the publication of *True Companions* and encouraged me in important ways to write a novel. Michelle Spinden, I'll always cherish the note you dropped in the mail, which ended with, "I hope you'll consider writing fiction." Ben Boss, thanks for telling me during our first meal out after Covid-19 lockdowns that it was my stories in *True Companions* that stood out to you the most. And Mike McCarthy, thank you for that affirmation of yours, "You keep taking your storytelling to the next level." It's one thing for a guy to have wild dreams; it's another thing entirely for his friends to be dreaming with him.

There are so many people to thank at IVP, some of them I know and some of them I don't. Among those I know are Cindy Bunch, my editor. Cindy, thank you for asking—twice—for a fictional version of the things I was trying to say and then giving me the freedom and the time to say them in a novel. Thank you, too, for your remarkable ability to know just where to push on a manuscript. I'm awed by how much better it became once you got your hands on it. And to the rest of the IVP team with whom I've been blessed to work directly—Lori Neff, Krista Clayton, Tara Burns, Allie Noble, Stephanie Seija, Maila Kue, Ellen Hsu, Rachel Hastings, Subaas Gurung—you are truly an incredible community of creatives. Thank you for the work you do every day to make it possible for me to create too.

To my readers—especially that core tribe of you we call the Lovable Learning Community—you are so graceful. You let me go silent for long periods of time so I can write out what is trying to be spoken through me. And then you dive in with gusto as we read through it and learn from it together. You all are one of the great, unexpected blessings of my life.

Finally and especially, thank you to my kids: Aidan, Quinn, and Caitlin. While I finished this book, I watched you perform in the all-state honors choir, your final musical of middle school, and your first concert band recital, respectively. With each performance, a phrase kept repeating within me: my heart is full, my heart is full, my heart is full.

And Kelly—my wife who understands me most of the time and believes in me all of the time—this book means a lot of things to me, but perhaps most of all it is a meditation on how much I'd still have to grow to ever let you go.

QUESTIONS FOR REFLECTION AND DISCUSSION

1. The book opens with Eli saying, "The past is behind us, but it is also, always, within us." What do you think about Eli's observation that the past can "feel dead and gone one moment and then, in the next, it can be very much living and breathing and *here*"? What are some common ways for the past to push its way into the present?

2. The imagery of a bridge is threaded throughout Eli's story as a symbol of the passage from death to resurrection. What were the "deaths" he was resisting early in his story? How might his future have been different if he had made different choices about these opportunities for transformation? What would you identify as his moments of resurrection?

3. When talking about therapy, Eli suggests that pain and hurt are inevitable, but unnecessary suffering can be avoided if we examine our hurts and flaws because it reduces the chances we will replicate them. Do you agree with him? How was Eli affected by avoiding versus approaching his hurts and flaws over the course of the story?

4. Eli acknowledges in the very first scene of the book that his loneliness is "both [his] greatest wound and [his] most dependable defense." Eli developed a number of defenses to protect himself from the loss of love or to preserve relationships with the ones he loved. Keeping secrets was his most obvious. What were Eli's other defenses? How did they help him at first? How did they hurt him eventually?

5. Six months past the deadline for his book, Elijah believes everyone is sick of him—Rebecca, Benjamin, and Jeff, specifically. Do you think this is true? How is Elijah's view of himself similar or different from others' views of him? How do his assumptions about what others want from him affect his relationships?

6. When Elijah departs his house for Bradford's Ferry, he chooses to leave his toothbrush behind because an empty toothbrush holder "looked like the end of a story whose conclusion I couldn't bring myself to consider." Then he observed, "We assert control in senseless ways when it's the only kind of control we can still assert." In what other ways did Eli attempt to exert control over his life? In what ways were these attempts successful or unsuccessful?

7. Why do you think Eli's old nightmare began recurring right after Rebecca left? What purpose did that dream serve over the course of the story? Do you believe dreams can be messengers from our unconscious or our soul, calling us in new directions or toward transformation?

8. What do you think about Father Lou's insight about the dark night of the soul being a time when God is waiting for a more honest conversation? Was Eli hiding from God as

well as from himself and others? How might a lack of honesty affect our relationship with God?

9. What is the significance of each of the conversations Eli had with people from his past? How did they encourage his unhiding? What lesson did he need to learn from each of them? Could those lessons have come from anyone, or did they need to come through those specific people?

10. Uncle Mark explains to Eli that his biggest blind spot is his truest, worthiest, most lovable self—his soul, his spirit. What do you think of this characterization of our biggest "blind spot"? How does Eli's story suggest we uncover or reconnect with our true self?

11. Eli is surprised by how we substitute "proxies for worth" for the worth of our true self. What are the examples of these proxies given in the book? What other proxies can you think of? Are some proxies more common than others? How do we discard these proxies and embrace our true worth?

12. Why did the memory of the night on the river with Johnny Mathers come to Eli when it did? How do you understand the difference between Elijah's and Benjamin's reactions that night while they waited for Johnny to reappear? What might it say about them and their respective stories?

13. Why did Eli's mom keep the secrets she did for so long? How did family secrets affect Eli's childhood and the adult he became? Do you believe keeping secrets in a family can have a generational impact as it did for the Campbells?

14. Eli frequently notices and experiences "thin spaces" in which time folds in on itself and the distinction between

past and present dissolves to some extent. Which thin spaces do you think were most influential in his transformation? Why? Do you believe thin spaces can exist outside of this story, in the real world?

15. What were the many expressions of love and grace that Eli was shown when he began unhiding? How might the story have gone differently if he had not been received in this way?

16. Eli becomes frustrated at first with Father Lou's explanation of forgiveness before eventually accepting it. What do you think of Father Lou's idea that "when you cut the rope of resentment that ties you to [the other], you will be freeing yourself, but you will also be freeing [them]"? In what ways does his explanation correspond to or differ from what you have been taught about forgiveness?

17. Near the end of Eli's final conversation with Father Lou, Father Lou paraphrases a quote from Henri Nouwen about how, in our loneliness, we are like two interlocked hands clinging to each other. Instead, to truly love each other, we must become like two hands folded so that we can move apart from each other, still touching at the fingertips but with space between us. How did you react to this and to Father's Lou's illustration about being held like this in the "cupped and loving hands of God"? Did the story's various reflections on what love is and is not have an effect on your own definition of love? Why or why not?

18. Near the end of the book, there are several scenes in which Eli appears to "hide" again—for instance, not telling Benjamin about the name of his lost brother and suppressing

his grief while saying goodbye to Rebecca's father. How were these hidings similar to or different from his hiding earlier in the book? Do you think you can hide for loving reasons? How does a person discern when it's okay to hide and when it's best to reveal oneself?

19. The book concludes with Eli holding Rebecca and Sarah "without holding on to them at all." The Epilogue does not reveal whether Eli and Rebecca stayed together. What do you think happened to their marriage, and why? Do you wish the conclusion to their story had been more explicit, or are you glad it's up to you to decide what happened?

20. How does Elijah's story resemble our cultural assumptions about a midlife crisis? Would you consider this a story of a midlife crisis? Why or why not? What did you think of Elijah's suggestion in the Epilogue that a midlife crisis can become a midlife awakening if we go on the inner journey it is calling us to rather than doubling down on all of our outward striving?